DOOMED

Ancient Legends Book Two

JAYDE SCOTT

Other young adult titles by Jayde Scott

A Job From Hell
Voodoo Kiss
Dead And Beyond
Forever And Beyond
Black Wood
Mortal Star

Jacket illustration by Shiela Oliveros
http://shielaoliveros.co.nr
shielaoliveros@gmail.com

Stock Images provided by and a huge thank you to the following
members of deviantart.com: black-ofelia-stock, caserta-stock, elandria,
liam-stock, mirrorimagestock, scully7491

ISBN: 1463711751
ISBN-13: 978-1463711757

For Foxy, Silver and Tabby

You taught me the true meaning of love …

Acknowledgments

My gratitude goes to my partner for the inspiration.
You're my rock.
A huge thank you to my editors and many beta readers.
Thank you to my critique partners, and in particular
Christine who always has an encouraging word ready.
And, last but not least, a huge thanks to all my
wonderful readers. I hope you'll enjoy this book as much
as I enjoyed writing it.

Chapter 1 - Family relations

I stood in the corner of the torture chamber, back pressed against the ancient stone. The air was hot, sucking every bit of oxygen out of my lungs. Bright rays seeped through the few loose stones in the wall, leaving a trail of whirled up dust particles in their wake. I sighed and pointed at the heavy mahogany door.

"How long is this going to take, Dad? You know I've to get to my job."

A guy hanging from long chains in the ceiling yelled like a pitchfork just stabbed him in the bum. I figured that was about the only answer I'd get. Groaning, I averted my gaze, hoping Dad, dressed in his usual business suit, gaze fixed on the guy undergoing some major torture, wouldn't notice, but of course he did.

"This is your job, Cassandra. Are you watching and *learning?*" he asked.

Nodding, I curled my lips into a forced smile, grateful Dad couldn't read my thoughts because we were blood-related. My stomach turned at the metallic smell of blood hitting my nostrils. You'd think after growing up there I would've been used to the whole shebang—torture, famine, death and so forth—but I still flinched and gritted my teeth. Truth be told, I'd rather do my nails and smell of YSL than dust, sweat and what else not. Even at King Louis XVI's court, which we were forced to visit as part of a history project at school, I was the one who stayed inside and ate all the chocolate truffles instead of joining the cheering crowd to watch the henchman decapitate France's traitors. Trouble was, Dad didn't quite agree with my pastime choices of shopping and doing my nails.

"Looky here, kiddo." Dad pointed at the poor soul who had probably made a few wrong choices in his life. "If you tickle that spot right under his solar plexus, he'll be in painful giggles for days. That's enough time to come up with the next step in his endless loop of torture. We have a reputation to maintain, got to be versatile."

Groaning, I rolled my eyes. I couldn't stand the yelping, shouting and crying any more, so I inched closer, holding my breath because the smell made me sick. "Dad?"

Dad's green eyes focused on me. "You know you're not supposed to call me that when we're at work."

I nodded, carefully preparing my words. "Right. Sorry, Lucifer. Do you think you could let me finish this for once?" I ran a hand through my frizzy red hair, which I did mean to straighten in the morning, but let's face it, with the heat down there I wouldn't have done my split ends any favor.

Dad cocked a brow. "You want to—"

Not really. "Uh—huh."

He beamed at me. "That's my girl. Want me to help you?" I rolled my eyes again. He held out his hands. "Okay, I was just checking. If you need anything, call me."

I waited until he disappeared out the torture chamber, then walked over to the guy dangling from some kick-ass chains, and tapped him on the shoulder to get his attention.

His eyes darted about; I could smell his fear, or maybe it was just the sickening odor of someone who hadn't showered in at least a week. Combine that with the heat, blood and a fair share of other body fluids, and you have a deadly combination.

I wrapped an arm around his neck, my sleeve barely touching his sweat-slicked skin. "Listen, mate. Here's the deal. I just got my nails done and I don't need them getting chipped when I practice one of these procedures from this little, old book." I held up my *Torture Techniques For Dummies* booklet, covering the Dummies part so he wouldn't think I was a complete beginner. "Do you think you could scream and moan a bit, you know, like you're in real pain?" I whispered.

He just stared at me, open-mouthed. I groaned inwardly. Was he dense or something?

"Yo," I hissed. "Either you do as I say, or the Big Boss's coming back. Trust me, you don't want that."

Dad's voice rang through the chamber, making me jump. "Less talking. More screaming!"

I groaned. Seriously, no pressure there. "Just warming up, Dad."

9

"Looks like you're the one that needs convincing," he roared. "Where's your Louis Vuitton handbag?"

"No, don't do anything rash, like cut my credit cards in half." I licked my finger, and then leafed through the pages. My finger landed on Impalement: A sharp pole is pushed through a victim's body while alive. Who in their right mind would ever practice something that barbaric, not to mention disgusting?

"Please yell," I whispered. The guy barely acknowledged me, so I held up the page to him, praying he could read. His eyes skimmed the large fonts, pupils widening. I could see I was finally getting somewhere.

"Oh, that looks painful." I sighed. "I've got goose bumps just thinking about a nasty procedure like that. If you don't start acting, I'm going to call my dad to show you how this little number works."

It took a few seconds for the message to kick in, but the guy finally let out an ear-piercing cry.

"Okay, cut it." I shot a last glance over my shoulder and turned back to him. "It's kind of late and I need to get to work. What do you say, you scream one more time, then fall into a nice coma? Doesn't have to be a deep one. They'll let you sleep for a few hours until I get back."

He nodded.

I counted to three and slipped out because I couldn't take it any longer. Dad thought one day I'd inherit the family business aka Hell, but I had other plans. I loved my customer service career. Soon, I'd have my own company and we'd give Amazon a run for their money.

Chapter 2 - Distros

The torture chamber was situated on the third plane, Acerbus. Hell had seven different dimensions, each coming with its own perks of physical agony and mental misery. By the time I reached our mansion on the first level to change for work, I'd be covered in grime, sweat and what else not. Before I wasted any more time, I took out my high-tech phone, and beamed myself onto the second upper plane, Distros, where the heat was still bearable. Usually, I tried to avoid it because Distros is one spooky place, but I had no choice than to travel through only one dimension at a time since I hadn't yet come up with the right programming on my phone.

Proud of myself, I peered at the tiny electronic item, which I invented in a rare moment of utter ingenuity. It looked like any other cell phone, albeit a very chic one in a sleek 'n silver way. But, based on its functionalities, it resembled an electronic genie. However, since I had designed it not long ago and it hadn't passed its beta stage, it was more unstable than *Windows Vista*. But I figured it'd have to do until I got my fallen angel powers for my eighteenth birthday, which was only a few weeks away. Until then, I might be immortal, meaning not much could really kill me, but absolutely useless without my phone since I had no superhuman powers, apart from being able to stop the time—but only once a year. Dad's rules sucked.

The wide plane was covered in a thick layer of grey dust blocking out the sun. A strong wind whirled the decaying leaves on the ground, blowing them toward the dilapidated cottages in the distance. Many deceased people lived in Distros, souls who would be accepted into Heaven once they sat out a certain amount of time for their petty crimes, such as lacking faith and having the wrong priorities in life. I knew for sure none of Dad's demon employees were around because Distros was home to our temporary visitors that didn't require torture for their sins, meaning there was almost no supervision. Dad figured, being there in that semi-darkness instead of with their loved ones was enough punishment already, so he didn't get involved.

As said, Distros gave me the creeps even more than the torture chambers in the lower planes. The emotional turmoil and suffering was too strong for an angel. So I didn't usually linger here, but today something made me hesitate.

"Hello?" My voice echoed in the vast space, cutting through the eerie silence like a knife.

The soft wail of a girl carried over from my right. Even though I knew better than to get involved, I headed toward the tiny lodge. She was sitting on the porch, her blonde head buried in her lap, strands of hair swaying in the wind. Behind her, a loose shutter thudded against the dirty wall of the house.

"Are you okay?" Stupid question, I know, given that she was dead and stuck in Hell. Of course she couldn't be okay when her mind kept recalling the still vivid memories of her life. Rubbing my upper arms, I took several tentative steps forward until I stopped several inches away from her. This was the nearest I'd ever been to a Distros ghost. The distress wafting from her was palpable in the air. My fallen angel side flickered to life, soaking up the chaos surrounding her, but for once I didn't feel like enjoying the thrill. There was nothing exciting about human suffering and emotional pain.

Her head rose, revealing a pale, chubby face with large blue eyes and thin lips. She couldn't be much younger than me, but the wet trails on her cheeks gave her the innocence of a child. But she must've done something to deserve being sent here.

"I haven't seen you before. Are you new?" she asked, wiping a plump hand over her cheeks.

I nodded because it was easier than disclosing my real identity. I figured she might not be so inclined to talk to me if she knew. "I'm Cass."

"Theo." She smiled and patted the floor next to her. I dropped down, tucking my legs under me to stave off the cold wafting from her skin. In spite of the high temperature outside, she was undoubtedly freezing like all the other ghosts on that plane.

As if on cue, a shudder ran down her arms, turning her flesh into goose bumps.

"Where do you live?" Theo asked, wrapping the thin shawl tighter around her slender body. I pointed vaguely behind me to the woods with their dying trees and copper grass. She bobbed her head, knowingly. "It's much nicer there than to the west. At least, you're not being constantly preyed on by the demon wolves."

She was talking about the guardians' helpers who made sure no one escaped Hell through the east gate.

"You were crying because of someone," I said, eager to change the subject.

"How do you know?"

I shrugged, considering how much to reveal. "I often see and hear what's going on in other people's minds." Apart from those related to me by blood, that is.

Theo's eyes grew wide open. "That's a cool gift to have. I bet I wouldn't be dead if I could do that."

She had been murdered in cold blood. Memories of a dark passage, an underground tunnel, flashed before my eyes. I shook my head to get rid of them, and they stopped, but not because I wanted them to. I couldn't yet control what or how much I saw.

Theo smiled bitterly.

"Why are you here?" I whispered.

She averted her gaze to stare at a large fissure in the ground. "I hurt someone very bad."

The pictures didn't come, so she was blocking them out of her memory. That wasn't the way Distros worked, meaning it was only a matter of time before they returned to haunt her.

"I just wish I could warn my sister," Theo continued.

"Why?"

She peered up from the ground, her blue gaze meeting mine. Her memories started flooding my mind. "Because she's dating his brother," Theo whispered.

Tremors ran up and down my spine as more images flashed before my open eyes. A sense of sadness grabbed hold of me, drawing me deep into a drowning pool of sorrow and regret. This was why angels weren't supposed to get too close to humans. We were too sensitive for our own good, enjoying celebration to excess, and killing ourselves over the melancholy in mortals.

I rose, pushing up on my arms to steady my shaking knees. My seventeen-year-old body felt aged by decades, my soul wounded, just like Theo's. It wasn't right that she be here, and yet it was because she took someone's life.

"I have to go." My hand reached out for her, stroking the almost white blonde hair.

"That's okay." She smiled, her lips trembled. Her eyes glazed over like a veil covering a window, hiding her very soul. She was in pain and lost in her past again. "Goodbye, Sofia. We shall meet again when you're dead, just like me."

Her sister's name was Sofia. The knowledge made me walk away briskly, the cold wind clearing my head a little. Twelve years ago, Mom had become friends with a Distros ghost, right before she left to resume her position as a seraph in heaven. One day she just disappeared because the pain became so strong she couldn't live here with Dad and me any more.

If Dad found out I conversed with one of the souls, I'd be in major trouble. Think locking me up for the next ten

years or, even worse, cancel my credit card. My meager
Skylife wage wasn't nearly enough to cover my apartment
costs. I knew I must forget Theo because there was
nothing I could do for her. Once she did her time, she'd
be welcomed into heaven. The knowledge consoled me for
all of five minutes during which I took a shower and
changed into a clean pair of jeans and a shirt. Then the
feeling of something not quite being right returned again.

Chapter 3 - Hearing voices

I arrived at my tiny cubicle with five minutes to spare during which I prepared to do what I always did: lean back and enjoy the atmosphere. Lines were ringing. Heads were nodding, eyes rolling; bored voices assured frustrated customers their orders would dispatch soon, and refunds would be issued within a week upon an item's return. No place offered more constant and diverse drama than the Skylife head quarters, where the customer service department was based. As part fallen angel, I thrived on chaos. It was better than chocolate.

The clock on my computer showed a minute to go. I smiled, soaking up the frayed nerves and the contained voices threatening to rise any minute.

"Cass? Are you all right? You look a bit flushed." It was my supervisor, Rick—a short, bald man in his mid-forties who hated his job but knew how to suck up so no one found out. Unfortunately, I did because I could read his mind.

I smirked. "You try coming from one hundred plus degrees to this. All that heat and steam—"

Rick nodded. "You went to a spa? I wish I could afford it. I've heard sauna's great for tension and stress relief."

If I told him I lived in hell, he'd fire me for being as loony as an apple in a banana tree. "Yeah, that's the ticket," I said. "A little R&R. My minute's up." I put on my headphones, signaling him our conversation was over. I was ready to answer my first call.

Rick shot me a doubtful look before he disappeared around the corner, counting the hours until he could return home to his lager and TV. The constant reminder in his mind drove me nuts.

"Skylife customer service. Cassandra speaking. How may I help you today?" My voice sounded confident and forthcoming; I'd repeated it so many times Dad said I recited it in my sleep.

"Listen, I'm enquiring about an order which should've been here a week ago. Where the heck is it?"

The guy sounded pissed off, irritation dripping from his deep voice. Somehow he seemed familiar, and yet I didn't pay attention as thick waves of pleasure washed over me. The promise of imminent drama made my skin tingle. For a second I felt guilty, and then I just shrugged it off. It wasn't my fault my dad's DNA coursed through my veins. I smiled and took his order number, my fingers gliding over the computer keyboard effortlessly. "Let me just check for you. Customer satisfaction is our priority." It was all a lie we were supposed to tell; the company only cared about the cash and profit margins. "Ah, here it is, sir. You ordered a few security items." Five cameras, sensors, movement detectors and mace—was he trying to fortify a bank? I cleared my throat and resumed my chirpy chatter. "The parcel was dispatched last Tuesday and should be with you shortly."

A pause on the line, then, "Ain't good enough, Mary Poppins. I need it now, otherwise I want my money back."

"I can assure you it will arrive within the stated delivery estimate. If not, we're more than happy to refund your payment. Now, have you visited our website lately? We have many items discounted up to fifty per cent."

He snorted. "I doubt I'll be ordering anything else soon since you can't seem able to deliver one parcel."

Someone was grumpy today. I smiled. "Of course, sir. I understand your concern. Is there anything else I can help you with?"

"Is the parcel sitting right here in my hands? No. It isn't. You haven't exactly helped. And your chirpy voice has made my headache worse," the guy said.

Boring. Hang up. This guy has LOSER written across his forehead.

Listening to several voices speaking at the same time was hard work. I groaned, wishing I could shoo away the tiny devil, Kinky, dressed in a black robe and sitting on my left shoulder, like an annoying fly. Ever since separating, my parents had adopted the habit of demonstrating their parental love by trying to outdo each other. It all started with Mom gifting me a little personal angel, Pinky, dressed in loose shorts that looked like diapers with a golden halo casting a glow over his blonde locks. Pinky took the place on my right shoulder and was supposed to teach me proper etiquette when Mom wasn't around. Of course Dad had to throw in a tiny devil by the name of Kinky, a personal demon with a beautiful face, dark eyes and hair as black as coal. Needless to say, Kinky was all that social etiquette wasn't about.

"Your parcel will arrive soon," I said, my focus returning to my customer. "As part of our endeavor to provide the best customer service in the world we offer our valued customers the possibility to rate the representative. From one to ten, how would you rate my service?" I made it sound like it was no biggie, but inside my head I was shaking and chanting, *Please, say ten, or else I won't be appraised advisor of the month.*

"Just get the parcel to me." The line disconnected.

I gulped, a hot flush washing over me as I peered around to make sure no one was listening. A dissatisfied customer wasn't exactly a sign of competence. Hopefully, my boss didn't record the call.

"Thank you for calling Skylife. Have a lovely day," I whispered. That was the risk of working in customer service, not being able to avoid the usual jerks. Fortunately for them, I had the patience of a saint, which came from my mother's side of the family.

The next few callers were more cooperative. Before I knew it, it was time for my lunch break. I headed for the nearest café to get a grand latte and a chocolate croissant, then returned to my desk and devoured the hot pastry, washing it down with the sickeningly sweet drink as I listened to the chatting voices around me. My half hour was barely over when my line rang again.

"Skylife customer service. Cassandra speaking. How may I help you?" I took a last sip of my coffee and almost spit it over my keyboard at the sound of the familiar voice.

"Any updates on my parcel yet?" There were more than a dozen other operators in this room. How the heck did he get directed to me?

"It's been only a few hours, sir. Please wait until tomorrow. I'm sure the post will deliver it first thing in the morning."

"Are you talking facts or are you just making an assumption?"

"I—" My eyes darted about, taking in the tiny desk littered with pens and loose sheets, as I considered whether to lie. If I told the truth, he'd never rate me a ten. "Someone told me."

There was a brief pause on the other end of the line. "You have the inside scoop from the dispatch department."

Huh? "Excuse me?"

"Come on, tell me what you know. Where is it? Is someone making this hard on me on purpose?"

What gave the idiot the impression a huge company like Skyline cared about a single shopper? "We want to keep our customers happy. Why don't you give me your number and I'll call you as soon as we know more?"

"You'll call?"

He sounded so hopeful, my smile returned. "Of course. We want you to get your items as quickly as possible. I'll make this a top priority."

"Okay." He repeated his number twice, just in case I was too dense to note it down properly the first time around. "Don't forget," he said before hanging up.

I'd never met anyone so obnoxious, but the line rang again and I forgot about him. Outside, darkness descended, carrying heavy clouds that promised a rainy night.

"I'm off," Rick whispered behind me. "See you after your holidays."

Nodding, I waved and responded to my last customer of the day.

"You never called even though you said you would," the same guy said.

"How—" It didn't matter why he got re-routed to me yet again. I needed to keep a professional attitude so, naturally, I told a lie. "Our dispatch department is still investigating. I promise I'll get back to you as soon as I know more. If there's nothing else—"

"Actually, there is." The guy took a deep breath. "You're located only a few miles away. Why don't you pop over and deliver the parcel yourself?"

For a moment, I stared at the phone, lost for words. In the twelve months I'd been working there, I received the weirdest requests, but none involved playing postman while being telephone stalked. My anger flared up and Kinky wasn't helping by making himself heard again.

Piss off, mate. Kinky had a point.

"I'm sorry, sir. I wish I could do that, but it's against company policy to visit a customer." I kept my smile in place even though I didn't feel like it.

"Not good enough. I need this parcel today. You don't seem very busy, so make yourself useful and bring it over."

Why, he was one infuriating guy. He could call himself lucky that I took my job very seriously. "I'm afraid that's not possible, sir."

"Why not?"

"Because it's against—"

"I want my parcel."

Kinky snorted. *Tell him to pop over and you'll shove it up his—*

Don't listen to Kinky. The poor man's desperate, Cassie. For all you know he might be trying to protect his pet cat from wild animals, Pinky said.

Kinky laughed into my eardrum. *More likely from your bad breath, you diaper-wearing, inflated—*

My customer said something I missed. Was that how a schizophrenic felt? I couldn't take it any more. "Shut up," I yelled. My work mates peered up from their computers screens. I smiled at them and pointed at the papers on my desk as thought that would explain my outburst.

The guy on the line took a sharp breath. "What did you just say to me?"

Kinky looked away, pouting. I slapped my hand against my left shoulder even though I must've tried a million times before and knew there was no chance in Hell I'd get rid of him. "Not you, sir. My colleague's been—" Breaking off, I rubbed my temples. "I'm sorry for the misunderstanding."

"Apology not accepted, unless you bring over my stuff."

Bring over my stuff, Kinky mocked. *Tell him, I'll pop over and put the mace—*

"But hurry up. The game's starting at seven and I don't want to be interrupted," the guy continued.

My blood was boiling. "What do you think I am? A delivery courier? Why don't you make use of all the waiting on your hands and get a life in the meantime? You'll thank me later."

For the first time in my promising career, I did the unspeakable and hung up on a customer, instantly regretting it. What was I thinking? I loved my job. If I got fired, Dad would request that I move back home and I'd rather not.

You see, as a child, I was always the odd one out. When other girls dressed in pink and white, I could only wear black and blood red—as in red with loads of blood splatters. It was my father's sense of fashion.

Other girls had puppies and fluffy kittens to cuddle. I had a beast of a hound with blazing red eyes and unnatural speed. Bruno was the stuff of nightmares, and would devour anything coming within a thirty-mile radius. At least, I was never bullied since the few kids that tried, disappeared forever. Dad said they moved home, but I knew better.

I always knew my parents weren't the usual sales clerk and nurse; Mother was a high-ranking angel, seraph to be more precise since she hated being called a mere angel. How she met and fell in love with someone like Lucifer was beyond me, but it goes to show love is blind. Once the infatuation's gone, so are the pink goggles. Now, when we all gathered for birthdays, they couldn't even pretend to like each other.

"See what you've done, Kinky?" I glowered at his smug smile. He shrugged and disappeared in a huge flame that sizzled. He was just hiding in my purse until the air cleared again and he resumed causing more mischief.

A clock struck six, ending my last working day. Taking a deep breath, I grabbed my bag and headed home. I drove through the crowded city like a maniac, barely halting at stop signs, and arrived at my one bed flat in record time. If Dad wasn't so stingy, I could afford at least a mansion, but he wasn't keen on his only child walking among mortals, and so he kept me on a very short financial leash.

I barely got out of my SUV, an expensive reminder of my family heirloom, when I smelled something in the air. Kneeling on the naked ground, I caught a whiff of a sweet scent I couldn't pinpoint. My heart fluttered in my chest, my legs turned to jelly. This sure beat even the turmoil at work.

Oh, this is good stuff. Kinky was back, his moaning interrupting my concentration.

"It's probably just drama, someone getting into big trouble," I whispered, unlocking the front door. The reflection of a guy mirrored in the glass. My breath caught in my throat, as I stood frozen to the spot. The hazel eyes, dark blond hair and golden skin disappeared again, and for a moment I wasn't sure whether I imagined seeing him.

You should get a piece of that, Kinky said.

You know you mustn't. Your mother would be very disappointed, Pinky said.

Kinky snorted. *Shut up, Stinky. You wouldn't know fun if it bit you in the—*

Don't you dare call me 'Stinky.' Unlike you, I bathe every day and—

"Shut up, both of you." I shook my head and headed up the stairs, eager to lock myself up in the privacy of my four walls. I might not be able to escape the irritating angel and devil sitting on my shoulders, but at least I could pretend.

Chapter 4 - The bond

"Cass?" Dallas's voice echoed through the corridor. I turned, my heart catching in my throat. Even though we met months ago and barely exchanged a word, I'd recognize his scent from a mile. Hundreds of thoughts raced through my mind. What was he doing in London? Did he live nearby? Was he seeing someone? Did he like chocolate?

I peered down at my crumpled denims, and ran a hand through my red, unruly hair, then turned to regard him.

Standing in the hall, a hesitant smile playing on his lips, he was staring straight back at me. His face looked pale against the black of his jacket; the fluorescent light cast a garish glow on his shiny hair. He inched closer, hesitant. "I'm Dallas. You probably don't remember me."

I did. How could I forget the face I'd been thinking of for the last few months? Granted, I could've called over some of Dad's demons and demand they track him down, but that wouldn't have been the brightest idea. For one, they might've decided to bite off a leg or two in the process, or worse—tell Dad about my new love interest. Dad didn't need to know I'd fallen for a mortal, and no less one that couldn't keep a job for longer than three months.

"I know who you are." My voice almost broke off. A hot rush washed over me. My vision blurred. I sniffled, then sneezed very unladylike. I gathered I must be coming down with a cold.

He beamed, nodding. "Want to grab a cup of coffee? I know it's late and..." He trailed off.

"Sounds great." I smiled and marched over to him, ready to head out again. No harm done in joining the guy for a drink. Dad would never find out. It wasn't like I was running off to marry Dallas, or anything.

* * *

"Sorry about the call," Dallas said as soon as we had taken our seats at a nearby café. "I didn't mean to come across like a total jack-off."

I frowned. "What?"

"I'm usually much friendlier, but I really need that security stuff."

My eyes scanned his features because I had no idea what he was talking about. Then it dawned on me. "You're the one pestering me all day."

"I'm sorry."

"Did you follow me?" My voice sounded thin, barely more than a whisper.

He winced, a tiny frown crossing his brows. "I guess you could call it that. I thought I'd pay Skylife a visit to complain when you walked out the door. Your hair seemed so familiar."

I couldn't blame him. A red, unruly mane wasn't very common in the land of *L'Oreal* and hair straighteners. I smirked. "I'm glad you remembered me for something."

He reached out, his hand stopping inches from my fingers. "How could I forget you? I love your style."

"Thank you. As Oscar Wilde once said, Be yourself; everyone else is already taken." My cheeks flushed. The guy obviously had a great fashion sense 'cause there weren't many people who understood my style of crumpled jeans and lots of color.

His eyes shimmered in the dim room. "I'm just glad we got to meet again."

One couldn't exactly call it an accident, more like accidental stalking. Come to think of it, it wasn't even accidental since he *chose* to follow me home. His insolence would have had any other girl fuming, but I was compelled to feel flattered. Guys weren't usually mesmerized by my hair, color or cut. And then my father's DNA came with a few perks as well, like causing uneasiness in the pit of a mortal's stomach if he so much as glanced at me from a distance in a crowded room. Naturally, some were more receptive than others. Dallas must belong to a rare species that was completely oblivious to the danger pouring from my every pore.

"Are you angry?" he asked.

I shook my head, mesmerized by his gaze, not to mention the bulging muscles. "Don't assume because I have red hair, I jump to being a hothead."

29

Dallas shook his head. "Never." I couldn't help but smile. His hazel eyes peered into my very soul as he continued, "Do you believe in love at first sight?"

I blinked, surprised at a guy asking such a question. "I don't." Or so I thought, until a few seconds ago. But I wasn't going to blurt that out.

"I don't follow pretty girls home, but you captivated me like no other I've ever met," Dallas said. "I had to talk to you, no matter what it took. I'm sorry."

"Water under the bridge." I laughed, feeling a slight pull toward him. "But you'll have to work on those telephone manners of yours."

Tell him to jump in the lake. I shook my head at Kinky who'd just made his grand appearance again.

"Let me make it up to, I insist. How about dinner at the place of your choice?" Dallas asked.

I looked at my watch, stalling for time. Did I really want to have dinner with a gorgeous yet mortal guy? Dad would be livid. "It's late."

"My telephone manners might suck, but my dinner manners are half-way decent. I do eat with my mouth closed and I've recently learned to use a fork." I laughed. Dallas's eyes sparkled with humor. "Listen, it's the least I can do for you. I won't be able to go to sleep knowing I treated you like crap. I'll look like a zombie tomorrow with big bloodshot eyes and—"

Say yes. We'll order lobster and let him foot the bill, Kinky said.

Dinner's very romantic, Pinky whispered. *Tell him he mustn't forget the flowers.*

Who needs flowers when she can smell him, you idiot? Kinky yelled.

"Shut up," I hissed.

Dallas frowned. "What?"

"I mean, *shut up*! I'd love dinner." I shot my two companions an imploring look, hoping they wouldn't ruin this date like they ruined everything else such as my life.

"What about right now?" Dallas cocked a brow, expectantly. "I don't have any plans."

I nodded and grabbed the menu, burying my face into the thick cover because I figured if I kept looking into those gorgeous gold-speckled eyes I might just faint. I'd never felt so drawn in before; he was making my head all dizzy. Something was wrong. Maybe the coffee was too strong, causing my blood pressure to jump through the roof.

It's the bond, Pinky squealed. *How magical that you should meet your soul mate this way.*

You don't want to be tied down for the rest of your life like some ball and chain, Kinky said.

Did he just say 'soul mate'? I blinked, my mind unable to comprehend Pinky's insinuation. It couldn't be. I'd know if Dallas was *the one*, my soul mate, the one given to me by Fate.

It's him. I can see the silver thread drawing you to one another. Pinky started clapping in my ear. *Look at you! You make such an adorable couple.*

"What are you having?" Dallas asked, eyes beaming, face glowing unnaturally. The thought of food made me nauseous. And I was never one to turn down a good steak. Dallas didn't seem to fare any better though. Tiny beads of sweat trickled down the side of his face. Maybe he was as

31

nervous as I was. When he noticed me staring, his cheeks grew red as though he was burning from the inside out.

"Is something wrong with your temperature?" I leaned forward and pressed my palm against his forehead. His skin felt like fire. Maybe I should run and get him an ice pack. Or pour out the glass of soda and dump the ice over his head. Boy, that'd make a great first impression on our very first so-called date.

He caught my hand and kissed my wrist. His soft lips made my whole body tingle; his hot breath grazed my skin as he whispered, "Never felt better." Something sparkled between us, the air crackled. A shiver ran down my spine. Dallas dropped my hand again. "I didn't realize what I was doing."

Something wasn't right. I had to get out of here. I jumped up mumbling, "I need to use the restroom."

"Cass," Dallas called after me, but I didn't stop.

Forcing my way through the crowded tables, I reached the cold bathroom and locked myself inside, then took out my phone, dizzy. I speed-dialed Aunt Krista's number because she was the only person who would know. I mean, the woman had been married a million times, so she had plenty of experience.

"Darling-girl, so good to hear from you." She sounded genuinely excited. I gathered I had her attention for all of ten seconds.

I took a deep, steadying breath. "Auntie, you know the bond? Have you ever felt it with anyone?"

She let out that high-pitched helium laughter of hers. "Of course I did."

My heart calmed down a little at the prospect of finding out what was going on. "What was it like?"

"Can't tell you before you're eighteen. Your father would kill me."

Ready to lie my way through this conversation, I rolled my eyes. She wouldn't know anyway. "I turned eighteen a while back."

"When?"

I shrugged even though she couldn't see me. "A few hundred years ago."

"Are you sure, darling?"

"Don't you think I know my date of birth?" I said. "Want me to fetch a demon to bring over my birth certificate? He'd be there in a jiffy." I bit my lip, hoping she bought my bluff.

"You're so lucky you don't look it," Aunt Krista said.

"Must be my DNA."

"You're right. When I was your age people thought I—"

I slapped my forehead, irritated. If I didn't stop her, the woman would chatter for hours. "Auntie, we were talking about the bond!"

"I know that. Let me think." She paused. "You know how everyone complains about a dizzy head when they have the flu?"

I tapped my chewed nails against the tiled wall. "Yes?"

"That's it."

"You mean, you compare the eternal bond between two people that are meant for one another with flu symptoms?" I laughed. "You're nuts."

"Not everyone has the same symptoms, and they usually go away after the first date. Why are you asking?" She sounded suspicious. I sat up straight, frantic, because she

33

mustn't know. If she talked to someone, Dad would find out in a heartbeat.

"Because I've sworn off men forever and have decided to become a nun. I need to know the feeling so I can run in the other direction, if the opportunity ever presents itself. Thanks, Auntie. See ya."

Aunt Selena laughed. "You young people. Your emotions are all over the place. You want to be a nun today, and tomorrow a racecar driver—"

I groaned inwardly. The woman could really go on for hours. I made a crackling sound into the phone. "Bad connection. Got to go." I hurried to hang up and returned to my seat.

Dallas's cheeks turned bright red as he stood and pulled the chair aside to make room for me, a frown crossing his face. "I thought you were making a run for the hills."

"Run? I'm already sweating a river." I wiped off my face with my sleeve. My stomach clenched at his sight. My fingers itched to touch his skin.

"Are you all right? You look like you're going to be sick any minute."

I felt like telling him he didn't look any better, but stopped myself. "The air's a bit stuffy."

He nodded, staring at me, wide-eyed, as he leaned over the table. The air crackled again. "Tell me about yourself. I want to know everything."

I leaned back, putting a bit of distance between us, but it didn't ease the tension inside me. "Is this a date or a job interview?"

He smiled. "I love a girl with a great sense of humor. Let's start over again. Do you live with your parents?"

I shook my head. "Not since last year. I moved out when I got my job."

"Where did you grow up then?"

I didn't even want to try and explain that one. "Let's go back to question number one." I peered around, searching for facts that would make me seem fascinating in his eyes. The trouble was, I wasn't fascinating. That was more Dad's thing. "I'm very spontaneous," I said.

"Really?" He walked around the table and occupied the seat next to me. My heart started to race. "Me, too. What's the most spontaneous thing you've ever done?"

"Let me think." I tapped a finger against my chin. What about the one time I climbed the Eiffel Tower in the middle of the night? Couldn't tell him because I was tipsy and only trying to impress one of Dad's demon shape shifters. Dad went ballistic. Come to think of it, every single thing I ever did involved something that would piss off my parents. "Oh, I know. I eat the weirdest food combinations, like vanilla ice cream with ketchup."

Dallas nodded, impressed. "That rocks. How about we top that?"

"I'm listening."

"What do you say we do something *really* spontaneous and shock everyone?"

I cocked a brow, my heartbeat speeding up at the prospect of drama. I liked him a lot already. "Like what?"

He shrugged. "Let's move in together."

Yeah, baby. Rent-free. We'll freeload off of him big time, Kinky said.

I laughed at Kinky. "What?" Talk about taking things slowly.

"It'd be fun to skip the dating part." His eyes shone, drawing me in. I was intrigued.

I cupped his face and lowered my voice to a mere whisper. "Who says you're even my type? And who knows if we'll ever date?"

He winked. "We've got chemistry, and that only means one thing."

"What?" My pulse raced faster. He recognized our bond and wasn't backing off.

He flashed me his movie star smile, all gleaming white teeth. "It's only a matter of time." He was so cocky I couldn't fight the attraction.

"You're—" I peered into his eyes, searching for a give-away sign that he was joking, or making fun of me, but there was none. I nodded, a hot flush of excitement washing over me again. Something pulled me forward until my lips almost brushed his. He was the one, I knew it. Dad would go bonkers. I was in big trouble, but as usual I couldn't resist causing drama. "Let's do it."

Grabbing my hands, he planted a kiss on the corner of my mouth. "I'll pack tonight. Your place looks bigger than mine."

Chapter 5 - Moving home

My heart still fluttered twelve hours later when Dallas arrived with countless bags and boxes, all stacked up in my little hallway. Saying goodbye the previous night felt awkward and surreal. But I was glad it happened because it gave me a whole night to think about the whole situation. Aunt Krista had been right; the flu symptoms magically disappeared, but I had other worries now. How could I agree to him moving in? Apart from Mom and Dad, I'd never lived with anyone else, let alone a guy. Where was he supposed to sleep?

Dallas wrapped his arm around my waist and pulled me close, gazing into my eyes. "So, where's my room?"

Using every ounce of my willpower, I eased away with a big grin. "Not where you're thinking."

He arched a brow. "And how would you know what I was thinking?"

Good question. No way was I telling him the truth, that I kind of sensed it because reading minds was part of my fallen angel abilities. "Good intuition." I pointed at the living room and hoped he'd be happy settling for the sofa. He might be a hot guy, but I wasn't doing anything with a miniature angel and devil watching the live performance from their first row seats.

He shrugged. "I guess I can settle for the couch."

The boxes started to pile up in the hall, taking so much space I could barely squeeze through to reach the kitchen, tumbling over an old rugged baseball with some faded scribbling on it. I held it up to Dallas. "Want me to toss this out?"

His expression changed to horror for a moment, waves of dread wafted from him. "Hell, no. I had to jump pretty high to catch that one. I actually knocked drinks all over some guy, but he let me off the hook because I was ten."

Sports? Seriously? I grumbled as I caught a glimpse of a white, plastic helmet inside another box. How much stuff did the guy have? If he continued this way I doubted I'd be able to find my few belongings among all his clutter.

"Why do you have so many things?" I muttered.

Dallas groaned under the weight of what resembled a huge casket. From the looks of it, it might as well be a coffin. And there I thought I was the strange one.

"What did you say, babe?" he asked.

"Nothing. Ever thought about opening a shop? You'd be rich in no time."

Dallas stopped his carrying stuff around, grinning. "Yeah, I might one day. I always figured I have amazing management and organizational abilities."

I shook my head, realizing that was exactly why people shouldn't move in together before knowing each other for a few months. But he did look handsome in his jeans and shirt, bulging arms peeking from underneath cotton sleeves. Besides, it was a new experience. As part fallen angel, I thrived on excitement.

It was midday when he finally finished carrying stuff around. The stocking and tidying up hadn't even started yet. I tried to ignore the cardboard boxes in every corner as I ordered pizza and let Dallas foot the bill.

He peeked inside the cartons. "You got cheese crust, right?"

"I'm more the thin-crust girl." I shot him an apologetic glance as I tossed a slice of salami and pepperoni on a plate, and then handed it to him.

"That's my favorite." As though to prove his point, he took a bite and choked on the spicy stuff.

I giggled even though I shouldn't, but his red face screamed drama and drama was the very essence of my being.

The phone rang. I hurried to answer without giving it much thought until it was too late.

"Cass, you should've been here an hour ago." Dad didn't sound too pleased. "How are you supposed to take over the family business when you can't ever make it on time?"

I groaned and slumped down on the floor, pressing my back against the wall. "Sorry, Dad. Something came up."

His voice turned all concerned. "What happened? Do you want me to pop over?"

"No!" I shook my head. "Don't come. It's nothing. Just women's troubles, that's all."

"Want me to send one of your aunts over?"

What was it with my parents and their inability to understand after spending twelve months in London and fending for myself, I was perfectly capable of dealing with an emergency or two? Particularly if that emergency involved a hot guy moving in and the need to keep it a secret.

"I don't think they could help," I said. "Besides, I'd rather talk to Mom."

"Oh." He paused for a moment. I could picture him covering the voice piece while he heated up hot stones under some poor soul's feet. Yeah, hearing Mom's name did that to him. Last time they met for coffee he caused an earthquake in Alaska. "I don't see how she could possibly help you," Dad said, slowly.

"Dad, don't even go there. I'll be right over, okay? See you in ten." I hung up and went in search of Dallas to tell him I might be away for a couple of hours, or days, depending on what Dad had in store for me.

Ten minutes later, I stood in the hall and took out my phone to open the portal when I realized I was in a relationship now, basically living with someone, so I'd have to be more careful how I used my phone.

I drove the SUV a few miles to a nearby shopping center parking lot and parked there. Stepping out, I whipped out my phone and punched in the code to open the portal. The air crackled; tiny flashes of lightning cut through the air inches from my face, waiting for me to squeeze through. Just as I took a step forward and pushed my hand in, a lady with thin, snow-white hair pulled into a bun, and deep wrinkles across her forehead, appeared around the corner, holding a leash. Thick glasses sat tight on the bridge of her nose, so she probably couldn't see a lot. But her little poodle, complete with pom-poms and colored ribbons, started to bark like crazy, pulling at his leash in my direction. The woman shot me a glare as though I had just maltreated the yapping, little thing. I shrugged and stepped through, noticing her eyes widen as I vanished into a yellow burst of light. The poor woman would probably end up thinking she had a screw loose in her head. Under normal circumstances, I would've waited until she disappeared, but not today. Dad needed me. Better not keep him waiting and risk him sending one of his demons to get me. He couldn't yet find out about Dallas.

* * *

My room was on the first floor of Dad's mansion, a huge place with marble floors and minimalist furniture. I made a beeline for the wall-to-wall walk-in cupboard to change into my one and only black business suit before joining Dad in his mahogany office. He rocked back in his leather chair, staring out the large window to the high lava mountains in the distance, steam rising from the geysers below.

"Dad?" I entered, only then knocking on the door. "What's up?"

He turned slowly, his green eyes burning with tiny flames, just like mine when I was angry or soaking in a bit of drama. His hair was combed back, giving his wrinkle-free face a strict impression.

"Look at this, kiddo." He pulled out his remote control and switched on the hidden plasma screen on the opposite paneled wall. I hopped on the polished table, minding the letter holder in the shape of a pitchfork, and peered at the images scrolling on the screen: candles spread across a stone floor next to countless unmoving bodies. The picture changed to a newspaper report blaming faith and a belief in the end of the world for a rise in suicides.

I shook my head. "So?"

"Of course, you wouldn't know." Dad groaned and switched off the screen. "I keep forgetting you're not old enough to understand what's happening out there." Dad started drumming his fingers on the table. "In my time, I was a feared man. Nowadays, mortals no longer believe I even exist."

"Why do you want them to fear you? They'll find out you exist soon enough."

"You don't understand, Cassie." He ran a hand through his thick, black locks I used to admire for hours as a child. "It's not the same once they're dead. Their lack of interest in my existence makes me feel insignificant."

Frowning, I inched closer. Was he depressed? Did he have a midlife crisis? Mom hinted something last time I visited her in Heaven, but the bright light gave me a headache, made worse by the constant choir music, so I didn't really pay attention to her chatter. I realized I should've. I laughed nervously. "Well, there's nothing you can do about it, so why don't you just forget it? Or even better, talk to a therapist."

"See, that's where you're wrong." Dad's lips curled into a huge smile, white teeth flashing as he pulled out a brown folder from a drawer and tossed it toward me. I caught it in mid-air, wondering whether he had come up with the idea of causing a few more catastrophes until mortals started to take him seriously again.

"What's this?" I peered at the folder, but didn't open it.

"That, my beloved daughter, is the answer to our problems."

Who said I had a problem? "And that would be?"

Dad laughed, eyes glinting. "Take a look."

I wasn't keen on it, but I opened the folder and skim the papers nonetheless, my eyes almost falling out of my head. Not literally, of course. "An advertising campaign is your big plan? You can't be serious."

"Why not?" His smile vanished. I had to tread carefully here. If he was depressed, thrashing his hopes might not be the best attempt at therapy.

My brain kicked into gear as I tried to come up with the least upsetting answer. Where did I even begin? "Because advertising is employed to sell a product. What exactly are you selling? A week of all-inclusive torture?"

He inclined his head. "You don't think that's an attractive offer?"

I threw my hands up. "Dad! This is a bad idea. You don't have a product or service. You don't need advertising, PR more likely. Why don't you hire a PR guru to *raise awareness*, improve your image, or whatever it is that you want to achieve?"

"Mm." He nodded, considering my advice for a moment. "I like that. I'll have both, advertising and PR. I'm thinking huge billboards and lots of media coverage."

43

I rolled my eyes because he didn't get anything I said. What was the point in explaining anyway when he was stubborn like a mule?

"How are you going to get the media coverage, Dad? It's not like journalists will queue out the door to interview you, will they?" He laughed as though I'd just recited the joke of the century. I narrowed my gaze, my sixth sense telling me he was up to something. "What's so funny?"

He kept guffawing; a tear ran down his cheek. I'd heard of bipolar disorder. Maybe, after years in this heat, he had turned bipolar, sobbing one moment, and suffering from hysteria the next. I waited until he'd calmed down enough to speak. "You should've just seen your face. Sorry." He cleared his throat. "The job's perfect for you to get accustomed with the family business."

"What?" I gaped. He couldn't be saying what I was thinking. Clearly, he didn't just suffer from bipolar disorder; he was also delusional.

Dad squeezed my shoulder. "Don't worry, we're not making you a mere *employee*. You're going to be the *project manager*. You will be running the whole operation, planning, implementing and evaluating our progress. How about that? Isn't that exciting?"

I was still gaping. How could he possibly think making Hell popular was exciting? "That's—" I scanned the floor, searching for words.

"No need to thank me. You've earned it. All the hard work's paid off, eh, kiddo?" He raised his brows, face glowing with pride. "I was thinking we could call it, *Looking for Fire, Thrills and Excitement? Why The Hell NOT?* Inventive, I know."

"More like corny," I mumbled. "Listen, what makes you think I have the necessary qualifications to bring your little project to fruition?" I regarded him intently as he bobbed his head slightly, the tiny glint from before returning.

"Well, you're smart and you know a lot about humans since you've chosen to live among them." He paused, grimacing for a moment. "Granted, I wasn't happy about it for a long time, but I see your point now. And, lastly, you work for that company."

"Skylife?"

He nodded.

I frowned because I couldn't make sense of his logic. "How does being with Skylife qualify me to lead a huge propaganda campaign?"

Dad shrugged. "You sell stuff to customers."

"I don't *sell* stuff," I yelled. "Dad, how many times do I have to tell you, working in customer service involves answering questions, not persuading someone to part with their money." I jumped from the table and walked to the window to put some space between us. The geysers outside spewed hot water into the sizzling air.

"I'm sorry. I keep forgetting." He looked so earnest I instantly regretted my outburst. The truth was, even after so many centuries he was still excited about the whole Hell business and would've been better off having a child who shared the same enthusiasm. I wished I could make him proud the way he deserved. For a moment, silence ensued between us and we avoided each other's gaze. Dad talked first. "You don't have to—"

This was my chance to repay him for all he'd done for me. I couldn't care less about Hell's popularity and brand recognition, but if it meant so much to him I'd do whatever it took to help him. Inching closer, I grabbed his hand, interrupting him. "It'd be my pleasure."

"You sure, Cassie?" His lips twitched as though he didn't dare hope.

I nodded. "I'd love to be your project manager."

"When you're done we'll promote you to second-in-command."

Laughing, I rolled my eyes. "Now, don't get too excited. I haven't finished my apprenticeship yet."

"About time you did," Dad said.

I didn't respond because I couldn't be bothered to trigger yet another argument. "When do I start?"

"Now. I'll send someone over to pack your bags." He didn't even blink as he opened the folder again, reading through the bullet points. "I've thought about a few companies we could hire for the billboards. You might want to give them a call and get a quote."

"Whoa!" I held up my hands. "Pack my bags? I can't move back here." What about Dallas, my job and the life I'd built for myself? He couldn't expect me to leave everything behind.

Dad peered at me; our gazes locked in that fierce yet silent battle that'd been going on between us ever since I realized he might seem intimidating, but that was just his job. In real life, he liked to let his hair down like everyone else.

"If something comes up, I can't afford not being able to get hold of you," Dad said.

I shook my head. "That's not going to happen. You always know where I am."

Dad cocked a brow. "I might consider getting rid of Kinky and that tiny angel. You know how much you always complain about them."

Kinky squirmed on my shoulder, but kept quiet as he always did in Dad's presence. I could sense his nervousness though. Apart from the job of being a companion, there wasn't much else a personal demon could do. Given Dad's reputation for getting rid of surplus baggage, who wouldn't start sweating? As much as I was tired of Kinky's antics, I wouldn't want him to *disappear*. Besides, he might just decide to spill the beans about Dallas. This was my chance to instill some much-needed respect into him.

"You'd get rid of them both?" I tapped a finger against my lips. "That's a temping offer." From the corner of my eye, I watched Kinky's eyes turn as big as saucers.

"Do we have a deal then?" Dad held out his hand.

I grabbed it and gave it a quick squeeze. "I'm moving back in for a week tops, and I'll keep Kinky for the time being. Let's see how he fares."

I left with the promise of moving my things that afternoon and arrived home to Dallas's still unpacked boxes cluttering the hall.

He gave me a peck on the cheek. "I missed you."

"Sorry I took so long."

"Water under the bridge." He smiled. "See, we have a lot in common. We even use the same expressions."

Forcing my lips into a grin, I pulled him on the sofa, unsure how to tell him I might be away for a while. Putting distance between us wasn't going to do our relationship any favors.

"What's wrong?" Dallas cupped my face, inching closer until our noses almost touched.

47

I took a deep breath, meeting his gaze. The warmth in his golden eyes sent shivers down my spine, my immortal body felt weak and dizzy. "I have to leave."

He blinked. "What?"

My heart sank. "I'm so sorry."

A thin line formed on his forehead. "Okay, I admit skipping the dating part was my idea, but I didn't agree on skipping the whole 'living together' thing."

"We're not skipping it."

He snorted. "Could've fooled me."

"A family emergency has come up. My father needs me to stay with him for a while."

"Oh, Cass. I'm so sorry. Is he okay?" He sounded so concerned, I felt bad for lying to him.

"Yes, he's fine. It's just the family business needs me. We might lose everything if I don't go down there and fix it."

Dallas nodded. "Sure, I understand. Do what you have to do. Family's everything. Besides, we can still see each other every day."

I hesitated. Leading the type of campaign Dad envisioned might take all my time, particularly since I had no idea what I was doing and needed to learn as I moved along.

"You probably don't know but I give killer back rubs, you know, to help you deal with all that stress," Dallas continued.

That sounded like divine. But visiting Hell? Unless he pierced a dagger into his heart, or someone like me took him down there, that wasn't going to happen. I squirmed. "It's not that easy."

"Why not? You don't want your father to meet me? I know I was sweating up a storm at the restaurant. It was a volcano in there. I promise not to sweat all over your dad."

I giggled inwardly. The poor lad could never handle Hell where it was a million times hotter. I shook my head. "It's not that."

"What then? Are you afraid of hopelessly falling in love with me?" He cocked a brow and pulled me closer. "You want to tell me, Cass. I can see it in your eyes. No one can resist my charms. Now, tell me the real reason."

How could I defy that confident smile? Or perseverance. "We're going to California."

"Oh." A shadow crossed his features, his forehead creased into a frown. "How long are we talking, babe?"

"A while."

He ran a hand through his hair and paused for a moment, as if pondering, avoiding my gaze. "There's email, video chat, telephones, and texting. We'll stay in touch. I'm not letting the most fantastic thing in my life get away."

I opened my mouth to speak when Kinky let out an exaggerated sigh. *He'll find someone else in a heartbeat.*

"No, he won't," I hissed.

"What?" Dallas asked.

I smiled. "Nothing."

A hottie like him? Kinky smacked his tongue.

He'll be faithful, Pinky said.

Don't listen to him. All he knows about mortals is what he's been spoon-fed on a fluffy, white cloud.

As usual, Kinky's argument made sense. He might not be the most congenial being, but he knew human nature better than an angel who used to spend most of his time

49

cheering along with Carry Grant while watching movies from the fifties. We barely knew each other but somehow, the idea of being away from Dallas wasn't an appealing one.

"Cass?" Dallas asked, giving my hand a squeeze. "Are you okay? Listen, babe, we have something so special...something that sizzles. We both can't deny it." My attention snapped back to him. He continued, "No other girl has ever taken my breath away like you have. Leaving before things have even properly started sucks. But you go do what you have to do. Your family depends on you. I promise I'll be waiting right here for you."

I took in his broad shoulders and toned quadriceps. Yeah, right. He'd find someone else in no time. "Want to come with me?" I blurted out before I could stop myself.

He laughed. "What?"

I shrugged. "It was just an idea."

"Sounds like a good one. I thought you'd never ask. California, here we come."

"I hope you like it *hot*."

"Are you kidding?" He jumped up like an excited kid, making my heart skip a beat. "The hotter the better. I can't wait to catch up on my tan."

"Pack plenty of suntan lotion...and your darkest pair of shades."

My pulse spiked as he inched closer and wrapped his arm around my waist, pulling me to his chest. I buried my head in the crevice of his armpit, breathing in the musky scent of his deodorant.

"When are we leaving?" Dallas asked.

"Tonight." I groaned inwardly because now we'd really have to fly to California to make this journey look authentic. I wished I could just tell him who I was and what we were doing, but there was no way in Hell he'd understand. So I beamed at him and jumped up, dragging him to his feet. "Come one. We've got lots of packing to do."

Chapter 6 – Disneyworld

"Ladies and gentlemen," the pilot announced through the intercom. "Thank you for flying Southwest Flight 156 to Los Angeles. We'll be landing shortly. I hope everyone had a pleasant journey. The weather here's ninety degrees, so make sure you get out your shades. Have a wonderful day and thank you for flying with us."

Dallas pushed his sunglasses down the brim of his nose. "California here we come." I laughed. He looked so adorable with that giant grin on his face.

The flight attendant's voice echoed through the aircraft, "Folks, please gather all of your belongings as you exit the plane. If you do leave something behind, please ensure it's something we want. And one last note, no leaving small children or ugly spouses."

Dallas chuckled.

The plane jerked and I hit my head against the seat. Were we landing or were we being shot down? I turned to face Dallas and pointed to his seat belt. "Fasten up tighter, babe, because it's going to be a very *bumpy* ride."

"Bring it on." Dallas flashed me his carefree grin, all white teeth gleaming.

My lips pressed together in a line. He had no idea what I was really talking about. A bumpy ride didn't even begin to describe my whacky family.

* * *

Sitting on the bed in a cheap motel in Los Angeles, I wondered what I'd been thinking dragging Dallas into my affairs. Since our flight landed two hours ago, I'd been brainstorming ways to smuggle Dallas into Hell without his knowing, but I had yet to come up with something useful.

Knock him over the head and drag him in there by his hair, Kinky suggested.

Pinky tsked. *Neanderthal.*

I ignored them because I just realized I had another problem I didn't consider while extending my invitation: how was I going to explain Dallas's arrival to Dad? What happened to my resolution to keep his existence a secret until I knew for sure our relationship was going somewhere? As usual, my big mouth had to speak before my lazy brain kicked into motion. It was too late to change plans now, so I'd have to find a way to prep Dad before he blew my cover and Dallas found out he dated Lucifer's daughter.

I knocked on the bathroom door. "Dallas? Are you remodeling the bathroom?" He'd been in there for ages. What took him so long?

"Just a second," he yelled back.

I returned to my place on the bed and started tapping my fingers on the brown covers. No one ever made me wait. He was lucky we had a connection, otherwise I might've been inclined to make him aware of this tiny detail in a rather unpleasant way. Like kicking the door open and pulling him out of there and into the scorching depths of my father's abode.

Ten long minutes later, he finally made his entrance, dressed in faded blue jeans, and a black shirt, showing off his muscles. His usual leather jacket was draped over his arm. A dog tag adorned his wrist. Why it took him an hour to slip into his attire was beyond me. While I found he looked absolutely hot, I doubted Dad would be particularly keen on the rocker style. He ran a hand through his dark, shaggy hair, making my heart melt.

Dallas stopped in front of me, brows drawn. I raised my brows. What was he waiting for?

"Well?" He held out his hands. "How do I look?"

"You're wearing that?" I pointed at the tight shirt.

"Well, yeah. It's my best outfit. I thought it'd make sense to keep it informal, but not too casual."

Not too casual? I laughed. "Great. Now can we go?" Dad had given me ten minutes and I was turning up twenty-four hours later. He'd be barking mad.

"Do you think I should change into something else?"

"No, you're fine. You'll make quite the impression, trust me." I jumped up and grabbed my phone when he pulled me close against his chest.

"I hope so," he whispered, touching my cheek. "You look beautiful."

This was it, the moment of our first kiss. Our gazes locked, blood rushed to my cheeks. My breathing caught in my throat. Before I could decide whether to try my latent abilities at mind manipulation and force his lips onto mine, he let go of me.

"I'm sorry. You know I want to kiss you more than anything, but I wouldn't want to be the reason why you're late. I want your dad to like me," Dallas said. "Settle for an IOU?"

Funny that he shouldn't want to be the reason for our lateness when he had just spent more than an hour in the bathroom to get ready. I turned to the door to hide my disappointment. The same moment, an idea popped into my head.

The rental car was parked across the street. Dallas held the door open for me as I jumped onto the driver's seat, and we speed through the mid-morning traffic, heading southeast.

"Have you been here before?" I asked, even though I imagined knowing the answer. Dallas was a born and bred Brit. I doubted he'd seen much beyond Scotland.

"I spent three months backpacking through the US, then another one in Canada. What about you?"

I daren't avert my gaze from the heavy traffic. "I've been to a few places. My father's always emphasized the importance of seeing the world." It wasn't a lie. Dad always said nothing was more important than being accustomed with your potential customers, which is why he had forced me to visit what he called the greatest battlefields on earth: from the Austria-Ottoman Wars in 1529, the Spanish Conquest of Peru in 1532, and the Napoleonic Wars in 1815. Throw in a few police chases and the odd suicide, and I'd basically seen it all.

"We have so much in common, we'll get on like a house on fire." Dallas made it sound like a joke, but I could sense the nervous undercurrents.

I leaned over and patted his knee. "Don't worry. He'll love you." I wished I could believe it, but truth was I'd never brought a boyfriend home before, let alone a mortal one. So, I had no idea how Dad would react.

"Is that Disneyworld?" Dallas pointed at the white towers in the distance.

"That's Cinderella's Castle." I craned my neck, wishing I could see more than just the towers, even though I had seen it a million times. The fairy tale castle located at the middle of the park was beyond magical, with beautiful, white walls, tiny windows and lots of sparkle. As a little girl I always dreamed of living in a place like that.

"What are we doing in Disneyworld?" The frown on Dallas's face told me he didn't share my enthusiasm.

I cleared my throat. "He lives there."

"You're pulling my leg. Does he work there?"

"He's a—" I hesitated, wishing I had made a list of plausible answers to possible questions. "He's managing the place."

"He runs Disneyworld?"

"Yep. Not bad, huh?" I cringed at how far-fetched my lie sounded. Who in their right mind would believe it?

Dallas fell silent. I peered over at him and noticed the scowl. Not good. Now he thought he was inadequate, lacking in the financial and educational department. Boy, what would he do when he found out I was an immortal queen destined to rule over Hell for the next billion years or so?

"He started as a cleaner and worked his way up," I said, realizing this lie sounded even more improbable than managing Disneyworld.

"Is Dad happy you're working in customer service?"

His question took me by surprise. I shrugged. "More or less. He thinks it's just a passing fancy until I join the family—" I stopped myself before I said more. "Let's just say Dad hopes I'll join the company."

"I suppose Dad wants you to join the team and skip the higher education."

"Something like that." I slowed down the car as we rolled into a parking lot. My fingers snapped the flip phone open as I kept his attention focused on me so he won't notice me opening the portal. "Is that what you envision for yourself?"

Dallas hesitated. "I don't know. Life's too exciting. There's so many things to see and do before I die."

Tanned people wearing Bermuda shorts and sweaty cotton tops were gathered in small groups, ambling toward the ticket admission in the distance. A few lingered around their vehicles, chatting or arguing. With my immortal eyes, I could see the door to the portal swirling around in a blur of bright colors. The air all around us smelled cleaned and crisp, like after a thunderstorm. Good thing humans couldn't see 'my gateway to Hell' with the naked eye. That certainly helped made the whole affair authentic, or so I thought until a loved up couple came dangerously close to the tiny particles. The air flickered, ready to suck them right in.

Oh, crap. I jumped out of the car and motioned Dallas to hurry up. We needed to get moving before someone passed through by accident and realized they might have bitten more than they could chew when they signed up for visiting *Disneyworld's Phantom Revenge* theme.

"Let's go." I locked the car and grabbed Dallas's arm, pulling him into the invisible shield a few inches away.

The strong energy crackled around us. I heard his gasp as we were drawn into the underworld. The temperature rose a few degrees; a hot gust hit us in the face. All moisture seemed to have evaporated from the atmosphere. No way would Dallas not notice the sudden and drastic change from concrete and chattering crowds to dirty ground and boulders everywhere. Although it pained me to spin yet more deceit between us, I whipped out my phone and punched in the order to knock him out.

My phone vibrated. An instant later, Dallas dropped to the ground. Kneeling next to him, I grabbed a bottle of water out of my purse and poured some over his face. His eyes blinked open, his hand wandered to his head. "What happened?"

I brushed his hair out of his eyes. "You fainted."

Sitting up, he peeled his shirt from his chest, fanning air as he looked around. "Last thing I remember is being outside of Disneyworld by the ticket booth. Where did everyone else go?"

This was the hardest part. If I made a big deal out of it, he might see through my bluff.

I gripped his hand. "I'm so sorry. We were taking the staff-only entrance where no visitors are allowed. You said you felt lightheaded, but followed me along the path, and then you just dropped. Are you okay?"

He smiled. "Of course I am. How about we keep my fainting episode between us?"

"My lips are sealed."

He rose to his feet. The confused look on his face betrayed he wasn't quite convinced though as he peered around him at nothing but boulders and dead trees. "We're going to have to stop at the gift shop and pick up one of those fan spray bottles. You know, the ones all the tourists carry around the theme parks. I didn't realize it was this hot today."

Yet another delay wasn't an option. I'd just key it into my phone and let it magically appear. Smiling, I nodded. "It's awful, isn't it? Imagine living here forever."

"I couldn't stand it."

"See why I left?" I could slap my forehead for my blunder. I was supposed to sell this place to him, make him want to spend the week here with me. "Look at the bright side, at least you'd never have to worry about heating bills."

He snorted. "Trust me, air conditioning isn't cheaper."

I pulled him around the huge characteristic boulders blocking the narrow path, which were called The Boulders of Hell on Dragon's Path—the only entrance on this dimension. The sun stood high on the pale blue horizon streaked with bands of red and orange. The earth glimmered red, a few flames leapt up from the ground. I hurried to stomp on them before Dallas noticed. The scarce trees adorning the narrow trail looked like black rubber, devoid of leaves, the dry bark was scorched in several places.

"You should really have your dad invest in some fertilizer," Dallas said.

"I'll get right on that." Nothing was growing in this place except my frustration of how I was going to pull this number off.

A few voices carried over from the left, where a large stone blocked our view of the forking street. Dallas stopped to listen, but his hearing wasn't good enough to make out the words.

A fox with beady red eyes darted past us. I jumped into Dallas's line of vision, but it was too late.

"What was that?" Dallas asked.

I shrugged. "Just the local wildlife."

"It had red eyes, Cass. I think it was foaming at the mouth, probably from rabies."

"I'm glad you worry about me. It's sweet, but I'm a big girl. I'll have Dad send out animal control." I touched his face. "Now, wait here. Okay? I'll be right back. Just need to tell the guards we're here."

He shook his head. "I wouldn't want anything happening to you."

I rolled my eyes. "Dad's the big boss, remember? He'll take care of it." Since he was the devil and all, which I didn't add because there was no point in spooking the poor guy when we had barely begun dating.

"If you're not back in five, I'm coming after you."

"Sounds like a deal." I smiled and rose on my toes to meet him halfway for a peck on the cheek. His lips brushed the corner of my mouth. An electric jolt rushed down my spine, making my skin tingle.

Peeking over my shoulder to make sure Dallas wasn't following, I dashed for the demons, hoping they were clever enough to take my threat of torture at face value for a change rather than question my authority and mess with me. Trouble was, the high ranked ones weren't particularly keen on my authority so they tended to challenge my position and push their boundaries, being only loyal to my dad.

Uh-uh, trouble ahead, Kinky said.

"What? Why?" I whispered when my gaze fell on one of the demons.

Oh, no, Pinky wailed. *You're going to be in so much trouble. For the sake of your loving parents, I wish you'd stop falling for the bad guys.*

Kinky snorted. *Puuuuhlease! In Hell, he's quite the catch.*

"Thrain!" I waved and he turned, shooting me an easy-going smile. There was a time when I fancied his green eyes, dark hair and toned body—until Dad found out I tried to date one of his shape shifters. He assigned Thrain to the lowest level of Hell and sent me to spend a few freezing weeks in the Himalayas to explore other options. I was ready to use that as an argument if Dad challenged my relationship with Dallas.

Thrain whooshed the chirping Levion demon away. The thin, green spirit bowed, eyes darting across the ground, as he skipped from one leg to the other. I was glad it wasn't a Beleth because Beleths were quite the talkative kind, and Dad would be hearing about my meeting with Thrain in a heartbeat. Beleths were also notorious for sucking up to Dad, eager to get his approval to climb up Hell's social ladder, so they liked to embellish the truth.

"Girl, you're a sight for sore eyes." Thrain grabbed my arm and pulled me to his chest, a dangerous glint playing in his eyes. He was up for fun, which made me feel guilty, even more so since my boyfriend stood a few feet away. So all the rumors flying around this place were true? I didn't believe them for a minute."

Keeping my distance, I nodded. "Yep, here I am in the flesh."

"And looking as hot as ever."

"Take it down a notch, will ya? You might piss off my new friend."

He cocked a brow. "Really? Is she as hot as you?"

"You'll meet *him* soon enough. Now if you could just go ahead and make sure no one's around when we pass through, I'd really appreciate it."

His jaw dropped. "Him?"

Was he jealous? I didn't think he was serious enough to get emotionally involved. I regarded his tattered jeans and disheveled hair. Pinky was right, I had a tendency to fall for bad boys. "How come you're back?"

He shrugged. "It was just a matter of time until Lucifer realized he couldn't possibly run this place without his best tracker."

I giggled. "I always thought you were better than *Google Maps*."

"Yes, you did, gorgeous." He moistened his lips, the tip of his tongue leaving a wet trail behind. I peered at it, and then away, embarrassed. Shouldn't that connection with Dallas make me stop noticing other people, particularly hot ex boyfriends? Maybe Dallas and I needed to seal it with a handshake or a first kiss, or something.

"Cass? Are you okay there?" Dallas yelled.

"Just a minute."

Thrain sniffed the air, amused. "You brought a mortal? I hope it's just personal luggage."

I ran a hand through my hair, wondering again whether he was jealous. "Nope. It's the real deal."

"With fluffy clouds, roses, symphonies and all?" Thrain whistled. "That's going to be one Shakespeare tragedy. I'd better book my seat in advance."

I slapped his arm. "Shut it, mate. Dallas and I will be very happy together."

He nodded, unconvinced. "I'm thrilled for you. So, tell me, does your dad know?"

I winced. "Not exactly."

"Does he even know the guy's trudging along?"

"Still working on it." Why all the interrogation? Then I remembered. Thrain might be a shape shifter and Dad's best tracker, but he was also a chaos demon, fallen just like Dad, so he was bound to have a flair for the dramatic, soak up tension where he could get it. I frowned. "Can you get your kick somewhere else?"

Thrain laughed. "It wasn't meant that way."

"Really?" I raised my brows.

"Want me to warm your dad up for you?"

I shook my head. "This is my battle. Just make sure the road's free."

"No problem." He winked. "We wouldn't want to frighten the poor boy."

Dallas wasn't a *boy*. Technically, he hadn't yet reached drinking age in the US, but half of the population hadn't. It wasn't a big deal.

"Get moving, or I swear I'll send you back to that place Dad had in mind for you." I pushed his shoulder as hard as I could. He barely budged from the spot.

"You know he would've eventually gotten used to the idea of us dating," Thrain whispered.

I stared at him, speechless for a moment. I knew where he was heading, and I didn't like it one bit. "Dad was right. You and I would never work out. You'll find the one meant for you."

He bowed slowly, an amused glint playing in his gaze. "Fair enough, Princess. If things don't work out with the boy over there, you know where to find me."

I nodded and watched him walk away, his shoulders straight, his leather coat swaying slightly in the scorching heat. There was a time when I would've given anything to hear those words, but now I only sighed and hurried back to Dallas, who was still waiting behind the huge boulders.

Chapter 7 - Hot as Hell

Dallas leaned against a twisted tree, drenched in sweat. His face showed red, ugly blotches, his eyes shone unnaturally bright. If I didn't know any better, I'd swear he was coming down with malaria. I shouldn't have left him in Hell's scorching heat, without a water bottle and at least half a dozen wet towels to cool his mortal body. I bit my lip hard. His suffering made my heart sink. It was all my fault.

"We'll get you inside," I whispered.

"Who's 'we'?" He laughed and wiped his soaked sleeve over his face. A moment later, wet pearls gathered again above his brows.

Oops. Another slip up. I was so used to Pinky and Kinky at my side, I always included them. "No one." Eager to change the subject, I pointed around the cairn formation. "We're almost there."

Dallas groaned but grabbed my hand in a clammy grip, following me as I pulled him along the trail. "Remind me never to even consider moving to California."

"It's not that bad."

He snorted. "Probably not if you're stuck at a floating pool bar, guzzling down ice-cold drinks with a soft breeze swaying your hair. I don't see that happening any time soon though."

I glanced at his crumpled shirt, wishing I had advised him to pack a change of clothes. Now I couldn't just beam over his baggage and pretend someone had couriered it over. Too many weird things had happened already. Maybe I'd find something else for him to wear before he met Dad in this damp attire.

"I could've saved myself the hour in the bathroom, huh?" Dallas said.

"Now that you're pointing it out, you're absolutely right." I shrugged. "You'd look awesome wrapped in a plastic bag with a tiara on your head."

He grinned. "I love spending time with you. You know that, right?"

My pulse gained in speed, my mouth turned dry. I nodded. "That's why we're here, to find out whether what we have is real."

"I don't doubt it for a minute. Do you?"

I winked. "Not yet." I took a step forward, hoping he got the hint. If Dad approved of our relationship instead of forwarding both of us to opposite sides of the world, we'd have to seal this deal once and for all. Since Auntie never mentioned how, I figured a kiss might be my best bet.

Dallas peered down at me, his eyes searching mine. I started counting the golden speckles, getting lost in their number. His lips inched closer until our noses almost meet. My stomach clenched and that feeling of floating outside my body returned. I held my breath, waiting for his lips to graze mine. Why was he delaying the inevitable?

My hand moved up his chest as I whispered, "Dallas." He smiled but didn't make a move.

"You must really be used to this heat. You're not sweating a drop," he said.

So much for our undying love and finally settling it all with a kiss. "Women don't sweat, they glow."

"It's hot like Hell. I'm sweating buckets."

A giant, blinking neon sign flashed in my head. Talking of Hell reminded me where we were. I might never get him out alive if we didn't strengthen our bond to show Dad our relationship was serious. Dallas meant well by wanting to make our first kiss special, but I figured he'd seize any opportunity available if he just knew what was at stake.

"I don't mind," I whispered. "As long as we're together nothing could bother me." My last attempt at signaling Dallas I wanted to be kissed ended in him peering at me, embarrassed. The magic was broken anyway, so I headed for Dad's four-story mansion carved into the red mountain cliff. Like a fata morgana, the air around it seemed to vibrate from the unbearable heat. We reached the tiny patch of front garden with its withered bushes and stone borders. The dry and cracked ground could've easily passed for the Sahara Desert. Smoke and steam rose from the zigzagging fissures, giving the impression of a snaking cobra.

The wrought iron gate squeaked when I pushed it open. Dad got a laugh out of that every time and refused to fix it. He liked the creepy factor. "This is where I grew up. Home, sweet home."

Dallas stared at the gothic Transylvanian castle, shimmering in red sandstone. The towers, spires, and colonnades glittered in the sun against the glaring blue sky. Specks of light danced off the giant stain-glass windows. "It reminds me a bit of *The Haunted Mansion*, right here in Disneyworld."

I laughed. Yeah, my dad loved the classical grandeur of Gothic. "Dad still thinks he's a kid. The creators had a blast designing this place. Since he borders a little on the eccentric side, he put on all the bells and whistles."

Dallas nodded, seemingly impressed. "You don't have a resident dragon living inside, do you?"

"Nope, but I had a hound until he grew almost as big as a room and started eating the furniture." I grinned, even though it was the truth.

"Can't wait to see this place at night." His gaze shifted to the monstrous stone gargoyles perched on each side of the steps. Whispers echoed in the air. I ran a hand across my lips for the guardians to zip it. They did, but not before Dallas jumped back.

"What's wrong?" I asked.

"Its eye opened! I swear it did."

I rolled my eyes and vowed to kick the demons into next week for scaring my boyfriend. "Did its wings start flapping too? Or did smoke come out of its mouth? It's only stone, babe. Let's get you something to drink. The heat's messing with your brain."

He let out a breath. "I must be making a terrible first impression. First, I faint, and now I'm seeing things. You must think I'm crazy."

I winked. "Never." If anyone was crazy, it was me—for bringing him here.

Grabbing his hand, I pulled him across the drawbridge. Dallas gazed down at the moat of flowing red lava. "Now that's a river."

"Don't get too close. The crocs bite."

"The special effects are beyond amazing. I wonder where the projector is."

"If I told you, the magic would be gone."

He smiled and pulled me closer. "When I'm with you, the magic's always here."

My heels clicked on the cobbled path as we made our way to the large double door. I grabbed the massive brass knobs and pushed the heavy wood panel open to reveal the hall with its marble floor, crystal candelabras and candleholders in every corner—and, most importantly, air conditioning.

Dallas hovered in the doorway so I said, "Come in. Don't be shy."

"Your dad sure likes candlelight, huh?"

I shrugged. "Not really, but I do. I had the house redecorated as soon as I could walk."

"You're officially hired to decorate our home," Dallas said.

Our home? He must be joking. Either that, or things were moving very fast. I certainly didn't mind. From the corner of my eye, I noticed Dallas wasn't smiling.

"I'd like that," I said, squeezing his hand.

"The air's cooler here. I feel already a thousand times better." He turned to face me, sending my stomach into somersaults. His gaze focused on my lips as he ran a finger down my cheek. I could hear his heart racing, drumming against his burly chest.

"Cass?" Dad's voice carried through the silence, making me jump a step back. Why wasn't he working? Torturing the next best sinner, or whining about how little respect mortals seemed to pay him nowadays?

"Wait in the library, okay? I need to change first," I yelled, pulling Dallas up the stairs to my room. I locked the door behind us and dropped on the bed with him next to me. "Why don't you take a shower while I get you a glass of water?" I pointed at the bathroom door. He nodded and left.

I got up again and headed downstairs in search of clothes for Dallas. Luckily, he was about the same size as Dad, maybe a few pounds lighter, so I figured there had to be plenty of stuff that fit him. I sneaked into Dad's walk-in dressing room and skimmed through the pants and shirts, then returned to my room with my find and a glass of water filled to the brim with ice cubes from the kitchen.

After the scorching heat Dallas had endured, I assumed he wasn't coming out of that shower anytime soon. Who could blame him? It suited me just fine since it gave me the perfect opportunity to catch a moment alone with Dad. I left everything on the dresser and joined Dad in the library.

"Dad?" Even though the door was open, I knocked on the wood to get his attention in case he hadn't noticed me.

He turned slowly, eyeing me up and down. "You said you needed to change. Where's your suit?"

"Couldn't be bothered. We need to talk." I sat on his desk, crossing my legs, the way I always did.

"Your mother used to fall for the wrong ones too."

"What?" I blinked, unsure whether I'd heard him right. Did he just mention Mom? And how did he find about my secret boyfriend? I guessed nothing slipped past his eyes.

Dad shook his head. "Never mind. Let's talk."

He knew. I could see it in his green eyes and the serious expression on his face. "Did Thrain spill the beans?"

"Thrain knows?" A shadow crossed Dad's features. "When did you two talk?"

Dad might be the devil and a master of disguise, but I could see right through his lie. "I saw him on my way here. And now I'm going to give him one swift kick that'll land him in Egypt or Africa. If he thinks what you did to him is bad, he has yet to see me in action."

"That's my girl." Dad leaned back, smiling. "He didn't tell me. I wish you'd stop underestimating your old father. I know everything, Cass."

I narrowed my gaze. "You're still watching me?"

"Of course I am. Do you honestly think I'd let my only child walk on Earth without constant supervision?"

"I won't have it." I shook my head. "Everyone has a right to privacy."

"That's not what this meeting is about though, is it?" Dad took a deep breath. "We agreed if you wanted to see someone regularly, you'd run it past me first."

I smirked. "You said if I wanted to date any of *your* guys blah, blah, blah."

"So you chose a mortal, and the best part is you brought him here to meet me." His tone was nonchalant, matter-of-fact. I didn't expect him to remain so calm.

I raised my chin defiantly. My temper threatened to flare any minute. "Dallas isn't just anyone. We have a bond."

Dad rose slowly, palms pressed against the polished desk. "You're talking about that wicked connection spawn by Fate herself in order to mess up everyone's life?" He scoffed. "Trust me, it doesn't mean a thing. As much as you want it to, it won't work, Cassie. So you'd better get out while it doesn't hurt so much."

Wrath choked up my throat. I narrowed my gaze. "How would you know?"

"Been there, done that."

"When?" He must be lying, which made me angry because, in spite of his reputation as a major trickster, Dad had never lied to me before.

He hesitated. "Been a while."

"When?" I leaned forward, staring at him.

"Before your time." He was avoiding a straight answer.

"Even before Mom?" Silence. "You're hiding something. Spit it out, Dad," I hissed. He couldn't be talking about Mom, or why else would he keep quiet about it?

"It's not important," Dad said, scowling.

"I want to know."

"Because you're curious."

I sneered. "I wonder who passed this particular trait onto me. Now that's a good question."

"Cass, just drop it. Please."

"I'll bug you until you tell me. Don't count on me forgetting because I won't. If you don't, I swear I'll join Mom and the seraphim troop in Heaven."

He sighed and dropped into his leather chair, gaze fixing on the fiery-red mountains in the distance. "It hurts to talk about it."

Changing tactics wasn't going to work its magic on me. "The sooner you open up, the better for your healing process."

Dad smiled. "No sympathy for your old man, then?"

I grinned. "None whatsoever."

"Okay, but you've been warned so don't blame me if you can't handle it." He took a sip of his sugary afternoon coffee.

Drumming my fingers against the smooth surface of his desk, I wondered whether I actually wanted him to reveal his secret. Of course there were other women before Mom, and some were yet to enter his life, but the knowledge didn't make the thought any easier to bear. Even though it had been years since my parents split up I still dreamed of a reconciliation, or at least a few hours without fighting.

"On the day I was sent down here, I met this beautiful woman. Five minutes with her and I knew she was the one," Dad said.

Just like me with Dallas. Dad had felt the bond...the connection. Leaning forward, I listened intently, because it was cute. I still wished he were talking about Mom though. "You were in love. What happened?"

Dad moistened his lips, his eyes glazed over as though he was in deep thought, reliving his past. "I tried to get a date for years, but she kept blowing me off."

"Your charm didn't work on her?" I laughed. "That's a first."

Dad nodded. "Still doesn't."

"You're still seeing her?" Did he cheat on Mom during all those years they were together?

"Not as often as I'd like to," Dad said.

"You—" My eyes threw daggers. I was lost for words. "You were thinking about her when you were with Mom. I'm going to tell her." I jumped up, knocking over his cup. The black liquid spilled onto Dad's papers. With an irritated flick of his hand, the stains disappeared, leaving behind white paper and no traces of what just happened.

"No, Cassie. It's not like that." Dad grabbed my hands, pulling me to face him. "Please, let sleeping dogs lie."

"She knows?" I don't believe it. No wonder she couldn't get fast enough out of Hell."

Dad avoided my gaze again. "You could say that."

In that case I'd rather not remind her and risk making her more upset, but that didn't mean I couldn't use the knowledge to my advantage. "I propose a deal. I'll keep quiet and you give Dallas a chance."

"Cass, you know I couldn't possibly agree. He's mortal; your time together is short. I don't want you to suffer when he grows old and dies."

I waved my hand around. "You're worried, got it. Now let's get back to business. I promise I won't tell Mom if you vow to like and accept Dallas."

"How could I when I don't even know him?"

I shrugged. "Who cares? Spend some time with him. Make him feel welcome. If he takes off because of something you do or say, I won't ever forgive you."

Dad laughed, eyes glinting. "You'll make an excellent second-in-command."

"So you keep saying." I rolled my eyes. "Promise, Dad."

He nodded. "All right. You have my word. I'll treat Dallas like I'd treat my own son."

Given Dad's constant pressure on me to do as he said, I wasn't sure treating Dallas like he was part of the family was a good thing. "Just don't go overboard."

"Done." Dad peered around. "Well, where did you hide him? Bring the boy over so we can start bonding before I change my mind."

Why did everyone keep calling him a boy? I jumped up, heading for the door, then stopped in my tracks. "I almost forgot. There's something else."

"What is it?" He sounded suspicious, slightly annoyed. "Please don't tell me I'm going to be a grandpa."

I puffed. "Fat chance. We haven't even kissed yet. You should know, since you have me spied on twenty-four hours a day."

Dad smiled, self-assured. "Yes, my invisible ghouls are my eyes and ears."

"Suck-ups."

"They're loyal." His green eyes flickered as he crossed his arms and leaned back, relaxed, as though a weight just lifted off his shoulders. "The fact that you and the boy haven't gone further than a peck on the cheek's the only reason why I haven't yet whisked him off to Dungeon 283."

"Dad! Are you bonkers?" Dungeon 283 was reserved for people like the bloodthirsty Roman emperor, Nero, and Ivan The Terrible. I grabbed his hand and gave it a squeeze, my gaze connecting with his as I whispered, "Dallas doesn't know who we are. Let's keep it that way."

"What do you mean?" Fake confusion crossed his face.

I sucked my lip, considering my words. No point in beating around the bush. "Dallas thinks we're in Disneyworld, California." Dad laughed. I held up my hand to stop him. "In fact, he thinks you're running the place. So, no talk about Hell, wrath, fire, demons, torture chambers, or anything else that might give us away."

"You're kidding."

"You are fit to rule this kingdom with your deceit. How did you pull it off, kiddo?"

I smirked, faking surprise. "What? You don't know? Oh, wait, you haven't gotten your daily report on me from your spies yet?"

"You know they report to me every night."

"Well, then I'll save you the trouble of reading." I rolled my eyes. "I flew him to California, took him to the amusement park entrance and opened the portal."

"Human bodies are not designed to take on that kind of trauma. In this dimension, the energy is too much for his mortal body. He should've been disintegrated. Did you have the portal set on human transportation?"

Did I? My mind went blank. I couldn't remember I even had that option on my phone. "Is that how it works?"

He arched a brow. "That's a 'no' then. There must be something special about him that he survived."

My secret plan almost fried my lovely new boyfriend. Maybe Fate was looking out for Dallas, after all. She must have a grand plan for him, or our bond kept him safe to travel where I was. I knew nothing about bringing humans into Hell and should've discussed it with Dad first. He could've given me the proper setting, but I couldn't take the chance he'd say no.

Dad's words snapped me out of my thoughts. "Back to my name, Cass. You can introduce me as Lucifer."

"Won't work." Thinking, I tapped a finger against my lips. "What about Luke from Lucifer, or Bob from Beelzebub?"

"No way, Cass. You said you wouldn't talk to your mother if I welcomed Dallas. That's a deal I'll keep, but being called something else other than what I am wasn't part of it." Dad shook his head vehemently. "It's bad enough we have to pretend we don't exist. If I let him call me Bob, I'll end up the laughingstock."

Damn, I should've bargained better. It was time for a change in scheme. I popped my eyes wide upon until they burned so they looked shiny and ready to burst into tears any minute. "Please, Daddy. I'll love you forever and ever if you do this. Besides, no one will know and it won't be for all eternity, just for a week or two until he returns home."

My lips started to quiver from the effort of keeping my aching eyes open. Dad looked away. His hesitation was a sign he was about to crumble under the pressure. I walked around his shiny desk, my heels clicking noisily on the wooden floor, and forced him to face me.

"All right. But only for a week," Dad said eventually. A week sounded like pure bliss. As the ever-optimistic chick, I knew anything could happen in a week, like Dad completely falling for Dallas's charm and morphing into his BFF.

I breathed out, relieved, and jumped into his open arms. "Thank you. Are you ready to meet the man of my dreams?"

Dad groaned. "Do I have a choice?"

Chapter 8 - Dinner small talk

I found Dallas inspecting the photos on my pin wall, which stretched from my cluttered dresser to the bay window across three quarters of the wall. Most of the pictures were snapshots of my parents and aunts; some were taken in front of famous places around the world. Luckily, Dallas had travelled extensively himself so he wouldn't feel inferior.

He didn't notice me standing in the doorway. I took a moment to gawk at him, marveling at how tall he was. Dad's slacks fit him like a glove, the shirt was a bit loose around his toned torso and broad shoulders, but it was barely noticeable. His brown hair had a shiny hue; the ends were darker where the moisture from the shower hadn't dried yet.

"Hey." I inched closer, wrapping my arm around his waist and pressing my cheek against his shoulder.

"I wasn't prying." He turned and shot me a lazy smile. His arms pulled me close. I could smell the sweet scent of my shower gel on his skin. "I figured you wanted me to change into these." He pointed at his clothes.

I winked. "You look cute."

"So do you." He leaned into my embrace, tracing my lips with his finger. My skin tingled, my breath caught in my throat. The air between us crackled. I wish this could be our first 'magical moment', especially since he looked so hot all cleaned up but Dad was waiting. And you don't keep Dad waiting...again.

I broke off first. "Dad wants to meet you."

Dallas nodded. "We shouldn't keep him waiting then."

"Having dinner with my Dad can be worse than going to a job interview. But don't be nervous. Just be yourself and he'll love you."

I pulled him down to peck him on the cheek before we joined Dad in the dining room. He greeted us at the door with a huge smile. I peered behind him and felt the heat drain from my face. A little Omnidus, dark as coal with tusks that reached up almost a foot, was setting the table. Spinning around, I grabbed Dallas's arm and yanked until his back was turned on Dad's maid demon.

"I'm B—" Dad cleared his throat. I glared at him. Seriously, how could it be this hard for him to spew out a fake name? Guess when it came down to pride, losing his identity sucked big time.

"Bill?" Dallas prompted.

I nudged him. "Bob."

"Short for Robert?" Dallas asked.

"He hates that name, babe."

"I'm Bob," Dad said, holding out his hand.

Dallas gave it a vigorous shake. "Dallas. Pleasure to meet you, sir."

"Please, call me Dad. All of Cass's boyfriends do."

Laughing, I slapped Dad's arm harder than intended. "He's just joking. I've never brought anyone home before."

"Which doesn't mean I didn't know about your boyfriends," Dad said. I glared at him, lest he keep embarrassing me, making me seem like a tart, but he changed the subject. "Dinner must be ready by now. Care to join us?"

From the corner of my eye, I noticed the Omnidus scurry through the connecting door into the adjoining kitchen. I grabbed Dallas's arm again and dragged him to the decked table. Our best china and silver shimmered in the dim light of the candelabra; three glass vases with red tulips, simple yet chic, built a beautiful contrast to the white brocade tablecloth.

"This is nice," I whispered. Dad winked, smiling. Maybe having the Omnidus around was a slip-up and he didn't mean to sabotage my relationship.

Dad poured cranberry juice into three glasses and handed us one. Dallas took a sip, insecure, as Dad focused his gaze on him. I knew this look. He was about to start the interrogation. He might as well strap Dallas to a lie detector and give him a polygraph test. As much as I would've liked to help the love of my life, this was one battle he had to fight for himself. If not, Dad would never take him seriously.

Eager to give them a minute alone, I got up mumbling, "I'll see about dinner. Be right back."

Dad nodded, but didn't look at me. I headed out the door, tuning in to the conversation, which started almost as soon as I closed the door behind me.

"So, how do you like it here in *California?*" Dad emphasized the last word like it was Chinese.

"It's nice. I've been here before."

"You're a well-travelled man then?" Dad asked.

"From one side of the globe to the other," Dallas said. "I've even climbed the Andean mountains for thirty five miles in Peru to the fortress of Machu Picchu."

"That's one of the Seven Wonders of the World," I said, returning to the room because I didn't like the direction this conversation was taking. "The Incas started building that around AD 1400. The Inca king, Tupaq Amaru, kidnapped my Aunt Krista for a virgin sacrifice in one of those temples without noticing she wasn't much of a virgin. Dad sent the Spanish on them who won in the end."

Dad grinned. "I was so proud of myself until I realized I had just wiped out an entire civilization."

I snorted. "How can anyone be proud of starting a war?" My gaze wandered from Dad's amused face to Dallas's questioning look when it dawned on me. Oops, I'd slipped. I burst out in a fit of laughter. "Just kidding."

"We almost had him," Dad said, trying to cover up for me.

Dallas laughed. "You two are such a riot."

"See, Dad? Dallas has been everywhere," I said, changing the subject. Unfortunately, I wasn't the only one to return to the topic at hand.

"You're a nomad?" I could hear the accusation in Dad's voice.

"I wouldn't call myself that, sir. I'd love to settle down one day."

Settling down? Dallas was digging himself an early grave here. Sucking in my breath, I signaled the Omnidus to bring over the cart with the first course. He bowed deeply and then scampered away.

"Who's ready for the first course?" I said. "I don't know about you, but I'm starving."

"Dallas was about to tell me his plans for the future," Dad said. "Isn't that interesting?"

I nodded and lifted the lids off the serving dishes. "Uh-uh. We have smoked salmon and salad. Yum."

Dad started shoving food onto Dallas's plate. Either he tried to fatten Dallas up like a Christmas goose, or it was an attempt at challenging his stomach's capacity until he threw up across the rug and made a dash for the nearest exit, too mortified to ever see me again. I wouldn't have any of it, so I grabbed the plate out of Dad's hand and placed it in front of me, then handed Dallas my own plate. "Thanks, Dad. You're a star."

A fake smile spread across his lips as he helped himself to a few slices of salmon. "You're welcome, sweetie." I dug in even though I wasn't hungry. Dad resumed the conversation. "Did Cass tell you she'd be leading our most important advertising campaign to date?"

"Really?" Dallas nodded and shot me a crooked smile. "That's fantastic. At such a young age it's a major achievement. You must be very proud of her."

"I am." Dad clicked his tongue. "She's carrying plenty of responsibility on her thin shoulders. To avoid any distractions, she's decided to move back home."

Dallas's eyes widened as he turned to meet my gaze. Putting my fork down, I peered at him from under my lashes. "Sorry, I meant to tell you."

He squeezed my hand. "No, it's okay. I don't need a babysitter while you work."

"Perhaps you could help out," Dad said.

Dallas shrugged. "Sure."

I glared at Dad. What was he doing? He knew well Dallas couldn't possibly contribute to our make-Hell-popular campaign. "I don't mind if you stay at the hotel and watch TV, or go to the beach."

"No, I'd love to help. This is bound to be so much more interesting than getting a tan," Dallas said.

Dad clapped his hands. "Fantastic. If you do well, I might even offer you a job."

I clasped my hands in my lap, digging my nails into the fragile skin of my arms. "Please don't make any concrete plans. You know I won't be staying forever, and Dallas isn't keen on the heat here."

Dad cocked his brows. "Really?"

Narrowing my gaze, I pointed at the still half-full plates. "Why don't you get the main course while I tell Dallas a bit about the campaign. You know, to brief him in."

Dad cleared the table in silence and left for the kitchen. Groaning, I started massaging my temples.

"It's not that bad," Dallas whispered. "Things are going better than I expected. Your dad's—"

"Shush, he can hear you," I whispered back.

Dallas shot me his easy going grin. "Not unless he has super sonic hearing."

"Let's just say he's never been a fan of headphones. His hearing's better than mine."

The door opened. Dad wheeled the cart in, heading straight for Dallas's chair. "I hope you like beefsteak."

"Sounds good to me." I smiled up at Dallas, only then noticing all color had drained from his face. My gaze moved to his plate where a puddle of blood had gathered around a piece of meat as large as my palm.

Dad slapped his shoulder, making Dallas sway a few inches in his seat. "Men like their steaks rare."

"That's disgusting, mate. You should fire the chef." I jumped to my feet, reaching for Dallas's plate when he held up a hand.

"No, that's exactly the way I eat it." I could tell from the panic in Dallas's eyes that he was lying, but I wasn't going to start an argument and emasculate him.

Dad slumped into his seat and started piercing the rare meat with a kitchen knife that wouldn't look out of place in a military base. "Where did we leave off?" He bit into a bloody piece, red liquid trickling onto his white collar. His teeth seemed to chew forever before he finished and swallowed the thing down.

"You were trying to scare my new boyfriend with your Dracula eating habits by sinking your teeth into a raw piece of meat like some ravenous werewolf."

Dad grabbed a linen napkin and wiped his mouth, grinning. "Where are my manners? I apologize."

Yeah, right.

"It's okay," Dallas said. "I don't scare easily."

But I did. Bile rose in my throat. I pushed the plate aside and took a sip of my water to calm my upset stomach before I ended up throwing all over the table. Dallas didn't seem to fare any better as he struggled raising the fork to his lips. How could he help with our project while being sick in the bathroom after Dad gave him E. coli or tapeworm infection on his first day in Hell?

"You don't have to eat that," I mouthed. Dallas smiled and popped the raw meat into his mouth, almost gagging. The grimace on his face made me so proud. He'd go through all of this for me. It made me feel special.

"Good, huh?" Dad said. "We usually have it once a week."

I nodded. "Yes, we do, but most of the time it doesn't look like it's been just cut off a cow and the chef forgot to turn on the oven."

Dad laughed. "Our Cass isn't keen on giving away the family recipe."

"What recipe?" I mumbled. "You slaughter it, and then slam it on a plate."

"No salt and pepper?" Dad put down his fork and turned to face Dallas, ready to resume his interrogation. "Back to you, son, what are your plans for the future?"

"So, Dallas." Dad put down his fork and turned to face him, ready to resume his interrogation. "What are your plans for the future?"

Dallas swallowed the half-chewed chunk in his mouth and tapped his napkin against his lips before he replied. "I was hoping to find a job that pays well."

"Really?" Dad nodded, seemingly impressed. "That's commendable, but I was thinking more in the line of your intentions regarding my daughter."

"Dad! We barely know each other." He was about to embarrass me again.

"You're my only child. I have a right to know."

Our gaze locked in a fierce battle again. We stared at each other in reticence, the promise of silent treatment versus keeping me away from the family fortune until I turned thirty passing between us. I spoke first.

"It's none of your business. Now, back off."

"I would like to ask for permission to date your daughter," Dallas said.

Dad laughed. "I thought you two skipped that step."

I gaped. How did Dad know that?

"You told him?" Dallas asked.

"She didn't. You see, son. I know everything. Nothing escapes me here in Hell."

Glaring at Dad, I nudged Dallas. "It's his nickname for this place because of the unbearable heat."

"We're going off topic, Cass." Dad folded his hands on the table, his eyes glued to Dallas. "You were telling me what you had in mind regarding my daughter."

"Cass is a fantastic girl. What we have is very special," Dallas said. "I've never felt this way before."

Grinning, I turned toward him, my brawl with Dad instantly forgotten. "Never ever?"

Dallas nodded, eyes sparkling. "I hope you feel the same way about me."

"Yes." My smile widened as I reached for his hand. A hot flush of love washed over me as his fingers clasped around mine, his thumb rubbing my skin. And then I noticed a bloodstain the size of a coin between his index and ring finger. Disgusted, I kept my smile in place because I wasn't going to complain about it. I'd make Dad pay for the steak later.

"Very touching," Dad said. "Let's get back to the topic though. Do your plans involve getting physically close to my daughter?"

"What?" I yelled. "No, Dallas, don't answer this one." I glared at Dad. "Why don't you arrange for your chef to prepare something edible while I call Mom? I bet she'd love to catch up. I could ask her about that old lady, you know, your soul mate."

Dad set his jaw. "Your mother's probably in bed by now, sweetie. You wouldn't want to disrupt her beauty sleep, would you?"

I grinned triumphantly. "Are you sure?"

"Positive." Dad got up and headed for the kitchen mumbling, "There must be some leftover chicken from last night."

"Don't forget dessert," I shouted after him, knowing he could hear me all too well.

"About before," Dallas started. " I want us to get to know each other and then see where it leads us. I've never given marriage one single thought, but it might happen one day, who knows?"

One day? Was he kidding? Didn't he know I'd been planning my wedding ever since I could crawl? I already had my dress designed, with all the details like pearls, silver threads and the whole shebang. Waiting for him to figure out whether marriage *might* feature in our cards wasn't an option.

"Marriage?" I laughed and slapped his arm. "Why would anyone want to hurry?"

Dad popped back in with a huge plate, the aroma of cheese and pepperoni invading my nostrils. "The chicken's gone, but I've just found a huge pizza in the oven. What are the odds, huh?"

Chapter 9 - It's called 'research'

In my absence, Dad had turned one of the bedrooms downstairs into my own home office with the usual huge glass table, sumptuous leather chair and bay window overlooking the erupting volcano skyline. I couldn't say I was unhappy. However, as much as I loved Dad, being with him 24/7 was more than I could bear so, naturally, I wanted to finish my job ASAP and get the hell out of there.

After spending the night in different rooms and a light breakfast with Dallas, I slumped into my chair and took a huge breath. Dad was quite the visionary, but he wasn't much of a planner. The campaign was supposed to turn him into the feared divinity he once was, but that dated back before my time. So, naturally, I neither knew anything beyond the distorted narration of supposed facts featured in books, nor did I actually care. I liked walking

Earth's surface unrecognized. Why Dad would want his face plastered across billboards in every major city was beyond me. Staring at the empty sheet in front of me, I wondered where even to begin.

A light knock on the door and Dallas entered. "Hey, can I make a phone call? Reception here's bad." Which wasn't surprising given we were still in Hell, hundred's of feet below Earth's surface.

"Sure. Use my phone." I tossed my gleaming cell toward him.

Dallas caught it in mid-air. "Thanks, babe." He headed back out, returning a minute later. "Do I need to dial anything to get an outside line?"

I gaped, flabbergasted at my own stupidity. Here I was, pretending we holidayed in California and Dad was a regular guy called Bob, and yet I passed my boyfriend the one item that could send him freezing in the ice-capped Himalaya with a Yeti on his butt or being swallowed whole by a forty-foot anaconda in the Amazon. Shuddering, I jumped up and snatched the phone out of his hand.

"Yes, but this model's particularly hard to handle. I had to take an induction course." I smiled, hoping I wasn't coming across as a total nutcase. "Let me do it for you."

I flipped the phone open and scrolled through the navigation. "Who are you calling?"

"No one."

"No one? Why would you need to use the phone then?" I regarded him intently.

Dallas buried his hands in his pockets, avoiding my probing gaze. "All right. I'm calling my sister."

"Amber?" I blinked, suspicion creeping up on me. Nothing wrong with calling one's family. He could've said so straight away...unless he wasn't telling the truth.

"Yep, the one and only." He moistened his lips and laughed nervously.

Why was he being so strange? What was he hiding? Was he cheating on me already?

He is, Kinky said. *Did you really expect a guy like him to be single?*

I shook my head lightly muttering, "You're right."

Kinky shrugged. *Don't worry; I'll help you chase him. As long as he's not wearing a ring on that finger, he's game.*

"He's what?" I mouthed.

Game, prey, available. Kinky rolled his eyes. *What's wrong with you? You're supposed to be the young and hip one. I feel like I'm talking to the old boss.*

He meant Dad, who couldn't hear him right now because he was in the lower levels of Hell, torturing a few souls. I made a mental note to tell Kinky I'd pass on the message.

"How's Amber?" I asked. "I haven't seen her in a long time. Not since—" Pausing, I cleared my throat because I didn't know how much Amber told her brother. He might not know after winning a paranormal race Amber was now stuck with the ability to communicate with the dead, and that the succubus deity Layla hunted her down because of Amber's bond with her boyfriend Aidan. It was all so complicated, I wished I could visit more often and gorge on the drama.

"Amber's fine, or so she says." Dallas nodded, averting his gaze again. "I don't know why she insists on staying in that creepy, old mansion with *Aidan*."

"She loves him." And they shared a bond so, naturally, they'd want to be together.

Dallas frowned. "I know, but he's hiding something. And one day, I intend to find out his secret."

I inched closer, sensing a change in his emotional undercurrents. A hot rush washed over me, my skin began to tingle as though hundreds of ants were crawling up and down my body. Was there chaos I didn't know about? Drama between Aidan and Dallas? I opened my mind, sending out my fallen angel vibes, only then realizing I couldn't read his thoughts.

"What do you mean?" I frowned irritated. Why couldn't I read his thoughts when no mortal secret ever remained hidden from me? At the periphery of my mind, I remembered my phone conversation with Aunt Krista during my very first date with Dallas. Right before I pretended the line went dead, she had thrown in some morsel of information about one not being able to read a soul mate's thoughts. I guess I should've listened more carefully.

Dallas ran a hand through his hair. "She just wants me to check in with her every now and then, that's all."

My mind picked up on something, but the picture was blurry. A loud ring pierced through my eardrum, making me flinch. His mental barrier blocked me off. No one could ever do that. My temper flared.

"Go on, then." I scrolled through my number directory and dialed, and then tossed the phone into Dallas's outstretched hand, glaring at him.

"Thanks." He turned his back on me and walked out. I felt a strong urge to chase after him, but Kinky's screech stopped me.

No!

"Why not?" I asked.

What if he catches you?

"He won't. No one ever does."

If you share a bond he'll know you're there.

I didn't think of that. "What am I supposed to do then? I need to know what's going on."

You mean you want *to know*, Pinky chimed in.

Honestly, what was wrong with being curious nowadays?

Send someone else to spy on him, Kinky said.

I peered around me, taking in the empty room and the scattered papers on my desk. "Who? There's no one about."

Kinky sighed. *I'll make the ultimate sacrifice and go.*

No way, Cassie. He'll just distort things to cause havoc, Pinky said.

Pinky had a point. The little devil liked drama just as much as I did. "You go and spy on him, Pinky," I said.

Kinky snorted. *If Dallas's hiding something, you know Pinky will never tell you so you won't get upset.*

He had a point too. I scanned the floor and gleaming surfaces as though an answer might magically appear.

Send the Omnidus, Kinky said.

I patted him lightly on the back. "You know you're starting to prove your worth." I focused my mind on the poor creature polishing the kitchen. He was a frightened, little thing, scurrying away at the first sign of mayhem, so I kept my order gentle, demanding that he follow Dallas from a distance without revealing himself, then report back to me.

Drumming my fingernails on the desk, I waited. Patience had never been one of my virtues, so the anticipating made me feel as though I was waddling through waist-deep mud pulling me down into a deep abyss. I didn't like the darkness down there because it symbolized unknowing and secrets which mocked my ability to sense every hidden layer of humanity.

A few minutes passed before Dallas popped back in. I curled my lips into a fake smile even though I would've rather jumped up from my seat and pounced on him, forcing him to spit it out.

"Is everything okay?" I cocked a brow. Surely, he must see the torture I was going through.

He nodded and placed the phone on the desk. "Yes, thanks. I'll pay you back for the call."

How when he didn't have a dime to his name? I waved my hand. "No need. I never know what to do with my free minutes anyway."

His smile didn't reach his eyes. Something bothered him. I wished I could threaten him into talking because my curiosity was killing me.

"I see you've started working on your Dad's campaign," Dallas said, skimming through my papers.

What made him think that? The sheets in front of me were all blank. I nodded enthusiastically. "Yes. Want to help me?"

He shrugged. "Sure. What do you want me to do?"

The Omnidus' thin voice invaded my mind, distracting me for a moment. He was waiting in the kitchen.

I cleared my throat and flicked through my notebook. "Why don't you start brainstorming ways to improve someone's popularity?" I paused, considering my words. "Let's say a company wanted you to be scared of their products, but in a good way."

Dallas raised his brows. "Huh? Scared in a good way?"

"They want to instill the utmost respect and awe." I bobbed my head, getting into it. "They want you to look up to them and realize how powerful they are."

"That's a strange marketing campaign for Disneyworld." Dallas slumped into the seat opposite from mine.

"It's still a work in progress. We have to come up with something original because everything else has been done before." I jumped to my feet, heading for the door. "Take your time. I'll be right back."

The hall was empty. Dad hadn't finished assigning the work for the day yet. I glanced over my shoulder to ensure no one was following, and then dashed for the kitchen, stopping in the doorway. The Omnidus waited under the counter, hidden from view. I squeezed next to him and peered at his bloodshot eyes gleaming with surprising sharpness.

"What did you find out?" I whispered.

"Boy talked about packet. Said it wasn't delivered." His red eyes trailed across the floor, his hands with skin dark as coal squirming in his lap. His voice sounded thin and high-pitched, breaking off in places as though he hadn't talked in a long time.

I leaned forward. "Did he say what parcel?"

The Omnidus shook his head. I figured it must be the one Dallas ordered from Skylife. Why was the security stuff so important? Was he in some kind of trouble? I focused back on the little demon. "Did he say anything else?"

"That he misses her. That going into the woods was his idea and he's very sorry."

So it had been Dallas's suggestion to go into the woods and steal the hidden gemstones, which turned Amber into a necromancer. Naturally, Dallas would now feel bad about it, but I still couldn't make sense of his need for several video cameras, mace and what else not. "He thinks he can protect her," I whispered.

"Pardon me, Princess?"

I grabbed the Omnidus' skinny hands, noticing his dry skin resembled parchment paper. "Dallas bought all the security stuff to protect his sister from all the immortality hungry idiots who think Amber's gift of communicating with the dead is the key to turning them into an undying deity."

The Omnidus nodded. "Yes, yes, Princess. And then he said he'd take care of himself and she needn't worry."

I tapped a finger against my lips. "Of course, she's worried something might happen to him as well. As long as she's a necromancer people will go to great lengths to get a piece of that, meaning they might come after him to get to her."

"He said he hasn't seen anyone and that he'll be staying in California until he's figured out what to do if they come. That's all, Princess."

"Thank you. You've been of great help." I smiled at the demon. He'd been in Dad's service for ages. Maybe it was time to promote him from kitchen helper to a more important position, a job function that would infuse reverence into his fellow demons rather than make them ridicule him at every opportunity.

He bowed deeply, his forehead reaching his naked feet with their thick soles and long, curled nails. "Anything, Princess."

"Would you like to leave the kitchen?"

"No, please. No." He shook his head, vehemently. Fear flickered in his eyes. "I did as you said. Please don't send me back to Scalov."

I laughed and patted his shoulder. "That's not what I meant. You've been a good servant. You've done a tremendous job around the house." His shaking became less violent, but angst lingered in his eyes. I continued, "You're too clever for your job." I was surprised Dad didn't see his intelligence. "I'll personally see to it that we find you a replacement. Someone who's worthy of your place and does the job just as well."

My praise wasn't lost on him. The softest hint of a smile crossed his features, disappearing just as quickly like a blown-out flame. "What am I supposed to do instead, Princess?"

"You'll be my personal assistant." I laughed at his surprised expression. The creased skin on his forehead softened visibly, giving him a more youthful appearance. I wondered how old he was.

"I'm honored, but I know nothing about serving someone as high as the boss's daughter."

I jumped to my feet and reached down to help him up from the uncomfortable tiles. "You'll learn. Now, get back to work before Dad returns. We wouldn't want to give him an excuse to deny our plea, would we?"

Chapter 10 - What's with the view

My spirits lifted as I returned to my office, finding Dallas leaned over a sheet of paper, scribbling in concentration. I was still mad he didn't trust me, but I also understood he had no idea who I was and only tried to protect me.

"You sure take your duties seriously." I traced a finger down his arm before I pointed at the countless bullet points. "Let me see what you came up with."

"Maybe when I'm done." He shot me a lazy smile and pulled me on his lap, planting a peck on my forehead. "I missed you."

"I missed you too."

His eyes shimmered. "You know what I just realized?"

"What?" I snuggled into his arms, inhaling the clean scent of his shower gel.

"I never knew there were erupting volcanoes in California," Dallas said.

Busted. Kinky laughed. *How are you going to explain this one? Wait! Let me grab my camcorder so I can record it for future reference.*

I grimaced. Granted, I didn't think of the possibility Dallas might look out the window, but it was nothing I couldn't fix. "It's all for show."

"Huh?"

Moistening my lips, I turned to face Dallas as I pointed at the highest peak, the flickering red flames giving the impression of a huge halo towering above it. "See that one over there? It's called Bursting Mountain. All kids are scared to death when they see it because it looks so real, but it's all plastic and special effects."

"You can do anything with lighting nowadays," Dallas said.

I nodded, thankful he bought my bluff. "Uh-huh."

"Since we're here we should visit it."

"Yes." I bobbed my head enthusiastically, and then grimaced. "Oh no. So sorry, babe, I forgot it's closed for renovations. Maybe another time."

"Why are the special effects on then?"

Gee, he missed nothing. "Thanks for mentioning it. I'll point it out to Dad. They might have forgotten to turn it off. What a waste of resources." Hopefully, Dallas forgot and never asked about it again. Otherwise, Dad might have to find a way to put out the volcanoes. I got up from his lap and returned to my chair, flicking through his notes.

"These are just suggestions," Dallas said. "I'm nowhere near a breakthrough yet."

"I like them." It was a lie. Organizing a Halloween party? Booking the spookiest hotel in the world for a launch party? He had to be kidding. Children might end up scared for five minutes, but that was about all the fear he'd get.

"This one's great." Dallas pointed at a few sentences squeezed near the edge. I leaned forward, squinting, as I tried to decipher his impossible handwriting.

"Jock thy Keeper? What's that?"

He laughed. "No, silly. Jack the Ripper. We could hire him."

"Nope." I shook my head. "Dad will never let him out of that dark dungeon. I hope he rots there for eternity. That nut tried to kill me because I knew his true identity."

"He's dead. Pulling my leg again? You're such a jokester." Amusement sparkled in Dallas's eyes.

I blinked, realizing my blunder. Dating a mortal was more difficult than I ever imagined. I had to keep all these secrets bottled up and sometimes they just spilled out of my mouth. When I dated down here in Hell, I could say what I wanted openly and *everyone* knew what I was talking about. "Of course it was just a joke. He's dead. I'm glad we'll never have to see that crazy dude."

"I wasn't talking about the real guy anyway," Dallas said. "Your dad could hire an actor to play him. Maybe even organize a whodunit in the style of Agatha Christie. Only, visitors will think there's a serial killer on the loose."

Jack the Ripper's picture still lingered at the back of my mind, making me shudder. Boy, did that bring back bad memories. In history class, we went back to London during the murders for a week of watching it all live, during which I had a really close encounter with Dr. Thomas Neill Cream aka Jack the Ripper. I tried to help Sherlock Holmes solve the case by revealing the killer's identity. Unfortunately, Sherlock was pig-headed and refused to believe me. He went down in history never solving the case. Sucks to be him. In Heaven, everyone still taunted him.

"What do you say?" Dallas prompted, jolting me out of my thoughts.

Nodding, I let the picture flash through my mind. The idea was quite original, but how would Dad fit into it? We could claim he was Jack the Ripper, but I couldn't quite see the connection to Hell.

"What do you think?" Dallas asked.

"Sounds great. I'll run it past him. He might want a few more options though. He's very hard to please."

"I'll get back to brainstorming then." Dallas gave my hand a quick squeeze before he resumed his scribbling.

Peering out the window, I gathered my thoughts. The conversation with the Omnidus zoomed through my mind. Dallas was keen on moving to California because he was scared of something or someone. With Hell, Dad's identity and Dallas's focus on turning his home into a fortress, there were too many secrets between us. How was this relationship supposed to work when we weren't honest to each other?

"What did Amber say?" I asked, hoping he might open up to me.

Dallas peered up from his notes. "What?"

I flicked open my phone, and then shut it again. "You never told me what your sister said."

He blinked. "I did."

"No, you didn't." Waiting, I crossed my arms over my chest. He didn't reply. "Was she upset because the parcel didn't arrive on time?"

"How do you know about the parcel?"

I rolled my eyes. "Dallas, you only called a million times to complain about it."

"Right. I forgot." He nodded, still tight-lipped.

I wished he'd share his worries with me instead of bottling up. Grabbing his hand, I forced him to look at me. "Why is she worried about you?"

What are you doing? Pinky hissed.

I grimaced, ignoring him.

"What makes you think she's worried?" Dallas asked.

There, now he's suspicious, Pinky said.

"You grew up together. When two people are this close, it's only natural to be concerned." Would he get the hint?

"Of course. We're very close, even more so now." Dallas sighed. "Let's get some work done before your father sacks us both."

Changing the topic wasn't going to work when I was as stubborn as a mule. "Last time I checked she left Scotland. Where's Aidan hiding her?"

Dallas's head snapped up, a frown crossing his brows. "What makes you think they're hiding?"

I groaned inwardly. If we kept going in circles like this we'd still be talking about it the following week. "Don't take it literally." Obviously, if I cared to find out where they hid I'd only need to give Thrain a call.

Dallas nodded, still avoiding a clear answer. "Okay, sorry."

My gaze searched his, the mental wall inside his head hindering my probing mind. Amber must've told him what happened, and Dallas kept it from me because he thought I was just a normal girl who couldn't handle the supernatural. I wished I could tell him I *was* the supernatural, but that might freak him out even more than having a necromancer in the family who could raise Great-grandma if she so desired.

I sighed. "Dallas, you know Amber and I go way back, right?" Way back was an exaggeration when we only met thrice a few months ago, but the truth didn't sound quite as indicative of my friendship with her. Dallas nodded so I continued, "To cut a long story short, she told me everything."

He gawked at me, disbelief reflecting in his magnificent eyes. "Really? She did? Even the last part?"

"Yes, she did. What happened back then is—" I whistled "—crazy stuff."

He laughed. "Loco. You could say that. I can't believe she told you. She said almost no one knew." No one? How about half of the supernatural world?

I got up and snuggled into his arms, brushing his hair off his forehead. His skin felt so warm and soft. "I'm one of the selected few. She trusts me implicitly." That was a lie too. Amber didn't tell me a thing. I had to read her mind.

Dallas buried his face into my hair mumbling against my throat, "I wish I could protect her. I'll never be able to sleep soundly knowing she isn't safe."

"She has Aidan."

He nodded. "I'm not sure about him." How could an immortal not be good enough to protect Amber? "I have some really bad news," Dallas continued.

I pushed his arms away to look at him. "What?"

"I'll have to leave as soon as possible. What we have is special, but I can't just leave my sister. I'm not ready for this until all the issues in her life are sorted out."

Dallas was so loyal to family. It amazed me. He'd do anything to protect the ones he loved. That instant I knew he'd fight for me too if it ever came down to it. He needed me now more than ever. I had connections he couldn't even dream of so, naturally, I'd stand by him. "I'm coming with you."

Dallas hesitated as though he was leading an inner battle whether to be honest with me. I guess his wish for honesty won. "No, that's not a good idea. Amber wasn't keen on us meeting again."

"What?" My anger flared up. Forget Layla, once I got hold of that wrench Amber I'd show her what a real immortal could do. I had every right to help protect the man I love, with or without Amber's blessing.

Dallas winced. "Her exact words were that you're trouble."

I snorted. "Me? That's a ridiculous insinuation. I've never been trouble in my *life*."

Pinky emerged on my shoulder. *May I remind you of that one time when you set Heaven on fire because you thought it'd be fun to watch the Cherubim run around like headless chickens?*

I was only five, and it never happened again.

"Please don't get upset. She didn't mean it like that," Dallas said.

106

"You bet she didn't." Amber might think she had the upper hand, but I wasn't going to give up on Dallas so easily. I smiled, sweetly. "I understand your concern, and if you want to leave I won't stand in your way."

"Thank you." He sounded relieved. How could that thought of leaving me ever *cross* his mind when we actually shared a bond?

"Did you know Disneyworld boasts more security than a prison? We have cameras everywhere. No face escapes the highly trained ex-marines living in the observation department."

"Really?"

Obviously, I had no idea, but I loved how gullible he was. My fingers brushed his cheek. I marveled at the softness of his skin. If Amber wasn't safe, neither was Dallas. I truly cared for Amber's safety, but I didn't want her problems taking away the man of my dreams. Surely, she would understand, particularly since she shared a bond with Aidan and knew how it all worked.

"Trust me on this one." I leaned closer whispering in his ear, "I'll share a secret with you, but don't ever tell anyone. It's so safe here, sometimes people placed under the witness protection scheme stay with us. We've never had an incident." I laughed inwardly. How could we have an incident with millions of guardian demons defending Hell with the help of their abilities?

"That's exactly what I'm looking for," Dallas said.

Putting on my poker face, I peered at him from under my lashes. "I should be mad at Amber for calling me trouble, but friends forgive and forget. If she needs my help, I'll be there for her."

Dallas smiled. "You mean she can stay here until they've figured out what to do?"

"What an excellent idea!" I popped my eyes wide open in fake surprise, hoping I wasn't going overboard. "Why didn't I think of it? You're so clever."

He tapped a finger against my nose. "Technically, babe, it was your idea."

"No, it wasn't. I would never take credit for your suggestion." I lowered my face until our noses met. "Why don't you call her and see what she has to say. Don't forget to mention you came up with it."

"What about your dad?"

I squirmed in his lap, stalking for time to make it seem like I was hesitating. "Don't worry about him. I'll figure something out." Retrieving the phone from my desk, I pressed it into his palm and winked. "Here, call her, and don't take no for an answer. There's a reason why even guys from the FBI come knocking on our door every now and then."

Chapter 11 - The curse

Dad didn't seem very happy to hear I was having yet more friends over.

"You're what?" He was pacing the study up and down; the frown on his forehead had been in place for the last two minutes, which was a new record given that we were neither at work, nor meeting Mom for lunch.

Pouting, I pressed my hands on my hips, ready to scream, beg or start giving him the silent treatment, all in this particular order. "You said I never bring anyone home, so there, I followed your advice."

"But, sweetie, I—" he ran a hand through his hair "— they're *mortals*."

"You say that like it's a crime. Are you discriminating against your main target audience? Besides, they're not mortal." I couldn't hold back a grin when I saw his jaw drop.

Dad's eyes narrowed suspiciously. "What are they?"

I shrugged. "This and that."

"No, Cass. If you want them to stay here you'll have to tell me the truth. Obviously, I could find out in a heartbeat anyway.

I laughed inwardly. If he could hear a heartbeat. Aidan was as dead as a doornail.

"Cass, are you listening?"

I nodded. "Sure. You were saying?"

"Why should I have to use my investigative skills? I want to hear the words out of your very own mouth." His voice sounded calm yet resolute. I sighed.

"All right, if you *must* know. Amber's a necromancer."

"And the boy?"

I winced. Nothing escaped Dad's heightened perception. "He's a—" I snapped my fingers, thinking. "What's another word for vampire?"

Dad groaned. "He's a vampire? In Hell? You know that's about the only species we don't have down here, and there's a reason for it."

"Come to think of it, I'm not keen on that word since Aidan neither drinks blood, nor shuns the sun." I started playing with the green tapestry on Dad's sofa, avoiding his gaze in the hope he wouldn't ask how I knew them.

"Good then, because we're not causing an eclipse just so he can venture out in search of his next snack."

I jumped up from my seat and hurried over to plop on his desk. "Dad, I told you he doesn't drink blood."

He peered at me unconvinced. "Is that what he told you?"

Really, he kind of underestimated me. "Nope. Obviously, I don't rely on hearsay. I know this for a fact because I attended the ancient ritual ceremony at the Shadowland cemetery."

"What?" Dad's jaw dropped. "I told you to never set foot on their cursed territory. They could use your blood for their rituals."

"You watch too many movies." At his shocked expression, I patted his hand. "I was only there for all of five minutes because Aidan agreed to retrieve an ancient ritual book from the Otherworld and give it to the Shadows in exchange for a ritual to free himself from the curse of blood. Since at that time I was still considering my career options, I thought it might be a good idea to assist everyone so it wouldn't turn into a bloodbath." Obviously, my plan was to pinch the book because I couldn't just leave something that powerful with all these wannabe immortals. The book was now stacked in a hidden compartment in my bedroom, but Dad needn't know.

"Where do you know these people from anyway?"

My chance to avoid this particular question evaporated into thin air. I shrugged again. "You know me, I travel quite a bit so, naturally, I get to meet the odd person. It's a small world."

Dad smirked. "Yes, well, they don't exactly advertise themselves on social networking sites."

I gawked, open-mouthed, because I never figured Dad knew one could use a computer for more than keying the number of souls entering Hell in an *Excel* document.

"You're surprised, huh?" He laughed. "Yes, your old man knows a thing or two about what's going on in the world. It doesn't mean I like it, but I'm clever enough to keep myself informed."

"That's great, Dad. Well done." Rolling my eyes, I slapped his shoulder. "Now, can we get on with it? The love of my life is waiting for me."

"They can't stay here, Cassie. Having a vampire around wouldn't be good publicity." Taking a sip of his coffee, Dad turned back to the folders occupying most of his massive desk, signaling me our conversation was over. Maybe for him, but not for me.

I smirked because it was time to skip the arguing and possible yelling, and move on to plan B, which involved begging, and maybe even shedding a few tears if I could squeeze them out. Truth was, I knew he was aware I manipulated him, but I didn't care. He should've thought about possible consequences before teaching me how to wrap Mom around my finger.

"Daddy?" I batted my lashes. "You know I'm really enjoying the last few moments we're getting to spend together. Soon I'll turn eighteen when it's time to leave the nest and fly away into the night."

"Stop being melodramatic, Cassie. It's not working. Not in this particular case." He sounded serious, but a glint of amusement flickered in his gaze.

I brushed a stray lock from my eyes as I continued unfazed, "You see, I might leave the nest sooner because Dallas needs to take care of his sister. Since he's the love of my life, I'm not letting him go. Will you miss me?" I pouted, praying for those tears to start flowing. They didn't.

"The love of your life?" Dad snorted. "You've known him for, what, two weeks?"

Not even, but Dad didn't need to know. "Haven't you ever heard of love at first sight?"

"Of course I have." Dad snapped his fingers. Thunder boomed and a brilliant bolt flashed over my head. "You have a better chance of getting struck by lightning."

I smiled. "Well then, call me one of the lucky ones."

"Who says you're lucky? Been there. Trust me, it's not all chocolate cake. " He snapped his fingers again and a dark rain cloud hovered above my head.

"Don't you dare," I hissed. Water didn't usually do my frizzy hair any favors. I couldn't risk looking like a drowned rat with my beloved around.

The cloud disappeared. Sighing, Dad started rolling his pen around his fingers. He was slowly losing his patience. It made sense to exalt my game. I pinched my thigh until it hurt, but the tears still wouldn't make their grand entrance.

"I'll give it two months," Dad muttered.

Ignoring his annoying wise apple attitude, I reached out and covered his hand with my palm. "I don't want to leave just yet and lose the last precious months we have left, but I must."

"Cass, I said stop the drama. You're turning eighteen, not entering a convent."

The first wet sensation reached the corner of my eye, but it was nowhere near enough to spill a fat, visible tear down my cheek. "Turning eighteen is a passage that changes everything. I've heard it can turn the most loving adolescent into a party animal, who's always too busy with drinking and hooking up to call home. Is that going to be my future? I'm scared."

Dad smiled. "I'll always know where you are."

I set my jaw. "No, you won't. If you plan to plant your GPS aka Thrain into my phone, I'll get rid of him and you won't see me for the next fifty years."

Dad grunted. "There's something I need to tell you, sweetie."

His tone promised bad news. I raised my brows. "What?" The clock on the wall struck a full hour. Seconds passed and yet he didn't respond. "Say it, Dad," I prompted.

He hesitated, avoiding my gaze. "Your aunt Patricia's the same age as you."

"So?"

"She's bound to her home."

I shrugged. "And? Get on with it."

Taking a deep breath, he turned to face me. "The same fate awaits you once you turn eighteen."

My jaw dropped. "What?" He couldn't be serious. "You mean I'll be bound to a haunted bakery for the rest of my life?"

Dad shook his head. "Not to the bakery. To Hell."

I laughed, figuring he must be winding me up. "Patricia's not eighteen yet."

"She inherited the bakery sooner than intended."

"But I don't want to live here." I jumped to my feet, knocking over a few folders in the process. "Do you have any idea how dreadful this place is? It's like being stuck in the Stone Ages without the rare excitement of being hunted down by the odd dinosaur."

Dad smirked. "Well, thank you for slanting off my life's work."

I pointed a finger at him. "It's *your* achievement, not mine. I have my own dreams to follow. You can't keep me here."

"You won't have a choice," he muttered.

In spite of the usual spats, until now I always thought Dad and I had a fantastic father-daughter relationship. I just realized I was wrong. I narrowed my gaze, my blood boiling. "That's it. You can finish that campaign yourself because I'm not helping you out any more."

"Don't blame me, Cassie. It's a curse even someone like me can't undo." Dad seemed pained, his expression betrayed suffering. I was upset, but something told me he wasn't ecstatic to relay the news either.

"Does Mom know about this?"

He nodded. Great. Everyone knew but me. Pulling my nose, I plopped back down on his desk wailing, "Why me and no one else I know?"

"Because Patricia and you are part—"

"Fallen," I finished.

Dad nodded. "Yes. There's this little misunderstanding that our kind gets out of control once we turn a certain age."

In other words, people thought we were promiscuous. Talk about clichés and being biased. "It never happened to you, or Aunt Krista and Selena."

"It's a new rule," Dad said. New could mean anything from a few hours to centuries in Dad's world. There was a more important question.

"Who put it in place?"

Dad pointed at the ceiling. For a moment, I didn't get it. And then it dawned on me. The big boss where Mom lived. I might be able to haggle with Dad, but in Heaven my little schemes stood no chance.

"So, what does this curse involve and why didn't Patricia tell me about it?" I asked.

"I asked her not to tell you so you wouldn't get upset." Dad sighed. "I wanted you to enjoy the time you had left before being tied to this *dreadful* place."

I nodded, suddenly putting two and two together. "That's why you agreed to letting me rent a flat and getting a job." His easy-going attitude, which sparked many fights between him and Mom in the last few years, made sense now. "How do I get rid of this curse?"

His pained expression returned again. "You can't. Only one person can free you."

"The person I'm connected to." Dallas's image popped into my mind. Dad might not believe he was *the one*, but I knew it. I laughed, feeling lightheaded as though a weight had just lifted off my chest. "I've found him already so it seems like I won't be here for long after all, Dad."

"Finding him isn't enough," Dad whispered. "You'll have to get married."

This was getting better by the minute. I knew all the hours spent planning my future wedding would come in handy one day. "Don't worry. I'll sort that out soon. It's only a matter of time."

"Don't count on it." Dad scoffed, annoyance crossing his face. It must be tough seeing his little girl grow up so quickly, but he'd have to suck it up and deal with his separation anxiety because I wasn't going to spend eternity in this heat.

That reminded me he still hadn't agreed to letting Dallas's sister and her emotionally detached boyfriend stay over. "Can Amber sleep in one of the bedrooms in the west wing? You won't even know she's here."

Dad shook his head. "No more guests. Look, kiddo, I have work to do."

What was wrong with him? Why was he so stubborn? My schemes never failed. Amber had to stay over for the sake of my relationship. "I'll stop pestering you if you let them stay here for a week."

"I'll think about it," Dad said, returning to his sheets. "Now, get back to that campaign. We haven't got all eternity."

Pouting, I headed for the kitchen to see whether lunch was ready, and then carried a tray with food up to my room where Dallas was having a nap because a coyote's yowling had kept him awake all night. There were no coyotes in Hell, so it could only be one of Dad's winged gatekeepers doing the nightshift on bringing in a few deceased souls. But Dallas needn't know.

I placed the tray on the night table and kneeled next to him on the bed, brushing his light brown hair from his warm cheek. Stirring, he opened his eyes, the golden speckles catching the rays of sun flooding in through the high bay window.

"You're back." He smiled and propped up on his elbow.

"Care for a bite?" Lifting the lid, I allowed the aroma of freshly baked bread to waft past me.

"You read my mind," he said. "I'm starving."

117

Yeah, I wish. I hadn't been able to read one thought since the second I met him. I ripped off a chunk and held it in front of his mouth until he bit into it. Watching him chew and swallow, I realized I'd have to come up with a solution even if it meant keeping Aidan and Amber hidden in a barn so Dad wouldn't find out.

"This is delicious, homemade just like my grandma used to make it." Dallas sat up and helped himself to a plate.

"My dad hired the best baker in California." I smiled, pleased that I had found something he seemed to like about this place. "He's come every day for the past five hundred—" I stopped, realizing my blunder. "—I mean, five years."

"She's fantastic. A bakery is one of my favorite places. I love creamy French éclairs and mini donuts with strawberries and whipped cream." He laughed. "Maybe I'll be a pastry chef one day."

"One of my aunts has a bakery. She'd love you." Something else that might just earn him brownie points with one of the relatives.

Dallas peered up, interested. "Does she live nearby?"

I shook my head. "She isn't keen on the weather. After she inherited the bakery she moved there for good and never visits." I didn't point out she couldn't visit, literally, since she was bound to that haunted place by blood until the curse was broken. Given the place was secluded in the Swiss Alps and no stranger ever got sidetracked there, it might be a long time before we saw her again.

"That's a shame," Dallas said. "I love my family and couldn't imagine not seeing them regularly." Which was why I'd do everything in my power to keep Amber with us so Dallas wouldn't leave.

"When's Amber coming?" I made it sound nonchalant as if I didn't really care, but my heart picked up in speed.

Dallas swallowed the chunk in his mouth before replying. "I forgot to tell you. Thanks for reminding me. She said she'd catch the first flight from London."

First flight? As if. Aidan could teleport, meaning he could close his eyes and transport her here within a few seconds. Only Dallas was naïve enough to believe his sister's plane could defy all rules of modern aviation by flying thousands of miles in the short timespan between breakfast and lunch. So his sister hadn't told him everything about the supernatural world after all. I wondered why. Besides, Amber's situation must be dire if she and Aidan were coming to Hell knowingly. "That's great. You can stay here and work on the campaign while I pick them up from the airport."

He shook his head. "I'll come with you."

I smirked. "Sure. Whatever you prefer."

"Your dad doesn't mind?" His inquiring gaze focused on me. For a moment, I felt as though he looked right through me into the very core of my being. I swallowed hard, considering my words so the lie would sound believable. The sensation passed when he took another bite and washed it down with a big gulp of orange juice.

"Dad's always been rather fond of guests. He said he'd be happy to let them stay in one of our cottages on the other side of Disneyworld."

Dallas frowned. "Is it safe there?"

"Yes." I nodded enthusiastically. "Even more so than here. All our special guests stay in a cottage. They're fancy

119

with lots of space and modern kitchen appliances. Amber will love it there."

"I hope so," Dallas whispered, pulling me close. His heartbeat throbbed like a drum, racing faster than mine. I raised my lips to his when my phone rang.

"It's them." I didn't even need to look to know. "Why don't you answer while I make sure the cottage's ready for their arrival?"

Dallas nodded and pressed the phone against his ear. I headed out in search of my future personal assistant.

Chapter 12 - You forgot to bring the dog

I found the Omnidus scrubbing the marble floor in the kitchen. The balcony doors hung wide open. A hot gust of air wafted in, sucking the last bit of oxygen out of the room. If I were mortal, I would've probably fainted by now.

Walking past the gleaming kitchen counters, all kept in black and white with marble surfaces, I hurried to close the door and turned on the air conditioning. The Omnidus bowed and maintained his position until I signaled him to rise. He stood, shooting me fleeting looks from under singed lashes. For the first time, I noticed he was clad in rags, grey and worn from years of washing. The pair of pantaloons frayed around the ankles, his dry skin peeked from under the gaping holes in his shirt.

I inched closer and placed a hesitant palm on his scrawny shoulder. "What's your name?"

"Ginny." His tone was even more high-pitched than before which made me conclude his nerves in my presence hadn't settled.

"Ginny," I repeated. "Do you remember we talked about a promotion?"

He nodded, eyes scurrying across the floor. Whatever happened to the little creature must have scarred him for life. I continued, "No one will ever hurt you again." I knew I was making promises that might be hard to keep, but I vowed to do my best and protect him. "I'm here with your first job assignment."

Ginny's eyes lit up. "Anything, Princess."

Admiring his work ethic, I grinned. "I'm expecting guests, so I need you to prepare one of our best cottages for them. We'll need a vase of fresh flowers on the dining room table with a pitcher of ice water. Set out extra hand towels, toilet paper, and soap." I squeezed Ginny's hands to make sure he was listening. "Lots of soap. We know Aidan needs to wash all that vampire stench off of him."

Ginny's hesitant smile disappeared. "A vampire."

I rolled my eyes. "I know what you're thinking. Like water would help, right? A girl can always try."

"I'm a kitchen aide, but I will do my best to meet your expectations," Ginny said. I beamed at him, pleased.

"Just pretend you're opening up a new hotel and you need to impress the guests. You'll have to strip the beds, scrub the bathroom and put out a nice welcome mat. Make it as chic yet cozy as possible."

"Yes, Princess."

I tapped a finger against my lips, my mind racing a hundred miles an hour. "Oh, and Amber gets pretty grouchy without her coffee, so put the coffeemaker on a timer to start up in the morning. Don't forget to stock the fridge. We'll also need to place a basket of shampoos, soaps and lotions near a giant stack of fresh towels. Air out the place and leave two robes out on top of the bed with some chocolates. Some black, fluffy slippers would be nice too."

"Chocolates?" Ginny asked.

"You're right. Add some candles and rose petals." I bit my lip. "No, cancel that part. That's overkill. Although, I'm sure those two could use a little romance. It's just that Aidan's a whole lot nicer when he's all floating and in love. Guess you can say he's more tolerable to be around."

Ginny nodded enthusiastically. "Yes, Princess."

I regarded him, wondering whether it might just be too much for him. "I know you're thinking I'm going overboard with all of this, but Amber and Aidan must be spoiled at all costs. I have to make the chick happy, and the vampire dude too. If she leaves, Dallas leaves with her...and my life is over...literally. I'm putting you in charge of the whole operation, so gather a few Operandes and get to work because you only have two hours. Can you do it?"

He bowed his head whispering, "No one will listen to me."

He was right, but I was Lucifer's daughter so, naturally, being resourceful ran in my DNA. "Don't worry about it. I'll make sure they do." I was almost out the door when I remembered Dad mustn't know. "One last request," I called over my shoulder. "You can't tell anyone."

I didn't wait for Ginny's answer because I knew he'd never dare cross me, or question my motives. Thrain, on the other hand, just might.

Back upstairs, Dallas had finished his conversation and was keen on recalling it. I held up a hand to stop him and muttered, "Sorry it took so long. Can you wait just a few more minutes?"

He nodded so I headed out again, panting from all the running around. When had I become this harried yet industrious person? It felt good to have an agenda that kept my mind too busy to contemplate the curse or its implications. Mind, I wasn't even bothered because I was certain Dallas was the one. Whatever this curse entailed, it'd never even stand a chance to manifest itself.

I'm so proud of my little protégé, Pinky whispered. Was he crying? I turned sharply, but the little angel averted his face. *The way you're trying to help that poor creature shows me Kinky's disgusting ways aren't rubbing off on you.*

Pinky's problem was his sense of reality was rather distorted. Hell was a place built on hierarchy and keeping up appearances. I peeked left and right to make sure no one snooped on us. "Now, don't get emotional on me," I hissed. "I'm not helping Ginny as much as I'm trying to help myself. Imagine being stuck here for the rest of your life." I shuddered.

Pinky gasped. *Good gracious. What a disaster. Your mother would be so upset.*

I closed my eyes and sent Thrain a message to meet me in the hall. A few minutes later, the door swung open and in he walked, a grin playing on his lips. "Miss me, gorgeous?"

"Don't get your hopes up, mate. You and I ain't happening. Are you alone?" I peered around him, lest his bulky physique hide one of his helpers.

"Why would I bring anyone along on our date?" He marched past me into the living room and sank into Dad's leather sofa, his dusty boots grazing the soft throw. His insolence was hard to bear, particularly since I was a girl who valued cleanliness. At times, however, it makes sense to sacrifice one's integrity for the sake of a higher cause, so I bit my lip and kept quiet.

"It's not a date," I hissed.

Thrain smirked, self-satisfied. "Still trying to deny the feelings you have for me that burn deeper and hotter than Hell itself?"

My jaw dropped. Seriously, could he be more in love with himself? "I asked you to meet me in the hall. How you got the idea this was a date is beyond me. Listen, I need you to do something."

He narrowed his gaze. "If it involves deceiving your father, I won't do it."

"Of course, you will. Who do you think will run this place one day?" I raised my chin a notch. "If you want to have a future in Hell, you'd better start sucking up to the second-in-command otherwise—" I trailed off, letting him fill in the blanks.

He smirked and shifted in his seat, rubbing his dirty clothes over the cream throw, which was my joy and pride since it fit the black décor perfectly. Counting to ten, I clenched my fists.

I could see him fighting with himself whether to believe me or not. "You said you'd never be interested in holding any sort of position in Hell."

"Times change. Let's just say I can see myself taking over Dad's position in a few years." I cleared my throat. "Now, listen. My personal assistant, Ginny, will require protection to finish his work assignment. Make sure you've got his back."

Thrain cocked a brow, amused. "I didn't know you had a personal assistant. Who is this Ginny? Another guy I should know about?"

I shrugged. "You know Dad's kitchen aide. I've promoted him."

Thrain laughed. "That's certainly a nice leap up the career ladder."

"You could say that. Can I count on you?" I infused as much authority into my voice as I could muster. "Or do I have to look elsewhere for an employee worthy of my trust and a long-lasting collaboration?"

He bowed deeply, his piercing gaze remained fixed on me. "Your wish is my command, Princess."

I didn't like the smug grin on his face. Drumming my fingers against my thigh, I inclined my head. "Well? Can you take it from here or do you need any more instructions?"

To my delight, he finally got up from my pretty sofa and headed out with another bow. Playing a role in Dad's business might not be part of my life plan, but the perks weren't to be disregarded. It was time for the next part of my plan, so I pushed the thought to the back of my mind and joined Dallas. He was sitting on the bed, waiting patiently. His eyes shone, the corners of his mouth twitched. My heart made a somersault. I pushed the empty plates aside and sat next to him, my thigh brushing his, sending shivers up and down my body.

"Sorry about the delay. I had to take care of some details. What did Amber say?"

He leaned into me and brushed a stray lock out of my face. "Their plane landed an hour or so ago."

I cleared my throat to stifle the laugher bubbling inside my throat. Yeah, right. I bet they were still packing in London.

"Are you all right?" Dallas asked, handing me a glass of water. I took a deep gulp and almost choked on it when he said, "She'll meet us outside Disneyworld's Entry B in fifteen minutes, which must be up by now. I don't understand why they didn't just take a taxi."

Maybe I should run the taxi into Hell idea past Dad. He might get a laugh out of that one. "Maybe they were broke and took the shuttle bus. I don't know about you, but I can't wait to see them." And get them out of my system so we could finally focus on our relationship again.

"Makes sense. What are we waiting for? Let's go!" Dallas jumped up from the bed. I laughed.

"You're not too excited or anything."

"Thanks for doing this." Dallas's face was mere inches from mine, his voice was low, his breathing came in short rasps. "I'm glad we get to spend more time together because I like you a lot." He laughed softly. "Ever since hearing your voice on the phone I knew I had to meet you. It wasn't an option, more like a need. Crazy, huh?"

Not really. "I'm glad you stalked me, otherwise we might not have met before I turn eighteen."

"Why? What happens when you turn eighteen?"

I shrugged. "Dad's been pestering me about moving back home. I was planning to come back in a few weeks."

"I'm glad I got to see you again before you disappeared forever," Dallas whispered. His hand wandered to my back as if to hold me in place. His lips parted. I held my breath, my mind devoid of thoughts, but my heart got the message and started racing.

They're about to kiss. Isn't that cute?

Pinky's voice jolted me out of the moment. I groaned inwardly and averted my gaze. How was a girl ever supposed to seal the deal and get the guy to fall head over heels for her with someone wrecking every attempt at bonding?

Clearing his throat, Dallas jumped up and held out his hand. "Ready to go?"

I intertwined my fingers with his, marveling at the electric jolt running up and down my arm. "Are you sure you don't want to wait here?"

He shook his head. "You've done enough already."

I smiled because I was about to do even more, for both his sister and myself. Even though the portal could be opened anywhere, we took the way we came so Dallas wouldn't get suspicious. We drove around until we found the right entry. I opened my phone. Now all I had to do was wait for the perfect moment to hit enter.

"Making a call, babe?" Dallas asked.

"Uh, no. I'm checking to see if my dad called." Dad had given me a new code to open the portal this time so Dallas wouldn't pass out when we stepped through. It was also Dad's idea that I present him with a love letter to keep his attention occupied so I wouldn't have to feign yet another Gulf of Mexico thunderstorm. I tapped his arm. "I wrote you something. It's in the glove department."

"Really?" He pulled out a red envelope and tore it open, hesitating.

"Well, read it," I prompted.

Gazing down, he started to read out loud. "My dearest Dallas, the day you came into my life changed my world...."

From the corner of my eye, I made sure his gaze remained lowered, then pressed enter. A moment later, the portal opened. My foot hit the pedal and we sped right in through the swirling vortex, rolling to a halt in front of a large group of tourists.

"That's the sweetest thing anyone has ever done for me," Dallas said. His smile made my pulse spike.

"I poured out my heart." Sort of. I poured out my heart...into a major *Google* search. No man would ever take Dallas's place. He was my true soul mate. I could feel it in my heart, I just wasn't very good at writing it all down without a bit of help from a search engine.

"Can't believe we got here so quickly," Dallas said, peering around.

"You were really engrossed into that letter." Craning my neck, I tried to peer over the chattering crowd. "Are they here yet?"

"Over there." Dallas pointed to a tall guy dressed in denims and a blue short-sleeved shirt. If it weren't for his pale skin, unnaturally black hair and bulging arms, he wouldn't look out of place among the tanned tourists. The tiny girl standing next to him seemed more human with her shoulder length brown hair and plump figure. With her glowing skin and smooth face, she looked nothing like a haunted necromancer suffering from the usual surges of insomnia, and seeing people where there should be none. I figured as soon as Aidan found a way to rid her of the Gift, she'd return to being the mortal she once was.

I killed the engine. Dallas jumped out of the car and headed for them. Heaving a sigh, I ambled after him. When we reached Amber and Aidan, Dallas put a hesitant palm on the small of my back. I waited for him to pull me closer, but he didn't.

"Thanks for having us," Amber said, smiling.

Aidan nodded. "Yes, we can't thank you enough. The situation is dire and I knew this would be the safest place for Amber."

I smiled. "That's what friends are for. You're not putting me out. Mi casa su casa."

"Picked up a little Spanish?" Dallas said.

"I speak many languages." And I wasn't even lying. We literally learned hundreds at school.

"What about Latin?" Amber asked with an innocent look on her face. We had barely met again a minute ago and she was already fletching her teeth, ready to attack me at the first opportunity. Why need enemies with friends like her?

"Yes, I know that one too." I regarded her intently, my eyes scanning her skinny jeans and thin top, baggy around the waist. Her eyes moved about too quickly, her hands were clasped in front of her, the knuckles white. They were hiding something. I took a deep breath as I tried to make sense of the various nervous undercurrents, then focused on her thoughts. Nothing there. Amber knew I could read her mind any time, so she was probably forcing herself not to think of what bothered her. Well, she'd slip eventually. "How do you like California?"

"It's hot," Amber said. "But it's nice to get away from rainy Britain for a while."

Aidan nodded again. The weather wasn't the only thing they were trying to escape.

"We're very lucky to have so much sun." I winked. "Come on. Let's get you home. You must be tired from your *flight*." I raised my brows, taking in their reactions.

Amber didn't even blink as she pointed at Dallas. "Can I have a moment with my brother, please?"

I shrugged. "Sure, mate."

Aidan turned to face me as though that might give them all the privacy they needed. I tossed Dallas the car keys and watched them stroll to the vehicle.

"California, eh?" Aidan whispered. "I don't know how you got Dallas to believe you, but I'm impressed."

I laughed. "Your lie about the flight isn't bad either. Dallas seems to think he knows almost everything there is to know about you. How much have you actually told him?"

"Let's just say he's safer not knowing all there is." Aidan leaned closer, piercing blue eyes glinting. "Can you take care of her while I sort out our—" he hesitated, considering his words "—problems?"

"You're not staying with her?" The slightest hint of hope hid behind my surprised tone. If I could get rid of the vampire, Dad might be more inclined to let a necromancer roam his realm.

"Only until she gets settled. I trust you and Dallas keep her good company."

131

Kinky snorted. *What are you? A chaperone?* I wished he'd just stop sneaking up on me, startling me every time.

"She'll be perfectly entertained here at Disneyworld," I said. "There's just one tiny thing you need to do. Can you pretend to be dead?"

He frowned. "What?"

I waved my hand. "You know, deceased, departed, lifeless, stiff, whacked."

"Your father doesn't know we're coming?"

"Don't be silly." I rolled my eyes, laughing. "Of course, he does."

"Why the need to pretend we're dead then?"

I scanned the faces surrounding us to make sure no one was listening as I whispered, "Hell comes with a few rules. Stay inside, don't draw any unnecessary attention to you, and at least pretend you're dead, if you aren't already."

"Anything else?" Aidan raised his brows, smiling. Even though we had been acquaintances for a long time, until then I hadn't really seen him so relaxed. Having found his mate was definitely good for him. I hoped the bond between Dallas and me would make me glow like this one day. Maybe after I got rid of that wicked curse.

I met his gaze again. "Dallas doesn't know anything about me. Let's keep it that way."

"You know Amber's worried about him? She thinks you'll break this heart."

"She shouldn't be." I shrugged. "I've never been more serious."

"What are you? Twenty?"

"Seventeen."

"Seriously?" Aidan groaned. "Amber was seventeen a few weeks ago. Do you have any idea how long it took me to persuade her I was even dating material?"

"I can imagine." In fact, I had watched it all live before my eyes because none of them could keep their thoughts to themselves. From the corner of my eye, I noticed Amber and Dallas making their way through the crowd. There was something about the way Amber moved that raised my suspicion. Her pace was too light, too graceful; her hair too bouncy and shiny, like a *Cover Girl* commercial, minus the skyscraper model and bony legs.

She isn't mortal, Kinky said.

It couldn't be. Aidan would never break the Council's rules and turn her. As though reading my thoughts, Kinky shrugged. *If you say so, but don't tell me I didn't warn you.*

"Ready to go?" I peered around. "Where's your luggage?"

Aidan stepped aside to reveal the two large suitcases behind him.

"Dang sister, did you pack a suitcase the size of California? The car's too small to fit us four and all that stuff," I said.

"It'll be okay," Amber said.

Groaning, Dallas lifted a suitcase and dropped it again. "Whoa. This thing weighs a ton. What do you have in there? Everything but the kitchen sink?"

Amber pointed to Aidan. "It's all his, I swear." I didn't believe her for a second.

"I told her not to bring ten pairs of heels," Aidan said.

Amber laughed. "What's the point of having all that muscle mass if you're not going to use it?" I peered from her loved up expression to Aidan's grin and his inflated ego from her compliment.

"Certainly not to carry your baggage," Dallas said, jolting them back down from their private pink cloud. Amber's cheeks turned bright red, and they averted their gaze from each other.

I winked at him. "Are you sure you're not hiding more around the corner?"

Amber shook her head. "Nope. We're ready to go."

"Looks like you're moving in," I muttered as I lifted the smallest of the bags to help the guys carry Amber's stuff to the car. "The only thing you forgot is the dog."

Chapter 13 - A desert's cooler

Ginny did a fantastic job. I peered in awe at the state of one of our cottages as I showed Amber and Aidan around. Soft rugs covered the wooden floors; white curtains gave the impression of privacy from prying eyes. What I liked best, however, was the new furniture, all kept in brown and cream with a tiny hint of color in the form of the odd painting on the wall. Granted, it'd never pass as a five star hotel, but it didn't resemble the servant accommodations it was before either.

Excusing myself, I left my guests trying out the large sofa in the living room and headed out the backdoor, eager to express my gratitude to my new assistant. A blast of oven-hot air blew in my face, reminding me of why I didn't want to spend the rest of my life down here in this pit. I glanced around but I didn't see Ginny. A rustling in the shriveled ivy hedges caught my attention. I peeked through and saw Ginny waiting behind a row of twisted trees with drooping limbs, wilting brown leaves and peeling bark. Smiling, I covered next to him and grabbed his hands. "You did it, Ginny."

"You like?" He grinned from ear to ear as I nodded.

"It's marvelous. Did Thrain or anyone else give you a hard time?"

Ginny shook his head, wide-eyed. I didn't know whether he was lying or his startled expression was just an indicator of being embarrassed at someone caring about his wellbeing. He bowed to kiss my hand, leaving a wet trail behind. I made a mental note to inform Dad it was time to find new kitchen help.

"Thank you," I said. "Now, there's something else I need you to do for me." He bobbed his head enthusiastically so I continued, "Have you ever been outside of Hell?"

What are you doing? Pinky hissed in my ear. *You know you're not allowed to let your father's demons roam the streets without his consent.*

Where was Kinky when I needed him to take care of my unsolicited conscience? "Go away," I whispered. "No one needs you here."

You know I can't. Cassie, think of your poor mother when she hears.

"Then don't tell her."

But you know I must since I hear everything you say.

"Get earplugs." I turned to face the annoying angel. "If you say a word, mate, I swear I'll put Kinky in charge and let him do whatever he wants with you. That's bound to cause you a bruise or two."

Pinky pouted. *You wouldn't!*

I raised my brows. "Try me. I'll have a jolly good time watching you cry and make everyone else up there in Heaven very sad. You know, one tiny, sad angel and the melancholy will spread like a bushfire. Imagine all the wailing for weeks. No more music, no more laughter and joy. Can you live with yourself for being the cause of so much sorrow?"

He gasped and disappeared in a puff of smoke. I hated causing Pinky more distress than necessary, but my plan depended on its surprise factor so the unfolding events seemed genuine.

Ginny was still staring at me. I inched closer and started whispering in his ear, revealing my plan step by step. He nodded a few times, but kept quiet. By the time I finished, I could see even he marveled at my inventiveness. "What do you say?" I asked, eager to hear his opinion. "Will it work?"

"Yes, Princess." The grin on his face was infectious.

"We mustn't make any mistakes. Don't let anyone see or catch you."

He nodded. I rummaged through my purse and offered him my old phone, an early prototype of my current one. Just as pretty, but with fewer functions. He grabbed it with shaking fingers. "You want me to hold it for you?"

"No, I want you to have it." The poor guy probably never received a gift in his entire life. I closed my hand around his. "Use it to open the portal and squeeze out of Hell, and back in. You can travel with it anywhere. Call me if there's a problem."

He peered at me. "But who's taking care of the kitchen in my absence?"

"Don't worry, I'll figure something out. This is far more important. You want to help me, right?"

"Yes." His voice rose until it turned into a long squeal. "Yes, I do, Princess."

"Then follow my orders." He bobbed his head in agreement. I held out my hand to my ear, imitating a phone. "If anything goes wrong, call me."

I watched Ginny scurry away before I joined the others. Dallas and Amber were sitting on the sofa, laughing as they recalled a story. Aidan was leaning against the wall, not joining in the conversation. I smiled at him before tapping Dallas on the shoulder to get his attention and said, "We should give them some privacy."

He looked startled as though the possibility of being a nuisance never crossed his mind. "Do they—"

I nodded.

"Let's catch up later then," Dallas said.

"Are you sure you don't want to stay with us?" Amber asked as she accompanied us to the door.

Dallas shook his head. "Thanks, but I'll pass." He defied her wishes. Either he was keen on spending time with me, or he had finally realized it was only a matter of time until the lovey-dovey couple made him feel superfluous.

Amber narrowed her gaze. "Why? Because her bed is softer than the one in the guest quarters? You always did like to play with fire. I hope you don't get burned."

I rolled my eyes. Any more hints about my identity from Amber and I was going to tape her mouth shut with a roll of duct tape.

"So, you two got big plans tonight?" Amber asked.

"Babe, you don't need to know that," Aidan said.

"I do. That's what nosey sisters are for."

They stared at each other in silence, entangled in their own personal battle. The lines around Aidan's mouth tightened as though it wasn't the first time they were having this conversation.

You still don't see it? Pinky asked.

I shook my head slightly so no one noticed.

Look at her stature.

What was he talking about? I raised my brows at him.

Pinky groaned. *She's too confident, as though nothing can touch her.*

If standing straight was his measure of evaluation, then every dancer and model out there must be immortal. I rolled my eyes and shushed him by flicking my hair back.

Aidan shrugged and turned away, losing the battle. Amber raised her thin eyebrows, a fake smile playing on her full lips. "Are you sleeping in the same room?"

"You'll be happy to hear Dallas and I stay on different floors," I said.

My answer seemed to please her because she backed off a little, or so I thought until she asked, "What a coincidence you met again, huh? What are you two up to?"

"Amber, you're being rude," Aidan hissed.

She shot him an irritated look. "I just want to know how my brother met the love of his life and what he's doing with all his time."

"Let's just say we're not wasting a minute watching television." Dallas winked at me. He was winding her up, which made me like him even more. Whatever Amber's problem was, I'd never been one to back off from an argument.

139

"Can we talk for a moment?" I grabbed her upper arm to pull. She didn't budge.

Told you, Pinky whispered. Slowly, his words started to make sense. When did he turn her? Someone *must've* warned him about the consequences. Dad would be so mad when he found out I brought home not one but two immortals.

"You're worried about him, I get it," I whispered as soon as we were outside.

She took a deep breath, eyes piercing into mine. "He doesn't know anything about your world which makes hanging out with you even more dangerous."

"Mate, you know nothing about me or my world," I hissed. "I helped you without asking questions, but that doesn't mean I don't know what's going on." That was a lie. In fact, I had no idea what was happening, but it was only a matter of time until I found out. "What makes you think hanging out with an angel's more dangerous than a bunch of vampires who're running from a jealous succubus goddess?"

"That's not all we're running from," Amber muttered. "You've no idea, Cass."

I inclined my head, taking in the nervous tinge wafting from her. "He's safe with me."

She sighed. "You're probably right. At least you're not going to kill him to hurt us. Just don't break his heart. He really likes you."

"I like him too." I grabbed her hand. "Stay here for as long as you want. I'll pop back in the next couple of days to sort out a few things."

"Like?"

140

I shrugged. "This and that. Just trust me."

Various emotions crossed her face. Curiosity, hesitation, even skepticism, but she didn't insist.

"Anything else you'd like to run past me?" I asked.

"Let me think." Amber stared out at the expansive wonderland of rock formations and cinder cones strewn across the barren landscape in a variety of colors, shapes and sizes. A puff of air made her jump. Huge plumes of sulfurous fumes and steam poured out through long cracks and fissures along the baked, dry desert ground. The sound of rumbling filled the air; a red light from the fountain of glowing lava shone in the distance.

"Anything?" I prompted.

She shook her head. "Not really. But I have a question or two." She pointed to a glowing cascade of lava way off to the east. "How did you explain"—she cleared her throat—"the fiery waterfall to Dallas?"

I smiled. "Special effects. It's Disneyworld, right?"

She grinned. "You might get away with that, but how do you explain the temperature?"

"Everyone knows it's hot in California."

"So what's with the heat anyway? This place reminds me of a desert," Amber said.

I snorted. "I believe you'll find a desert's cooler."

"That's California for you." She laughed and we returned to the cottage. I could see from the faint smile on Aidan's face he eavesdropped on our conversation. The problem with vampires is they have too many abilities for their own good.

* * *

We arrived at Dad's mansion with half an hour to spare before dinner. Ginny wasn't here so, to avoid provoking Dad's suspicion, I decided to play waitress tonight. Lucky for me, Dad didn't join us.

"How's the campaign going?" Dallas asked.

I took a bite of my Chicken Tikka masala, burning my tongue. The trouble with Hell was, even the food never cooled down.

"Are you okay, babe?"

I nodded, swallowing down the chunk with a mouthful of water. "I'm fine. In case you haven't noticed, we've been away all day. I didn't get a chance to spend time on brainstorming."

"I've been thinking about something that could really make an impression on prospective visitors."

He had no idea. Hell never failed to leave an impression, particularly not when Dad showed up in his business suit, carrying his briefcase aka torture instruments box with him.

"What do you have in mind?"

Enthusiasm sparked in Dallas's gaze. He put down his fork and grabbed my hand. "Imagine this: darkness, creepy music. Suddenly, a masked guy with an axe jumps from behind a bush. People will be scared to death."

If they don't laugh themselves into an early grave, Kinky muttered.

I smiled. "How did you come up with that?"

"You like it?"

I nodded. "Yes, but how does it fit in with Disneyworld?"

142

"Don't you see, babe?" Shaking his head, he moistened his lips. "What's more sensational than a mad murderer?"

One had to admire his zeal and dedication. "Disneyworld's about fairy tales, princesses and castles."

Dallas held up a hand, interrupting me. "You forget *Freaky Friday*."

He couldn't be serious. "Please correct me if I'm wrong, but I thought the scariest part of that movie was a teenager being stuck in a middle-aged woman's body and the boyfriend trying to make out with one's mother. Did the mass murderer escape my attention?"

"You have a point." Dallas picked up his fork and resumed eating, speaking with his mouth full. "I'll come up with something else."

"I'm sure you'll do."

He peered at me, smirking. "You're winding me up."

"No." I shook my head, taking in his sparkling eyes and rosy cheeks. "I'd never do that. I love your ideas."

His fingers closed around mine, drawing circles. The sensation travelled up my arm and down my body, settling in the pit of my stomach. "What did Amber tell you about their situation?"

The sudden change in topic took me off-guard. "Nothing."

"She didn't tell you why they needed to leave London for a while?"

I shook my head, hoping my expression looked innocent enough. "Did they rob a bank?"

He laughed, but I could see a frown forming on his smooth forehead. "Trust me, I wish it was the case."

"Do you want to tell me about it?" This was his chance to open up to me and establish the sort of trust that defines whether a relationship is long-term material. If he betrayed Amber's secret, I knew he saw me as someone he'd like to keep in his life. I might even be inclined to share with him a few details about my own life.

My palms started to sweat, this time not from the heat. Dallas ran his fingers through his hair, hesitating. Eventually, he grimaced. "I can't. She wouldn't want me to."

I wished I could yell that I knew everything already, so what was the big deal? But that wouldn't help us make progress in our relationship either. Fortunately, my big plan would go into action tomorrow. Soon, he'd be bound to realize it was time to leave the family nest and start a new life with me as his top priority, hence, no more secrets or words unspoken. Nothing against Amber, but she stood in the way of our predestined bond.

Patting his hand, I smiled. "I understand. I'd never want you to do something behind her back and betray her trust. It wouldn't be right."

"You're so gorgeous." He touched my arm, leaving a tingling sensation behind. "Let's do something together, something romantic. Just the two of us."

Romance sounded great. "Tomorrow?"

"Or today." He raised his brows meaningfully. Whatever he meant, I'd have to shatter his hopes because I wasn't that kind of girl.

"We could head to LA tomorrow, do a Hollywood tour if you're into movie stars. I know where a few of them live." I didn't mention that I stalked half of them into their mansions in the hope of a flash of inspiration regarding my next career move. After trying my hand at being a personal shopper, which failed because people had no taste, I came up with the idea of gathering work experience at Skylife and then taking on the *Amazon* imperium.

"Hollywood isn't my thing," Dallas said. "We could go shopping though."

My jaw dropped. A guy offering to go shopping was about as rare as catching a snowflake in the Amazon Rainforest. Come to think of it, maybe it wasn't such a rarity after all given that Dallas owned twice as much stuff, and I was already the hoarding kind, collecting whatever junk I could find. No wonder my clatter didn't bother him.

I nodded. "Great. Let's leave right after lunch so we have enough time to crash Rodeo Drive." Ginny should be finished with all preparations.

We ate our dinner chattering about this and that, then snuggled on the sofa in the living room. I had no idea where Dad was, but I couldn't shake off the feeling he was avoiding us. Maybe he had started to see the bond between Dallas and me, and kept away to give us privacy.

Who was I fooling? He didn't seem to take a liking to Dallas during our only dinner together. Knowing Dad, he was plotting the demise of my blossoming relationship this instant. If so, he underestimated me because I was already a step ahead.

Chapter 14 - Wrong turn

Dad didn't turn up for breakfast either, but he left a cryptic message mentioning something about finding one of the gates open. I instructed the chef to employ new kitchen help and clean up himself in the meantime, then retreated to my office. Dallas had left for the cottage to spend time with his sister. It suited me just fine because I'd rather work to take my mind off my plan. The anticipation kept me awake most of the night already.

The campaign was still stuck in stage one aka brainstorming. I spent half an hour staring at the towering plumes of dark grey smoke rising from the volcanoes in the distance, trying to decide what the patterns in the dark swirls looked like, then another ten minutes peering between my screen and the empty sheets spread across my entire work surface.

Hell didn't feature in the 'Top 10 Destinations to Visit'. Heaven might be the more obvious choice. How did one make the one place popular that had been slandered for centuries? Even if the right advertising could change people's perception of what it was like to live down here, Dad's reputation as a trickster would be hard to shift.

Still no idea? You've been spending hours on this assignment and it's getting boring. Kinky leaned over my shoulder, making me jump.

"Could you stop creeping up on me like that?" I frowned. "May I remind you I've been busy with more important issues?"

Like hiding two vampires in Hell? Your dad will be so proud.

"Shush. They'll be gone before he knows it." I started flicking through my papers in the hope he understood how busy I was and made a beeline for the door, or my purse. But Kinky had never been the perceptive kind.

The idea with the murderer wasn't even a bad one. We could send a few demons up there and offer people the opportunity to hide in Hell. Once they see how lovely it is down here, they won't want to leave.

"That's sneaky." I rolled my eyes. "How is your little plan of misleading mortals into coming down here helping Dad's reputation?"

Kinky shrugged. *You don't want to acknowledge how grand my plan is because you're so competitive.*

What about inviting some journalists over? Pinky asked. *They could have dinner with your father.*

My jaw dropped. I stared at him unbelieving. "Pinky, who in their right mind would accept an invitation to dine with," I held up my hands, imitating direct speech quotes, "*the devil?*"

I know a few, Kinky said.

"Go away, you two. I need time to think and you're not helping."

She's jealous because she can't keep up with my imagination, Kinky whispered.

"Go away," I yelled. "If you don't disappear this instant, I swear I'll find a new job for you—feeding my lovely pet."

That beast of a hound? You're so mean. I was only trying to help. Kinky scoffed and disappeared.

I pointed at the self-satisfied Pinky. "You too." Shooting me a pained look, he vanished in his usual puff of white smoke.

The room fell silent again. I took a long, deep breath before I dared return to my work. My muse didn't seem to want to honor me with her presence today. I spent hours jotting down half-baked ideas, then tossed them into my mental wastebasket. I was even starting to consider giving Pinky's dinner invitation a chance, just to have at least one plan to show off.

By midday I gave up and headed for the cottage to pick up the man of my dreams. Dad's campaign might not take shape the way I hoped, but at least my relationship flourished, and soon we'd take it to the next level. No curse would keep me bound to this place, devoid of a social life, with Dad as the only company. I shivered. Nothing against Dad, but his ideas of fun involved working from dawn until dusk, and watching lower demons feed the hound guarding Hell's main gate who was quite prone to biting off a limb or two in the process.

Dallas chattered all the way to at The Boulders of Hell on Dragon's Path where I pulled out my phone to open

148

the portal. As though sensing what was about to happen, he frowned before we stepped past the stones and through the invisible portal, reminding me of a conditioned pet that feared the electric shock right before he was being served dinner. Soon, he'd start questioning the sudden presence of charged particles in the air. From then on, it was only a matter of time until he suspected a connection between the electric jolts and me flipping open my phone.

"Did you feel that? My hair's standing." Dallas shuddered.

"It's the Golf of Mexico. There's probably a thunderstorm in South America. Happens all the time." I put the phone back in my pocket. "You'll get used to it."

He frowned. "It's only when I'm in this particular place, nowhere else." He was quicker than I gave him credit for.

"Really?" I peered at him, faking surprise. "Are you sure, babe? Maybe you're just standing in a particular spot, or you're overly sensitive to the thunder and lighting. Some people complain about a strange sense in their bones right before the onset of rain."

Rolling his eyes, he pulled me closer. "That's called arthritis. I'm pretty sure I don't suffer from that condition just yet."

"Perhaps you will in the future. Make sure you drink your glass of milk every day."

"You're not taking me seriously, Cass."

I smiled and cuddled against him. A blue spark flickered where our skin met. He flinched. "Got to love static electricity," I said, lest he start asking questions.

"If you say so," he mumbled.

I guided him to a car, hoping he wouldn't notice it wasn't the same as our rental which one of Dad's employees returned the day before.

"Everyone around here's used to this phenomenon. Maybe it's time to stop paying attention to it. So man up and get used to it."

"Oh, I'll man up all right." Grinning, he reached out to grab me. I jumped into the driver's seat and shut the door. "Quick reflexes," Dallas said, seemingly impressed.

"Yep. Now, get in." I chuckled and adjusted the rear-view mirror, then started the engine as he got in. Time to change the subject before his inquisitive mind focused back on the portal. "Did Amber say anything about us dating?"

"She's cool with it."

"That's what she said?" I pulled out of the parking lot, barely paying attention to the crowded street because my heart was racing in my chest. Usually, I couldn't care less what anyone thought, but Amber played a huge part in Dallas's life and could influence his decisions.

"She said you're great and that she's okay with it if we start seeing each other."

I smirked. "How nice of her."

"I'd rather my girlfriend got along with my family," Dallas said. "It saves drama."

Drama was exciting. The more tension, the better. Who wouldn't want a piece of that? "Did you also mention that on our very first date, we decided to skip the dating and move in together? And that it was completely your idea?"

He laughed. "I think I left out the tiny details."

"You're right. Your family approving of me is the most important thing in this relationship." If he noticed the sarcasm in my voice, he didn't comment on it.

Turning the car, I changed lanes and drove past a petrol station into a broad road with dilapidated buildings towering on both sides. Small shops advertised cheap haircuts and designer clothes, all knockoffs of *Gucci* and *Prada* available for a fragment of the runway price. Children played on the sidewalks next to women clad in tiny shorts and tank tops. As we passed a dark alley, I was sure I heard gunshots and people screaming.

Dallas snorted. "So this is where the stars shop in Beverly Hills? It doesn't look like Rodeo Drive."

"Only the ones that plummet at the box office." I peered at a guy in what looked like a trench coat selling fake *Rolex* watches in front of a fast-food restaurant. "I'm taking a shortcut." From the corner of my eye, I spotted a frown on his face. Amber must've said something because he was more suspicious than before.

Two beady, yellow eyes glowed in the headlights. I hit the brake hard. The car came to a standstill, throwing us forward, as an animal as big as a dog scurried by and into the maze of trashcans.

Dallas shot me an irritated glance. "Come on, Cass. What's with all the back alley shortcuts? I'd rather not get eaten alive by giant sewer rats."

He looked so cute with that expression on his face. "Don't tell me a big, tough guy like yourself is afraid of a little dog?"

"You call that thing little?" Snorting, he looked up at a graffiti image splashed across the concrete wall of a building. Big block letters in a rainbow of colors glared out at us. "Great. We're in gang territory. Can't you just take the main road like everyone else? I'd rather we didn't end up dead somewhere in a gutter."

"Or a wheelie bin." I laughed. "Relax and embrace your inner thug."

"If someone comes near us with a tire iron, I can fight if I have to. Trust me, I'm no wimp."

Definitely hit a soft spot there. I leaned over and squeezed his hand. "I've been here a million times and know my way around." Which was true. Not even New York boasted the same amount of drama and human emotion so, naturally, I came here often.

"If you say so," he muttered.

We stopped at the traffic lights. A group of youngsters crossed the street, yelling and shoving, proud of a crime they'd just committed. I focused and saw hazy pictures flashing through my mind. Raiding a building. Stealing half a pound of drugs. I closed my eyes, slowly inhaling their elation caused by a surge in adrenaline. There was something else though. The air around them darkened, carrying the imminent scent of disaster and pain. Unbeknown to them, they were about to die.

"We shouldn't be here," Dallas whispered. "Please just drive."

I opened my eyes again and turned to face him, only now noticing the color had drained from his cheeks. The bond was slowly making him sense a bit of how I felt. He wasn't used to having a sixth sense so, naturally, he didn't know how to handle it, or so I thought.

The lights changed to green, but the youngsters lingered in the middle of the street. Two large, hooded figures appeared on the sidewalk behind them and pulled out guns. My knees started to tremble, but not from fear.

Dallas opened the car door when I grabbed his arm. "What are you doing? Are you crazy?"

"Those are just boys, Cass. I can't watch them die and not do a thing. Stay here, call the police, and lock the doors."

A sense of thrill washed over me. I could barely discern his words. The hooded figures raised their guns and aimed.

Don't let him go, Kinky shouted in my eardrum. Since when was he shying away from a bit of drama? *You'll lose him if he gets stabbed or shot.*

I peered at Dallas's face, still scared and confused but willing to risk his life to save someone else's. Kinky was right. If Dallas got hurt, I'd lose the love of my life and I'd be bound to Hell forever.

"Pinky, stop them," I whispered even though helping defied every rule in Heaven and Hell. Literally. Not even I was allowed to intervene in such a situation without authorization from a higher source like Dad, or the other big guy who happened to be Mom's boss.

How? Pinky wailed. *I don't have the power.*

Tell them to be nice and love each other, Kinky said. *If you mess up, you'll be stuck in Hell with Cass forever.*

Oh, no. Tears shimmered in Pinky's eyes.

Is he going to cry? Kinky mocked.

I don't want to be stuck in Hell. Pinky's thin voice turned into a long howl. The poor mite was terrified at the outlook just as much as I was.

"What are you waiting for? Get out there!" I muttered under my breath. Pinky sighed and disappeared.

Dallas yanked his arm away and fled out the door. A horn honked, then another. The youngsters started to shout obscenities at a *Rolls Royce* with gold flames on the sides and hood, magenta spokes, chrome rims, and dark-tinted windows. I rolled my eyes. A towering giant with the biggest arms I'd ever seen in my entire life walked toward Dallas swinging a tire iron. My heart leapt in my chest. I was surprised the guy didn't fall over with the ton of gold necklaces he wore around his neck like *Mr. T.* from the *A-team*. I had to do something, but what? Freezing time would've been a good choice, but I couldn't. I only have the power to do that once a year, and I already used that option up at lunch with Mom and Dad when their arguing gave me a headache.

Rushing toward them, I craned my neck to get a better glimpse when I noticed the shiny halo hovering in mid-air. One of the hooded guys held up a hand to the other as Pinky whispered in his ear. Seconds ticked by. Nothing happened. Dallas squared his shoulders, exchanging a heated conversation with the muscular man. Something about, 'Leave the kids alone and get the hell of here.' The man shoved him hard, but it wasn't enough to deter Dallas. He shoved him back. I was happy my man wasn't a wimp and could handle himself, but this guy was dangerous and could pull out a knife. Dallas's tough guy act was no match against a blade of steel. We needed to get away before a fight erupted resulting in a shooting.

"Get rid of the kids...now!" I whispered, knowing Pinky could hear me.

The lights changed from green to red. The hooded figures hesitated; their agitation was palpable in the air.

JAYDE SCOTT

The youngsters started shoving the driver. It was a matter of seconds before they took out whatever weapons they were carrying and caused yet another atrocity in our already brutal world.

If I had to, I'd jump in there and claw out everyone's eyes before they lay a single hand on the love of my life. Who was I kidding? There was also the problem of stepping into the heart of the drama. The currents could be too strong and I might not have the willpower to protest and stop what was about to take place. No matter how much I wanted to, my fallen angel nature wouldn't let me.

A thud clanked on the ground. The muscular guy had dropped his tire iron and hugged Dallas, mumbling something like, "I'm a lover, not a fighter."

Dallas eased from his arms. "I don't swing that way, man."

I inched closer and pulled Dallas away, shouting over my shoulder, "Yeah, he loves you, too. Got to go. It's been a blast."

"Thanks, dude," the guy said.

"Cass!" Dallas yelled. "Get back in the car."

I smiled and jumped into the driver's seat. "Looks like you diffused the situation."

He shook his head. "That was weird. One minute the guy wanted to kill me and the next he wanted to hug me like I was his best friend."

"Got to love crazy California, huh?"

I started the engine as the hooded figures put away their guns and turned on their heel. Pinky appeared on my shoulder, his eyes were filled with pride.

"Didn't you forget something?" I muttered.

"Oh, thanks. My wallet fell out of my pocket." Dallas reached down to pick it up.

I was talking to Pinky. "What about them?" I whispered.

Pinky whimpered and vanished again, only to materialize over the youngsters' heads a moment later. His eyes were closed, his arms wide-open, stretched out to the side as though in meditation.

Why's he praying? Kinky said.

I shook my head, signaling that I didn't know. He must be appealing to the youngsters' conscience. I could only hope they had one. But it wasn't the youths who backed off. Holding out his hands in a peace sign, the driver turned away and walked slowly to his vehicle. The shouting continued, but the crowd of kids slowly dissipated as the lights changed from red to green again. I revved the car and sped off. The deep lines around Dallas's mouth told me he was still confused what just happened. Too bad he was about to experience another surprise within the next ten minutes.

Chapter 15 - Otherworld this way

"Please tell me you're not taking yet another shortcut," Dallas said.

I killed the engine. "We're getting out."

He narrowed his gaze and peered out the window at the busy street with rundown housing complexes to both sides. "Why here?"

"Because we wouldn't find a parking space on Rodeo Drive. It's only a minute or two away. Walking's healthy." Smiling, I jumped out of the car and shot a fleeting look at the dirty alley to our right. Next to it, the dark brown building with its boarded windows and peeling plaster gave it an even more menacing flair.

"Maybe we could shop another day," Dallas said. But he followed me out nonetheless. His gaze swept over the rundown area, lingering on a group of tourists emerging from a house on the other side of the road. One would think, after living in London for most of his life and travelling to so many countries, he should be unperturbed by crowds, but as usual Dallas proved any cliché wrong.

"If you could settle down anywhere in the world, where would it be?" I asked, inching closer.

He hesitated, his eyes still darting about uneasily. "If I tell you, can we go there this very second?"

"Maybe."

"Your air-conditioned house."

I turned to face him. "You're so full of it. You hate the heat in California."

"Well, I'm thinking I'm loving your house right now. Watching the game on TV with a bowl of popcorn and an ice cold drink with you snuggled up in my arms sounds like heaven."

"You don't like cities very much, do you?" I grinned and held out my hand. He grabbed it and grimaced.

"I abhor them. It's like being caged in with nothing but dust and exhaust fumes to breathe."

I waited for the traffic to slow down and stop at the traffic lights before I pulled him across the street. "Rodeo Drive's right over there. You can smell *Gucci* and *Armani* from here, or so it's said."

"Really?" He shot me an amused look. "All I can smell is the bins over there and rotting garbage spilling out of them." He stopped and took a whiff. "I think someone's having cabbage for lunch."

I winked. "Maybe it's *Chanel's* new perfume."

"If it is, don't expect to get it as a Christmas present." He wrapped his arm around me, pulling me against his chest. His gaze glazed over, lingering on my lips. He wanted to kiss me. I groaned inwardly. Seriously? This was the most perfect moment he could find for our first kiss, surrounded by waste and smog?

I pulled away, disgusted by the aroma of onions wafting past. "We came here to shop, so shopping's all you're getting."

He grabbed my hand, pulling me back into his embrace as he whispered, "I thought you'd appreciate a guy who shared the same interests."

That's why he offered we pay Rodeo Drive a visit? A smile spread across my lips. "I thought by agreeing to come here I was doing you a favor."

"You're not into shopping either." His mouth moved closer, his hot breath caressed my cheek, making it tingle. I felt a strong pull toward him, hurrying me to pull him close and never let go. My emotions overwhelmed me, making me choke on my breath.

"I love shopping, just not with a hot guy on my arm. That's too distractive." A soft gust ruffled my hair. I didn't turn. Behind me, footsteps thudded closer. I still didn't turn.

Dallas attention snapped into place. He raised his gaze slowly. Peering over my shoulder, he whispered, "Don't move."

"Why?" I mouthed.

"Hand over your purse," a male voice said.

Dallas swallowed hard. Beads of sweat gathered across his forehead. "Do as he says, babe."

Turning, I shook my head. My gaze fell on the little man about forty with teeth black as coal, dressed in dusty rags. His shirt showed tiny holes across the chest, dark hair peering out from beneath. I raised my chin defiantly. "If you think I'll just give you my belongings, you're mistaken."

The man inched closer, holding up a knife, his wrist shaking. "I'll hurt you if you don't."

"Babe, just give him the purse," Dallas hissed. "I'll get you a new one."

I took a step forward, staring into the man's bloodshot eyes. "No. You'll have to find someone else because I'm not playing victim."

His irises enlarged. I nodded to reinforce my words.

"She doesn't mean it, sir." Dallas stepped behind me, placing a hand on my shoulder as he whispered, "What are you doing? Move away from him."

"Don't worry. I've got it all under control." Smiling, I reached into my bag, my fingers closing around my phone.

"Put your hands where I can see them," the man yelled.

"Are you out of your mind?" Dallas whispered.

I shook my head. "Are you scared of what I might be hiding in here?"

The man raised his knife to my chest. "Hand over your purse. Now!"

Dallas stepped between the knife and me, pushing me behind him. His neck was bathed in sweat, the thin material of his shirt's glued to his back. "If you're going to hold a knife up to somebody, do it to me and not to a defenseless woman."

The guy glared. "You're just begging me to slash your pretty little face. Not so sure Girlfriend here would ever want to step out in public with you again."

Dallas squared his shoulders. "You take one more step and I guarantee you'll be the one having social phobias when I'm done with you. Your friends will have to call you Scar Face." That was a good one. Soaking up every morsel of drama, I peered at the mugger, waiting for his reply.

"I'm going to beat you into a pulp. We'll see who protects her then."

"You'll have to kill me first before you ever get to touch her." I could see Dallas's muscles tense, ready to attack. He was so handsome and brave. Although I was perfectly capable of taking care of myself, pride rose in my chest at the knowledge my boyfriend would defend me with his life.

I rose on my toes to peer over his shoulder, then winked. Our aggressor lunged forward. At the same time, I pressed a few buttons on my phone. The earth trembled beneath our feet, a gust of wind knocked Dallas to the side. He collapsed against the garbage bins. Our aggressor shot me an anxious glance and took off the way he came.

Dallas stirred, groaning. Lying next to him, I closed my eyes and put on a pained expression.

"Cass?" His hand brushed over my cheek to my throat, feeling for a pulse.

My eyes fluttered open. "Dallas?" I whispered. "Don't leave me."

"Are you hurt?" His voice betrayed his concern; his fingers hurried across my skin, checking for wounds.

I raised my hand to my head, and dropped it again as though I was too faint to move. "What happened?"

"Attempted mugging. Can you walk?"

"I think so." Groaning, I pushed up on my elbows.

Dallas helped me to my feet whispering, "You'll be okay. Let's get back to the car and I'll drive you to a hospital."

Taking slow steps, it took us a while to reach the main road. A man dressed in an expensive designer business suit sporting a Rolex watch was talking on his phone. We walked past without paying him any attention.

The car was still parked on the side of the road. Dallas held out his hand. "Can I have the keys, please?"

I rummaged in my purse, then shook my head. "I must have dropped them."

He groaned. "This day can't get any worse. Wait here."

I watched him walk over to the chattering man and tap him on the shoulder to get his attention. The man continued talking without so much as a glance at Dallas.

"Sir!" I yelled. "Please, can you call an ambulance? We were just mugged."

The man still didn't react.

Dallas turned to me, frowning. I inched closer until my arm brushed the man's suit.

"The rich moron's ignoring me. Does he think he's too good for us?" Annoyance was palpable in Dallas's tone.

I shook my head. "No, I don't think so."

"What do you mean?"

"Look." I waved my hand in front of the man's face. His eyes didn't move, he didn't even blink.

"Is he blind?" Dallas asked.

I stepped closer and cocked my head. "He could still hear us."

"Yeah, my mouth's pretty big." A frown settled between Dallas's brows. "Maybe he's hard of hearing too."

That's called distorted reasoning. How did he even come up with his explanations? "He couldn't talk on the phone if he were."

162

Dallas nodded. "Right. What's his problem then?"

Turning to face him, I grabbed his hand. "He can't see or hear us."

"I can see that. There's got to be a rational explanation." Dallas leaned over and yelled in the man's ear, "Hello? Is anyone home?"

"That won't help much." I moistened my lips, soaking up every bit of tension wafting from him as the meaning of my words slowly started to sink in.

"Let's find someone else then, someone who can hear and see us." His unconscious might have gotten the message, but his consciousness was still in denial. He needed to say it first to believe it.

I squeezed his hand hard. "Dallas, listen to me. It doesn't make sense that another person wouldn't see or hear us. There's only one probable explanation, and you know it."

His eyes widened. Disbelief crossed his features, followed by dismay. "We're dead?"

I breathed out, relieved his brain made an appearance and finally opened shop for the day. For a moment, I thought he might quote an alien invasion as the more likely possibility.

"Maybe not dead—" I hesitated "—yet. For all we know, our bodies could be hooked up to a life support machine in a hospital while a group of renowned surgeons perform major surgery."

Kinky appeared on my shoulder. *Renowned surgeons in a hospital? That doesn't make sense. Wouldn't you be hovering in mid-air next to your body then?*

I slapped my shoulder mere inches from the annoying, little devil.

"You mean we're returning to the crime scene in the hope to find a psychic that will help us catch the murderer." Dallas nodded, alarm pouring out of him in huge, hot waves. His shirt was soaked with sweat. "That definitely sounds like something I'd do. I could never rest knowing the same fate could befall another poor guy taking his girlfriend shopping."

"You'd definitely be the poltergeist type. You'd be a cute one." I turned my back on him so he wouldn't notice the delighted expression on my face. The guy with the phone walked down the street, still not paying attention to us.

You're milking it for all it's worth, I've got to give you that, Kinky said.

"So would you."

"No, you'd be cuter." I leaned against his chest.

"You'd be a stunner," Dallas whispered, his lips lowering onto mine again.

Hey, focus, Kinky yelled in my ear, making me jump back.

Clearing my throat, I said, "So we're kinda dying then."

"I don't get it." Dallas rubbed a hand over his neck. "The last thing I remember is him jumping toward me, but not the pain or the knife in my gut."

"The dude had reflexes like Bruce Lee. We didn't even know what hit us." I shot him a weak grin. Time to change the subject. "I should've given him the purse, but the way you stood up for me was amazing. I'll never forget that."

He inched closer and pressed his lips against my forehead. "I'd do it again if I had to. I'm not going to let anything happen to the most precious thing in the world."

164

I bit my lip so I wouldn't gush out words of undying love. His words definitely struck a chord with me.

He pondered for a moment as if still contemplating the situation. I could almost see his brain putting two and two together. That's when reality finally struck. "But why us? Why today? I'm too young to die," Dallas said. I knew the self-satisfaction of standing up against a criminal wouldn't last long.

"It must be fate. Maybe a higher calling." I reached for his hand and pulled. He stood his ground.

"What are you doing?" he asked. "We can't leave."

"Why not?"

"Because we have to wait for the white light to tell us what to do next." He looked so convinced, I almost laughed.

I motioned to the sky. "Don't you think if there was a white light, it'd have arrived already?"

"Maybe it got held up at the traffic lights." He grinned. "I get your point. Where do you want to go then?"

I shrugged. "Don't know. Let's head down the street."

"One would think once dead you shouldn't feel the smoldering heat. I'm going to suffocate soon." He paused for effect. "Wait, I can't because I'm already dead."

"We're still bound to the physical plane, which means we feel what our bodies feel."

"Great." Dallas started walking down the street. I followed a step behind. "I still think someone should be here to greet us," he muttered. "Like my dead aunt Mildred. Bless her soul."

He was one tough guy to figure out. I thought going on a fast paced murder chase might be more his thing. If I knew meeting the clichéd blond angel clad in a white nightgown with a halo on his head meant so much to him, I would've arranged that instead. I was glad to find he wasn't freaked out though. He clearly had potential as my boyfriend, what with being Lucifer's daughter and all.

"We're supposed to do something before someone greets us," I said.

"Catching the culprit, I thought we figured that out already."

"Maybe." I pointed at the closest road sign, white with neon green letters. "That's a weird name for a street."

"Where?" Dallas stopped and followed my line of vision. "Lovers Bay."

"There's two of us. Maybe it's an indicator to head that way."

"If you think so," he said.

We turned right into a narrow alley with a patch of green grass and tall trees to both sides. Dark leaves swayed in the soft breeze. The three-story apartment buildings looked well maintained but deserted. A couple walked past, ignoring us.

"They didn't see us either." I peered at Dallas to catch his reaction.

He ignored my remark and pointed at another neon street sign a few feet to the right. "Otherworld this way—two together. That's strange."

"I think it's a message." We crossed the street and stopped in front of it.

"What's it supposed to say?" Dallas asked.

"No idea." I rolled my eyes behind his back.

It's called denial, Kinky said, appearing on my shoulder. *He doesn't want to see it, which reveals a lot about his attitude toward you and your relationship.*

"Hush," I mouthed silently, figuring not everyone's wired to know exactly when and how they want to get married. "Come on." I pulled Dallas through another side street until we reached a park and stopped under a tree, a few inches away from a bench. I scanned the place to make sure no one was around, but Ginny had done a great job here too.

Two tiny birds chirped from the branch above us. "Aren't they cute?" I whispered.

"What?" Dallas looked up, frowning. "Oh, you're talking about the birds. Don't make a hasty move so they don't fly over our heads and leave us a present in our hair."

The boy has no romantic bone in his body.

"The way they snuggle up to each other, they look so happy," I said, unfazed by Pinky's remark. The birds flew away, landing on top of another sign in the distance. "I think they want us to follow."

Dallas groaned. "You don't believe in a white angelic light, but you think a couple of birds are some sort of clue."

I playfully nudged him in the ribs to get his attention and pointed at a tree with low-hanging branches, which looked in dire need of some water. "What does the sign over there say?"

"Otherworldly retreat. Enter here. Honorable couples only." Squinting, Dallas spun around in a slow circle. "We are a couple. That should be our entrance, but I don't see anything."

I shook my head. "Technically, we aren't a couple since we haven't even kissed."

"Let's do it then." He pulled me to his chest, knocking the breath out of my lungs. There was barely time to blink before his lips lowered onto mine. The air around us crackled, a hot flush travelled up my body, making my head spin. His lips were smooth as they caressed mine, pressing gently, while his hands cupped my face, drawing me closer. My knees threatened to buckle under me. The earth seemed to quake beneath our feet, making my head spin.

Why do we need to see this? Pinky squealed.

Yes, get a room, Kinky yelled into my eardrum.

I broke free from Dallas's embrace and cleared my throat, beaming. Dallas's cheeks were on fire, the glint in his eyes told me he found our kiss just as special as I did.

"Do you think we'll get in now?" he asked.

"Don't know. We can try. What are we looking for anyway?"

"A door or portal, maybe a boat."

I raised my brows, but didn't comment.

A boat? Kinky laughed. *Unless it runs on wheels, he'll have to pull it into Heaven himself.*

"Where is it?" Dallas felt the air for a door. "We're a couple, so why can't we get in?"

"Maybe there's another requirement," I prompted.

"What could it be?"

Sensing it might take a while, I dropped down on the grass, leaning my back against a tree, and peered at the empty houses in the distance from the direction we'd just come from. At this speed, I'd be stuck with Dad for the rest of my life.

"It says 'honorable'."

Doesn't seem to ring a bell. Maybe use a synonym, Pinky said.

"A proper, respectable relationship." I smiled at Dallas. He shook his head.

"That's exactly what we have so it must be something else."

"In some cultures it's not respectable to date someone without a promise," I said.

He frowned. "Like?"

I held up my ring finger.

"Oh." For a fleeting moment, panic crossed his features, replaced by a huge grin. "Well, if that's what it takes."

He kneeled down, reaching for my hand, and wrapped a thin branch around my finger. Granted, it looked nothing like a ring, but my heart skipped a beat nonetheless.

"What are you doing?" I whispered.

"You mean the world to me and I know what I feel is real. I cannot go another minute without knowing you are in my life forever. Cass—" he moistened his lips "—I know this sounds crazy since we've only been dating for a few days, but it's the right thing to do. I know you're *the one.* Please don't say 'no' before you've given it enough thought. Do you want to marry me?"

Even though Ginny and I had been planning this moment ever since Dad mentioned the curse, I was overwhelmed by emotion. My breath caught in my throat.

He cocked a brow. "Please?"

I nodded and jumped into his open arms. "Yes. I love you so much."

"I love you too." He pulled me into his arms and planted a kiss on my lips, his eyes twinkling. "I'll get you a real ring as soon as—"

"We find a jeweler?" I laughed and pulled away slightly to meet his gaze, my heart hammering in my chest.

It's cheating, Pinky said.

No, it's not, Kinky said.

Yes, it is. She pushed him.

No, she didn't.

Kinky was right. I wasn't cheating. My little scheme wasn't meant to deceive Dallas because there was nothing to deceive. Our bond would've led to marriage sooner or later anyway. Behind Dallas's back, I pulled out my phone and punched in numbers and letters. The ground shook, the air crackled like a burning log. Dallas stiffened. "Not again."

I broke free from our embrace and pointed a few feet away. "Is that what you were looking for?"

He turned, a smile spread across his lips as he peered at the large, golden gate stretching into the white clouds above, steam rising a few inches above the ground.

"Is that Heaven?" Dallas asked in awe.

"The sign says Otherworld."

Dallas shrugged. "Sounds good enough to me as long as we get to escape this heat."

"Hope dies last," I muttered, pulling him through the portal back to Hell.

Chapter 16 – Doomed

The portal spewed us out at The Boulders of Hell on Dragon's Path. Dad's mansion was hidden behind the two boulders blocking the stony path. From here, it was only a five-minute walk, which should give me enough time to come up with an explanation. I never figured my plan to get Dallas to ask for my hand would work so, naturally, I didn't contemplate my next step.

"That's weird," Dallas said, peering at a jumble of black rocks in the dry lava beds.

"What?"

"We're back in Disneyworld."

"No!" I faked surprise as I turned to face him, wide-eyed. "Maybe the portal took us back to the place we're supposed to visit."

"Or Disneyworld *is* the Otherworld. I'm destined to spend eternity in an oven. How awesome is that? Let's see whether anyone can sense us. I know the perfect person," Dallas said.

He was talking about his necromancer sister. Visiting her could blow my entire plan so that wasn't going to happen. Plan A coming right up—tears. "I need to see Dad first." My lips started to quiver; my eyes filled with unshed tears. "He must be devastated after hearing what happened to his only child."

"Of course. You're right, babe," Dallas said, rubbing a hand over my back. "Just remember he won't be able to see or hear you."

We reached the mansion in silence. I instructed Dallas to wait in the hall while I headed upstairs in search of Dad. I found him in his office, leaned over countless sheets spread across his huge mahogany desk.

I peeked over my shoulder before I closed the door behind me and hopped on my usual spot on top of his papers.

"Cassie, where have you been?" He pointed at the large smudge of dirt on my arm I didn't notice in all the upheaval. I grabbed a tissue from his box and started rubbing my skin. "Something's wrong. The guards have reported that—"

"Shush. Dallas might be listening." I leaned closer, ignoring his frown. "I've found a way to get rid of the curse."

"The curse?"

"Yes, the one that will bind me to this place once I turn eighteen."

"You mean to your *home*," Dad said.

172

I waved my hand. "Let's not start a debate here. We haven't much time. There's something you need to do for me." He cocked a brow. I continued, "Dallas and I are getting married, but he thinks we're dead, or dying in a hospital."

Dad jumped up from his seat. "You're what?"

"Hush, what did I tell you," I hissed. "Sit down and keep quiet, Dad."

Taking a deep breath, he did as I said. "You're too young to marry. And to a mortal? Cass, what were you thinking? How did you even get him to propose? The kid said marriage didn't feature in his life plan yet."

"It's obvious you've been eavesdropping on our conversation." Pausing, I glared at him. "I don't appreciate that. Dallas was a little confused before, but now he's ready to take our relationship to the next level."

Dad groaned. "What did you say about a hospital?"

I flicked my hair back, sorting through my thoughts. "We had a bit of an accident, so he thinks we're deadly wounded. I need you to pretend you have taken care of our battered bodies for the last day or so."

He laughed. "Stop it right there. That's even too crazy for your old man."

I sighed. "Dad, do you want to see me happy?" He nodded, amused. "Then do as I say. I will use my phone to knock him out so you can carry him to his room. When he wakes up tell him how devastated you were, how you pulled some strings to get the best doctors in the world to save your only child and her adored boyfriend. Make sure you have some major dark bags under your eyes to show off. I'd be most grateful if you could shed a tear or two as well. Got it?"

He bobbed his head, smirking.

"What's so funny?" I snapped.

"It's just—" he shook his head and wiped a tear from the corner of his eye "—you've definitely inherited my inventiveness. I'm so proud of you."

"Well, I knew that DNA of yours had to come in handy one day."

"He still doesn't know, does he?" Dad said. Avoiding his gaze, I shrugged. "When are you going to tell him?"

"Soon." I started drumming my fingers on the polished armrest of my chair.

"You know he'll freak. You're lucky if he doesn't run away without so much as a glance back."

I stared at my stilettoed boots, wondering whether to get a second pair because they were so comfortable and currently on sale. It sure beat thinking about Dallas's reaction when he discovered my identity, or Dad's, for that matter.

"Come here, kiddo." Dad pulled me into a tight hug. I snuggled against his chest and breathed in his aftershave, letting myself fall back in time and feel like the little girl who always knew she was different.

There were so many things I'd rather not think about right now so I did what I always did: focus on taking one step at a time. I pulled out my phone, punched in the numbers to knock Dallas out, and hurried downstairs. Dallas was lying on the floor, unconscious. Dad threw him over his shoulder like he weighed nothing and carried him to the guestroom Dallas had occupied the last couple of days.

The blinds were drawn, the bed was made. One of Dad's demons must've aired this morning after we left. Every surface was clean and tidy; it looked nothing like a sickbed.

I tucked Dallas in, wiping a stray strand of hair from his forehead. He seemed so peaceful and serene, I could spend hours just staring at the way his breathing made his broad chest move up and down.

"He'll wake up soon," Dad said.

"I know." Taking a deep breath, I glanced up at Dad. "This doesn't look authentic."

Dad peered around and nodded. "What about now?" My nostrils flared, catching a whiff of medicine and disinfectant. The red, satin sheets changed to white cotton, torn in several places. I even noticed a bug crawling across the tiled, naked floor where a thick, soft rug had just been a minute ago. Gee, I couldn't wait to get my powers. Then I'd finally be able to do all of this and more with a snap of my fingers, instead of relying on my often malfunctioning phone.

I laughed and slapped Dad's hand. "Stop it." The cotton changed back to red satin, the bug disappeared.

"Better?"

"Keep the medical scent," I said. "Can we have more flowers and maybe a get-well-soon card from you? Thank you."

"Want me to write it in fancy cursive? Maybe add a few kisses and hearts?" Smiling, Dad rubbed a hand over my back.

Dallas's eyes fluttered open. He took in the room, confused. "Bob? Cass? What happened?"

175

"You, son, barely escaped the narrow clutches of death." Dad threw me an amused glance.

"I was downstairs a minute ago," Dallas said.

"That's not possible." I grabbed his hand. "Babe, you were in and out of a coma for—"

"Days," Dad continued.

"Hours," I said, shooting him a warning look. Obviously, the moment Dallas talked to Amber he'd find out he hadn't been knocked out for days. "We've been so worried, we've lost track of time."

"But we were together. We talked." Dallas's eyes grew wide. I figured my little story would haunt the poor guy for all eternity. I almost felt bad, until I realized I'd be by his side to make sure he recovered. Seeing it from that perspective, he got a great deal.

I wiped a fake tear from my eye. "We were in a place we should never have visited at this young age. Dad cried nonstop."

Dad nodded. "Yes, and then I laughed." I glared at him. He cleared his throat and continued, "I laughed because I had depleted all tears. Now that you're alive again, you should enjoy your lives instead of getting married."

"Dad!" I elbowed him in the ribs. "Don't you see it? We're only alive *because* we fulfilled our duty, which was to realize that we're meant to be together."

"Yes," Dad said. "I'm sure you're made for one another and you'll make a wonderful married couple *one day*. Just not in the next ten years or so."

Dallas peered from Dad to me then back to Dad.

"You can't tell me what to do," I hissed.

"I'm still your father," he whispered.

"What's the big deal anyway?"

"You're too young."

I smiled at Dallas. "You said we'd get a ring as soon as we found a jeweler. Well, there's no need for it. I'm sure Mom won't mind if I use hers. It's not like she needs it anymore."

"Cass, no!" Dad whispered.

I pushed out my jaw. "Stop me, then." He peered at me, unbelieving. Why was Dad being so difficult? Surely he understood the magnitude of the curse. I wouldn't let it ruin my life like it ruined Aunt Patricia's. The poor girl had to lean out the window to catch a ray of sun. I didn't see myself stuck in my room for the rest of my life, with Dad as my only company.

I planted a kiss on Dallas's cheek. "I'm so glad you're back. Let's arrange a family meeting so everyone can meet and discuss wedding presents."

"Whatever you want, babe." Dallas nodded, insecure.

"Can't wait. It'll be a blast." I threw Dad a triumphant look. He sighed and got up. I was inclined to believe I'd won this particular battle, until Dad turned with a smug grin.

"Don't make any hasty plans, sweetie. You and Dallas can't marry just yet."

I narrowed my gaze. "Why's that?"

Dad buried his hands in his pockets, stalking for time. "Because part of your family heirloom says you need your aunts' consent."

"That won't be a problem."

"You sure?" The corners of Dad's mouth twitched. I could see he savored every minute of this. "You seem to forget they've never been able to agree on anything in their entire life."

I stared at the tiles on the floor, dumbstruck. Dad was right. The problem wasn't so much a difference in taste but rather unwillingness to compromise. Their constant bickering reminded me of a malignant version of loving to disagree. It had become so pronounced that they kept changing their mind on issues in order to avoid adopting the same stance as the others. If one agreed, at least one of the others wouldn't. Basically, I was doomed.

Chapter 17 - Raising the dead

A family reunion to drop the news of my imminent marriage didn't seem like a good idea just yet. Not before I had a chance to talk to my aunts individually and explain why agreeing for a change could save me from major depression and an early midlife crisis.

My three aunts, Patricia, Krista and Selena, were Dad's sisters. Patricia was the youngest, Selena the eldest. In between came Krista. She had been married a million times—not literally, of course. But, given that she'd had more spouses than I cared to remember, it might as well be. She knew what it was like to find *the one*, so I decided to pay her a visit right after seeing Patricia.

Outside, it was still dim, but the first morning rays seeped through the drawn brocade curtains, casting a soft glow on my crimson spread. In half an hour, the world would be bathed in shimmering brightness, earth cracking

DOOMED

from the relentless heat. I was lying in my huge four-poster bed, contemplating my next steps, when a knock on the door echoed through the large room, and Dallas walked in. Ever since our pretend-accident, he seemed shaky on his feet, as though his perfectly healthy body suffered pain.

"You're awake." He cuddled on the bed next to me and pulled me to his chest, brushing my hair out of my face. His fingers moved gingerly over my skin, leaving a tingling sensation, like a hundred butterflies fluttering their delicate wings against my cheek.

I smiled. "Are you feeling better?"

"Maybe a little." He caught my lips in a fleeting kiss. "Your dad asked how the campaign's coming along. He said it'd be nice if he didn't have to wait for all eternity. Isn't he funny?"

I smirked. "Hilarious."

"He also said you couldn't visit your aunts before he saw some progress."

Groaning, I pulled the covers aside and jumped out of bed right into my fluffy, pink slippers. "Let's get to work then."

Dallas placed his hand on my arm, stopping me. "He said something else."

"Really?" Irritated, I stared at the blooming pink tulips on my dresser that weren't there a day ago.

"He asked me to invite Amber and Aidan for dinner. We're having—" Dallas cringed as he finished his sentence "—beef steak."

"Again?" Crap! Dad was onto me. My heart skipped a beat. I turned away from Dallas so he wouldn't see my shocked expression. Did Dad know about the vampires hiding in Hell? He couldn't possibly when he never frequented Distros. And yet something made me lose my cool.

"I think it's a good idea, but maybe talk to the chef and see if he can burn the meat to a crisp this time. Amber's not a fan of blood and gore." Dallas would eat raw meat to prove a point to Dad, but he wouldn't make his poor sister suffer the same fate too. Boy, did he coddle her.

"Maybe another time." I bit my lip to keep me from making a sarcastic comment. He sure did go out on a limb for his baby sis. What was she on? VIP status? I might as well roll out the red carpet and bow down at her feet. Oh, wait. I was already doing that. The girl had it made; everyone at her beck and call. Aidan on her arm, Dallas at her side and me at her feet even though she couldn't wait to ruin my relationship with Dallas. She was just lucky she happened to be the love of my life's sister. Like it or not, she was family...or soon to be, so I decided to suck it up a little longer.

Irritated, I tossed the tulips into the wastepaper basket and went to take a shower, then slipped into a pair of skinny jeans and a tank top in my walk-in closet, leaving my curly hair to dry naturally.

Dallas was still lying on the bed, waiting.

"Ready to go?" I asked.

He stood and followed, stopping in front of my office. "You know what's strange? Even though someone knocked me down, I have no bruises."

Yet another detail escaping my mind. Dad would call it sloppy. Smiling, I turned. "He didn't kick us. It was more of a shove and then we fell, hitting our heads in the process." Dallas nodded, unconvinced. I pulled him into the bright room and shut the door. "Can we get to work, please?"

He nodded and dropped into his chair. I rummaged through the sheets until I found the one with the previous brainstorming session's notes. In my distorted memory, there were countless bullet points. In reality, there were less than a half dozen.

"Still nothing, huh?" Dallas said. Reminding me of that tiny detail wasn't exactly going to help kick-start my motivation. Dallas grabbed the paper out of my hand and started reading. "I told Amber about the campaign, and she said she'd be happy to help."

My heart pounded. "You spoke to your sister?"

"Yeah, I called her."

"What did she say about the mugger and everything that happened?" If Dallas spilled the beans, I was screwed. Amber would drag him out of Hell in a heartbeat, and I'd lose him and end up cursed to Hell for eternity.

"Don't worry. I didn't say a word. I wasn't in the mood for a long sisterly lecture. She's quite fond of those." I let out a long sigh. "So can she help us with our project?" he asked.

"What could she possibly do?"

He eyed me carefully, hesitation crossing his face. An instant later, it disappeared again, and I knew he wasn't ready to spill the beans yet. "She suggested an event."

For the sake of my sanity, I hoped he'd stop advocating bringing people down here or trying to scare them to death. "Did she mention what kind of event she had in mind?"

"Yes, and it's a good one too. Promise you'll give it a chance."

I looked up at his smiling face. His gorgeous, speckled eyes shimmered, but there was a tight line around his mouth that wasn't there before. Aidan asked Amber not to get involved in our relationship so she found another way to push her controlling presence into our lives whether we wanted it or not. If I declined her help, Dallas would end up thinking I was rude. I couldn't let him think badly of me when I hadn't even dropped the bomb about my true identity yet. On the other hand, I wasn't keen on making a promise I had no intention to keep either.

"I promise I'll run it past Dad. How about that?"

"Good enough," Dallas said. "We were thinking about a ghost theme with psychics. Visitors could pay to talk to the dead." His hand closed around mine. "I know it's a lot of work, but we're all here to help."

"It's great. I love it. Let's see what Dad thinks though." He seemed so enthusiastic and confident about his idea, how could I shatter his hopes?

"Amber's a great actress. She'll be happy to play the psychic role."

I nodded, smiling. She was a necromancer; talking to the dead came with the job description. Of course she'd nail the part.

"Thanks for letting her be part of this. She's gone through a lot recently," Dallas said.

"Dad's having the last word."

His fingers started drawing circles in my palm, sending small jolts up my arm. "You know how much I adore you, right?" His voice was soft, promising. Nodding, I raised my fingers and trailed them down his cheek. He was so beautiful, it broke my heart because I knew he wasn't like me. His existence had a shelf life. I'd been trying to ignore this fact ever since Dad mentioned it.

I was lost in his golden gaze, peering right into his soul. We kept so many secrets from one another, and yet I doubted I'd ever felt closer to anyone in my entire life. We were connected by a silver thread we couldn't see, and that scared me because I feared it might rip any minute. How can you protect something you can't see?

"I don't ever want to lose you," Dallas said. His voice came even lower than before. Melancholy filled the air, like a thin, dark veil concealing the future ahead.

"Prove it. My birthday's in a few weeks."

"Cass, you know I can't buy you fancy diamonds and what else you women like. Heck, I can't even give you a house like this." He motioned around. "But I can give you my undying love. I want us to get married when you turn eighteen or as soon as your dad's okay with it."

"Why wait?" I couldn't stop the goofy grin forming on my face. I'd never been so happy. "It's the perfect birthday present ever. Nothing would make me happier than being your wife...before I turn eighteen."

If he was surprised by the sudden hurry, he didn't say so. Maybe he felt the urgency in my tone.

"I'd like that." Dallas smiled. A tiny dimple I didn't notice before appeared on his right cheek.

This is even worse than the newly wed shows on TV, Kinky said.

They're in love, Pinky said, wiping away a tear. *Isn't it cute?*

Did he just say television? That was the idea I'd been waiting for. Why bring people down here when we could deliver Hell into their living rooms? "We're doing a TV show," I whispered. Ignoring Dallas's questioning look, I grabbed a sheet of paper and started scribbling.

"I see your muse has just arrived." Dallas stood and pointed at the door, amused. "See you later, babe."

"Thanks." I barely raised my gaze from my notes, lest my idea miraculously evaporate into thin air and I was forced to start from scratch.

An hour later, my proposal was ready for Dad. My heart hammered in my chest as I made my way to his office, hoping he was in there for a change because I'd rather not leave the comfort of air-conditioning to chase him around Hell. I pushed the mahogany door open and peered into the empty room. Of course I could wait until he got home for dinner, but I'd be wasting another couple of hours, which I didn't have. Sorting out Dad's campaign so I could move on to my wedding issues was my top priority.

I couldn't call him on the phone because he didn't like being disturbed at work. Face to face I stood a greater chance of appeasing him enough with my campaign plan to tell me the whereabouts of my aunts. Why he insisted on making Hell the next top travel destination was beyond me. Let's face it, with its reputation of being home to mass murderers and the likes, who in their right mind would want to spend a week down here, let alone all eternity?

The entrance door downstairs opened and Dad's heavy footsteps thudded up the stairs. Seeing me, he stopped and smiled.

"Finished for the day already?" I asked.

He sighed. "I might be if my lovely daughter gave me a helping hand."

"My campaign proposal's ready."

He cocked a brow, impressed. "You didn't waste time then."

Guess that's what happens when you're fighting against the clock to beat a curse that'll chain you to the pits of Hell forever. "You know me, Dad. I'm a go-getter kind of gal."

"That's the spirit." He held the door to his office open. I walked past and spread my sheets across his desk. "What did you have in mind?" Dad asked, taking a seat opposite from me.

Even though I knew anyone in their right mind would consider my idea as beyond creative, my heart hammered harder. "You never really told me why you want this. Why is it so important to you?"

"If you really want to know—" he averted my gaze, gathering his thoughts "—I want your mother to come back."

I stared at him, unsure whether I'd heard him right. "Mom hasn't set foot here in thirteen years."

He nodded. "About time she did."

"Why would you even want that? The last time you met for lunch the earth shook and swallowed up half of a continent."

"That was one little earthquake, Cass."

I snorted. "Little? Smashed buildings and cracked roads stretched for hundreds of miles. It rated a 8.9-magnitude on the Richter scale. It was a miracle no one was killed."

He heaved a sigh. "I lost control. I'm sorry."

"Maybe you're sorry, but my point is, you two don't even get along."

"That's not true, Cass." He smirked. "Her heart ached from the suffering down here, and her teasing friends weren't helping. She was slowly dying inside. You don't know what it's like for a seraph to see her burning core slowly fading. If I could prove this place isn't as awful as everyone makes it out to be, she might give it another chance."

"I know what it's like Dad. You forget I'm half seraph." I set my jaw, fighting against the anger rising inside me. The truth was Mom left us because she couldn't deal with the reproach coming from the other seraphim who couldn't accept Mom's love affair with Dad. Their disapproval might've stopped one day if she chose to hold on for a little longer.

Dad walked around the desk and wrapped his arm around me, pulling me closer. I pressed my face against his chest and breathed in his aftershave, wondering why he'd still hang on to someone who left him so many years ago.

"Don't be angry," Dad whispered. "Not everyone's the same. Your mother will never be as strong as you are."

"Is that why she chose you?"

"It wasn't a choice."

I watched him return to his seat, pondering his cryptic reply. His expression was guarded again. He cleared his throat. "The campaign—"

"Right." I started flicking through my notes, suddenly insecure. "I hope you like it."

"I'm sure I will," Dad said.

"Judging from my research, mortals seem to have a distorted view of what Hell's really about. They seem to think all we do is coax innocents into giving up their souls so we can torture them forever. That's not what Hell's about. We're just as honorable and important as Heaven. Innocents have nothing to fear." I paused to make sure I hadn't lost Dad's attention yet. He nodded encouragingly, so I continued, "As you know, we can't invite people over to see for themselves how important this place is, but there are other means to reach them."

I stood, my voice no longer shaking. "We'll talk to people right where they're most open and willing to listen: in the comfort of their homes."

"How could we possibly do that?" Dad asked.

"I'm thinking about hosting a reality show." Smiling, I held out a sheet of paper with countless bullet points. He started reading as I continued. "We have so many souls down here; people who regret their transgressions; people who would love to get a brief moment with a loved one in order to communicate a last message or say goodbye."

Dad shook his head lightly. "Cass, most of our *visitors* aren't nice people."

"You're talking about the lower planes. We'd never even consider them. But what about Distros?" I squeezed his hand to make sure he was listening. "There's this girl, Theo. I know she isn't a bad person just because she hurt someone who wanted to harm her. It was self defense."

"How do you know her?" Dad's gaze narrowed.

I waved my hand. "It's not important. Let's just say what matters here is that she doesn't hate this place. She understands why it's necessary to be here, and she wants a last chance to talk to her sister and warn her. If you only got to know her, I'm sure she'd even consider saying something nice about you."

He shook his head again.

"Dad," I drew a deep breath, "isn't it what you wanted? That people start saying nice things about you? This is your chance. Grab it!"

"No, Cass." Dad's frown told me he was about to play stubborn again. "I won't let you go on national TV and shout out into the world who you are. What will Dallas say?"

His words caught me off guard. I never thought of that. I peered at the purple tulips in the vase on Dad's desk, taking in the perfect shape of their petals, as I tried to imagine Dallas's reaction. He wouldn't be pleased. He might even be mortified, embarrassed to be seen with me. I couldn't have that, and yet I saw this campaign as something other than a means to raise Dad's popularity. I could ease people's suffering so they may find closure, both the deceased and the living. Basically, this might just be my new purpose in life.

"I know someone who can help," I said, softly. "Amber's a necromancer and she's agreed to get involved."

"She's keen on exhibiting her skills on TV?" Dad snorted. "That's even worse than hanging a blinking banner over her head and shouting it from a rooftop."

"She said she'd love to," I lied. "Give us a shot, please. You won't be disappointed."

Dad sighed. For a moment, we sat in silence. Chewing on my inner lip, I held my breath as I wait for his answer.

"We'll do it," Dad said, unconvinced. "I realize you're a grown up now. It's about time I trusted you more."

I jumped into his arms and planted a kiss on his cheek. "Thanks, Dad. You'll be so proud of me."

"Even more so than I am already?" Dad whispered. "I doubt that's possible, sweetie."

Chapter 18 - Breaking rules

Raising a child in Hell is a family business, meaning everyone, including the great-great aunt, chime in as they see fit, calling at the most inconvenient times to scold or praise. Getting married was a huge deal so, naturally, sending an invitation wouldn't do the trick. Dallas and I would have to see everyone individually to get their blessing.

My aunts lived a rather modern life, traveling and marrying mortals, seeking careers and trying to blend in. Dad, being the conventional one in the family, had always been keen on keeping me away from them. Apart from the morsel of information Dad had passed my way throughout the years and what I'd read on the usual birthday and Christmas card, I didn't know much about their lives. Before I could dive into this adventure though, I had to ensure I kept my promises to Dad.

I waited until Dad returned to work before descending into Distros, marveling how nothing ever seemed changed down here. The quietness was even more disconcerting than the last time I visited with Dallas. I decided to call on Amber first because she was a key player in my campaign, then move on to Theo. If the girl didn't agree to participate, I'd have no problems finding another ghost, but a necromancer might be tougher to hire.

The little hut was bathed in silence. I knocked and listened for any movement, or stray thought, giving away Amber's presence, but nothing stirred.

She's right behind you, Kinky said a moment before I felt a soft breeze on my neck, barely more than a mortal's last breath.

I turned slowly, ignoring my racing heart, and smiled. "Here you are."

Amber opened the door and let me walk past into the tidy living room. Given how little she cared for cleaning, I figured it must be Aidan's doing.

"Cop a squat and I'll make you a cup of tea. We can have some girl talk." She gazed at me. "Wait. I can sense you're not here to talk about my newest pair of shoes. What can I do for you, Cass?"

The frostiness in her voice didn't go unnoticed. I wondered whether Dallas told her about our engagement. If so, it wasn't in her nature to keep quiet. Knowing her, she was more likely to scream and kick, and maybe even pour a glass of holy water over my head like she did to Aidan when she found out he was a vampire.

"Dallas mentioned you'd be happy to help with my campaign," I said.

"Of course, as long as it's really about promoting Disneyworld." She smiled, but it didn't reach her eyes.

"It's not." My heart started hammering again. "Did Dallas tell you we're getting married?" Smirking, she averted her gaze. I guessed that was an affirmative then. "You're not keen on the idea," I continued, unfazed. "It's okay. I can't blame you for not having a very good opinion of the devil's daughter."

Amber sat next to me and grabbed my hand, dropping it just as quickly. For a moment, silence ensued as though she needed to prepare her words. "You're not what I expected," she said, eventually.

"How so?"

She hesitated again, gaze sweeping over the old paperback on the side table. "You really seem to like Dallas. You're helping us hide here even though you don't know our reasons." She looked up, frowning. "You don't know the reasons, do you?"

I shook my head, only now remembering I meant to find out and then forgot.

"Why are you doing this?" Amber continued. "What are you gaining from all of this? Shouldn't you be—"

"Screwing you over?" I laughed. "See, that's why we need to set straight a few clichés about Hell. I'm helping you because I want Dallas to focus on our relationship rather than worry about your safety all the time."

She nodded. "Fair enough. I didn't know he was that worried. We would've never told him anything if his own life wasn't at stake."

"Does he know you're a vampire?"

Peering at me, she barely blinked. "What gave me away?"

"Call it intuition." Amber nodded as if impressed. "So, answer the question, did you spill to your brother?"

"Dallas knows I can talk to the dead, but I might have left out a few tiny details." She avoided my gaze.

"Like being a blood sucker."

A glint of anger flashed in her eyes. "I don't drink blood. I—"

Grinning, I held up a hand. "I'm kidding. I was there to witness the ritual, remember? And I certainly broke every rule." Like stealing the book from right under everyone's nose. Apart from Aidan, no one even saw me. That still had me giggling a few weeks later. Taking stuff every now and then was the easiest and most harmless way to please my fallen angel nature.

"Thanks for not telling Dallas about any of that. He would've freaked. I only mentioned my gift—" she raised her brows "—or should I say 'curse' because he wouldn't leave it alone. He knew something was wrong and I cracked under the pressure. You don't know Dallas. He won't let up until he has the truth in his hands."

I could only hope he wouldn't find out 'my truth' then. Inching closer, I soaked up the various emotional undercurrents wafting from her. "But you didn't tell him about me. Why?"

She shrugged. "That's your job."

I nodded. "Thanks for understanding."

"Never said I did." She sighed. "You're helping us, so I'm going to return the favor because I'd rather not owe you. What is it you want me to do?"

"Well—" I ran a hand through my unruly hair. "I was thinking of a reality show to increase Hell's popularity."

Amber snorted. "A television reality show? You mean one that's full of drama and mayhem? You want more people down here?"

"The reason's more delicate." I hesitated, hoping she wouldn't persist, but the prying personality trait must run in Dallas's family.

"As you can see, I have all day," Amber said.

I wasn't comfortable talking about Dad's affairs, but I feared if I didn't open up I'd never get to sorting out my other issues. "You must promise you won't tell anyone." I waited until Amber nodded, then continued, "Dad wants Mom back."

"Wait, I thought your mother was dead."

"Just because she's in Heaven doesn't mean she's dead." I rolled my eyes. "She's an angel." Amber cocked a brow. I held up a hand to stop any more questions. "I was hoping you could help me host a it."

She stared at me, amused. "You mean something like *Big Brother?*"

I cringed. "More like a mixture between a talk and a family reunion show."

"Sounds great." She glanced at the door as though she was expecting another visitor. I only now realized Aidan wasn't here.

"Where's Aidan?" I asked, frowning. "You're supposed to stay inside."

"He needed to stretch his legs."

She's lying. I didn't need Kinky to tell me that.

I know where he is, Pinky said. *Snooping around the place. He's looking for something, but I don't know what.*

I freed my mind as I dove into Amber's head, searching for whatever secret she was trying to hide. But whatever

195

her intentions were, she fought to keep them out of her consciousness. "If you have questions, you could just ask," I said.

"You'd better not get involved, Cass."

As in, mind your own business. Compared to the other layers of Hell, Distros was a small place. If Theo didn't know what Aidan was up to, someone else would. I smiled and changed the subject. "Are you up for raising the dead?" Amber shot me a surprised look. I shrugged. "What? You need practice, I need someone who has enough presence to divert the attention from me. It's a win-win situation for both of us."

"Who will see it?"

"A local network will be broadcasting it." I didn't tell her that my plan included intercepting every single TV station in the world so everyone with a TV set would watch the show.

If she knew, she might just get her fangs all in a twist. Kinky laughed at his own joke. *Fangs. Get it?*

I bit my lip hard so I wouldn't join in the hysteria.

"Aidan wouldn't be happy," Amber said.

I shrugged. "Then don't tell him."

"I can't do it." She moistened her lips, averting her gaze. Guilt could be a terrible weapon, and I was all for using it.

"We have a strict no-vampires rule in Hell. Dad doesn't know you're here, but it's only a matter of time until he finds out."

She peered at me, frowning. "You think he'll kick us out?"

196

I tilted my head, raising my brows meaningfully. "That, or worse. You're not safe out there, and you know it. Now if you were to help out Dad, he might be more inclined to let you stay here until you've sorted out your issues."

"You don't understand. The one who's chasing us won't give up so easily. It might never be over."

"Layla will eventually get bored of you stealing her boyfriend," I said. What was one missing vampire from an entire harem? The truth was, if Amber didn't unknowingly enter a paranormal race and win the necromancer ability, she wouldn't have the entire Lore court hunting her.

"I didn't steal him," Amber hissed. "He never dated her. It's more of a fatal attraction—something like, 'if I can't have him, no one can.' Anyway, I'm not talking about Layla."

I raised my brows. "Who else is stronger than Aidan?"

"The one who turned him," Amber whispered.

"Rebecca?" I laughed. Yet another of Aidan's jealous exes. The guy sure knew how to pick them. "She's stuck in vampire limbo." I knew that because I saw her through the eyes of Dad's winged demons aka gatekeepers. Amber entered the Otherworld to retrieve Layla's spell book so Aidan could perform a ritual that would help him live without a need for blood or constant darkness. Rebecca almost killed Amber before Aidan turned his beloved to save her life, or so I figured. But, of course, I might miss a few pieces of the puzzle. Rebecca should still be dead, burned to the bone by Dad's demons.

Amber shook her head. "She found a way out, and now she's hell-bent on revenge. If that crazy psychopath can't get to us, then she'll try for her next target. Somebody we care about. Somebody who's mortal and easy to kill."

"Dallas," I whispered.

"Yes," said Amber.

My heart dropped. "No! She'll never touch him. Not while I'm alive. I won't let her. I know a few tricks to keep that psycho away." My nails dig into my palms until my skin burned. "I don't believe it. How is she still alive? None of this makes sense. She died in that fire."

"Aidan believes she didn't."

Losing Dallas scared me to death, but I needed to keep a clear head here. Aidan was wrong. "It must be someone else because Dad's demons turned her into roast beef."

"You're probably right. We don't know." Amber grabbed my hand and leaned closer, her gaze connecting with mine. "That's why we need to stay here until Aidan finds out what's going on."

"Then you'd better put the necromancer in you to good use." I paused and squeezed her hand. "Dallas's natural charm must run in the family. You'll be an instant hit with viewers."

Her laugher rang through the air like a chime. "I like your style."

"Do we have a deal?"

She shook my outstretched hand. "Deal."

I spent another five minutes engaged in small talk, then left with the promise to send someone over tomorrow so she could work on her script. Of course she had to have a cocky comeback line.

"I thought reality shows were unscripted."

"You don't really believe that? Reality is an illusion. Do you watch *The Hills*? Trust me, all reality shows are scripted...and some very, very bad." I knew because I had stalked most of these so-called stars, but Amber needn't know that.

"Hmm. Guess you learn something new everyday." Taking me by surprise, she leaned to air-kiss me on the cheek. I waved goodbye and shut the door. Had I just tamed the dragon and she was about to welcome me into the family? Maybe Dallas was the charming one, but it seemed like I wasn't bad either.

* * *

Theo's house was situated on the other side of Distros. I didn't want to waste my time walking through the woods, so I programmed her name into my phone and beamed myself on her porch.

She was sitting on the cold wooden floor again, her blonde hair swaying in the wind.

"Hello," I said, taking two hesitant steps, lest I scare her.

She looked up, confused, and for a moment I doubted she remembered me. Then a tiny flame of recognition flickered in her pale, blue eyes.

"Cass," she whispered, holding out her hand.

I grabbed it tight and sat down next to her. "Listen, there's something you need to do for me." She nodded, so I continued, "I know a necromancer who can reach your sister, but you'll have to trust me."

Her eyes threatened to pop out of their sockets. "Are we running away from here?"

I shook my head. "Let's just say, we're on temporary leave."

"I'm in," she said, taking me by surprise.

199

"You don't want to know what's involved?"

She smiled. "I prayed for a chance to warn Sofia before dying. You don't look like us, so you must be one of the guards, or maybe you're my guardian angel. I don't care. I'd do anything to have my last wish fulfilled."

"Thank you." I pressed her skinny body to my chest whispering, "If you do a good job your sister will be safe."

What are you doing? Pinky hissed. *You can't promise that because you're not allowed to intervene.*

I smiled at the naïve, little angel sitting on my shoulder. One day I'd be running this place, making my own rules. I might as well start now.

Chapter 19 – Deadly

Aunt Patricia lived in a picturesque village situated in the snow covered Swiss Alps. I wished I could just beam ourselves up there instead of freezing in the gondola riding up at the speed of a snail. I buttoned up the top button on my long *Fendi* coat, leaving the last one open because I thought it might be stylish when another shiver ran across my spine. Then I changed my mind. Screw fashion. I wasn't turning into an ice cube to look 'cute.'

The cable car jerked and I stumbled backwards. I bit my lip hard as the aerial car groaned and creaked a few times. I wasn't a big fan of cars supported by cables from up above. If one of those snapped, we'd fall hundreds of feet. I'd survive, but Dallas wouldn't be so lucky. Even though my toes probably had frostbite, or were already completely frozen and in desperate need of an ice pick or blow dryer, I tried to distract myself with the breathtaking view. Jutting, snow-covered peaks stood out against the deep blue sky and glistened in the sunlight. The 360-degree panoramic view reflected on the surface of Lake Geneva over a misty fog bank. This would make the perfect picture for a screensaver. I made a mental note to get one for Dad to help him relax a little.

Dallas's arms were wrapped around my waist, pulling me against him, making my body tingle at being so close to him. He leaned forward and brushed my cheek, his breath building mist clouds as he spoke. "Thanks for inviting me. This winter paradise is beyond magical."

"Totally." I rolled my eyes, thankful he couldn't see me since my back was pressed against his chest. Who in their right mind would find running around in the cold with a red, runny nose and purple fingers magical? Why couldn't Patricia inherit a cocktail bar in Hawaii, or a five-star luxury hotel in the Caribbean instead of a bakery in a place that wasn't even on *Google Maps*? The only thing I wanted to do with him in this cold was snuggling together under the covers and feeding each other chocolate. We hadn't had a private moment ever since arriving in Hell. But with Dad around, I wasn't even sure I wanted one.

Sighing, I turned to face Dallas. "Listen, I think it's only fair to warn you that Patricia's a very nice girl, but she's a little strange."

"Really? In what way?"

I stared at the golden speckles in his eyes. He glanced at me attentively, as though he truly listened, and brushed a stray lock out of my eyes. Something, like electromagnetic waves, pulsated between us. "Well." I moistened my lips. "She doesn't leave the house very often."

"So she isn't into socializing." Dallas shrugged. "Big deal. Not everyone's a party animal."

I could live with his explanation, except that it was time to stop creating more secrets between us. He'd have to know the truth eventually, so I might as well start tossing little morsels his way. "It's not just that."

He leaned into me and kissed my lips gently. "Don't worry, babe. We all have one or two eccentric family members. I won't judge."

How could I possibly explain I had a whole bunch of them? Patricia was the least of my worries. I couldn't wait until he met Aunt Krista.

"Just remember that when you meet the rest of my family," I muttered.

The sun hid behind heavy, grey clouds. The gondola finally came to a halt and we stepped out, sinking into a thick blanket of snow that reached up to my hip. We were surrounded by white. Even the whitewashed walls blended in with the snow-covered mountains in the distance.

Groaning, I trudged forward, my arms shoveling the snow aside, as we moved forward to reach the tiny village stretching against the darkening sky. It'd be easier if I just melted my way through, but that'd probably freak Dallas out big time, so I had no choice than to keep torturing my aching muscles until we reached what looked like a paved street. I thought fighting our way through the snow was the worst that could happen, until I slipped on the thick ice, almost landing on my butt.

"What a great workout, huh?" Dallas laughed. How could he be so high-spirited when I was getting grumpier by the minute?

"I'm loving every minute of it," I mumbled.

How can Patricia stand this teeth-clattering, brain-numbing cold? Kinky said, shivering in his black robe. Staring up at the impenetrable structure with four towers and all natural stone, reminding me of a miniature of a medieval church or castle, I wondered about the same thing. Let's just say I was thankful she inherited the darn place and not I. If I were bound to this part of the world I doubted I'd ever leave the warmth of my bed, let alone prepare hot buns for hungry folks at five o'clock in the morning.

"Is that it?" Dallas pointed at a high chimney with white fumes snaking in the wind.

I nodded and quickened my pace, eager to slip my numb feet into a pair of fluffy slippers, preferably the ones you can warm up in a microwave oven. The slippery path led us right to Patricia's red painted front door. The windowpanes hung open. White curtains with tiny red hearts peeked from behind. A large wooden pane above the door advertised 'Magic Cupcakes'. I hoped they were magic indeed because I was starving.

I grabbed the brass knock shaped in the form of a doughnut and knocked as Dallas rubbed his gloved hands, probably looking forward to a mug of hot chocolate just as much as I was.

"Coming," Patricia called from inside a moment before the door burst open and she stood in the doorway, clad in a long medieval dress with a golden cord wrapped around her chubby waist. The dark green color complemented her red hair and emerald eyes.

"Looks like the house isn't the only thing trapped in the Middle Ages." I smiled and stepped in.

Patricia wrapped her arms around me, pulling me into a tight hug. "I've missed you, Grumpy."

"Patty, this is my fiancé, Dallas." I pointed behind me. For a moment, Patricia stood frozen to the spot, eyes wide. The milky skin on her smooth forehead creased into a thin line.

"Nice to meet you," Dallas said, holding out his hand.

"So that's why you're here. For a moment I was inclined to believe you'd brace the snow outside to see *me*." Cupping his hand, she turned to face me. A wide grin replaced her frown. "You need our blessing."

I rolled my eyes, playfully. "Don't be ridiculous. Obviously, I'm old enough to do what I want. So Dad told you."

She shook her head. "Nope. He said revealing the big secret would take away the surprise factor, and where's the fun in that?"

I bet he was watching us through his third eye or phone or whatever he used to spy on others nowadays, laughing his head off. Once my mission was over he'd see I was capable of as much manipulation as he. Maybe even more so since I was about to trick my own family who was probably expecting it already.

"You look so much alike, it's uncanny," Dallas said.

"We did before I inherited this place." Patricia pointed at her round hips and growing bust. "You're probably wondering whether I fell into a bag of chocolate croissants and had to eat my way out."

"I couldn't blame your comfort eating. You're probably just stressed. What with all the baking." I shivered at the thought of all the washing up at the crack of dawn.

"It's not just the baking." She rolled her eyes. "It gets kind of lonely in here with Prince Rasputin as my only company."

"Who's Prince Rasputin?" Dallas whispered.

Grinning, I pointed at the black Persian cat behind Patricia. He was lying on the rug in front of the hearth, tummy up, legs and arms spread to the side.

Dallas nodded and returned my smile.

"You look great," I said. "I'd kill for your curves."

She winked. "No need to do something that drastic. I'll just bake you a mean batch of chocolate truffle cupcakes. Come on in. Your luggage's just—"

"Arrived with the courier service. They're fast, aren't they?" I shot her a meaningful glance, lest she give away one of Dad's demons brought over our travel bags.

"Yep." She smiled. "And they're so cheap. A real bargain."

I motioned Dallas to take off his jacket, then closed the door behind him.

"This is nice," he said, peering around.

"I guess, if one's into bricks and medieval towers," Patricia said. "Actually, it's not that bad, or so I thought until I realized I can't ever leave."

"There's no one else to feed the village," I explained to Dallas. He nodded sympathetically.

"Surely, people can cook for themselves at home," Dallas said.

I inclined my head. "You'd be surprised."

"Please, have a seat. I'll get you something to eat." Patricia pointed at a velvet sofa in the color of rusty leaves, then disappeared into the adjoining kitchen. I peered at the thick carpets covering most of the wall and the heavy, dark furniture. This stuff must be worth a fortune on *eBay*.

"I'll be right back," I said before hurrying after Patty. I found her leaning over a kitchen counter, arranging warm muffins on a silver tray. The aroma of cinnamon and cardamom invaded my nostrils. My stomach made an unladylike sound.

"He's mortal, isn't he?" Patricia asked. "I can smell his scent from a mile away."

I nodded. "He's also the one."

"How do you know?" She didn't look up, but her voice dripped with doubt.

"I can feel it."

"It's that easy to recognize the bond then?" She walked over to the stone ovens stretching from the floor almost to the ceiling and peered inside at the leaping flames, mumbling, "Almost ready."

Following her line of vision, I noticed large baking trays with cupcakes, cookies and what else not peering from between the flames. "When did you learn to do all of this? Last time I remember you didn't even know how to boil an egg."

She smiled. "Honestly, most of the time I've no idea what I'm doing." She pointed at the large, leather bound book covering half of a counter. "I just toss all ingredients a bowl, pour the dough into a tray and slip it into the oven. After half an hour, I take it out and everything tastes marvelous. This is my new caramel covered hot bun with raisins. Try it." She tossed a large brown thing with white sprinkling my way. I took a tentative bite. It was surprisingly good, and then the slightest aroma of chili tickled my taste buds.

"Are there chocolate chips in here?" I asked.

She nodded, amused. "With a soft chili cranberry filling. Don't ask me how I did it."

I took another bite, bobbing my head appreciatively, then put the muffin aside. "Are you happy?"

For a brief second, I saw sadness in her eyes. "As happy as one can be."

"Have you ever tried running?"

"Once." She shook her head. "And never again, that's for sure."

"What happened?"

Patty moistened her lips, her gaze a million miles away. "I was fed up with this place so I packed a suitcase and walked out the door with Prince Rasputin in a kitty-cat carrier. When I entered town something strange happened."

My eyes widened. "What?"

"People glared and their voices throttled into deep, menacing growls, like they were possessed or something. A woman lurched at me with a butcher knife. Some guy tried to take down Prince Rasputin and me with a hammer. I was scared to death."

Inching forward, I squeezed her hand sympathetically. "Patty, that's horrible."

She nodded. "Yeah, you could say that. The entire town was after me!"

"But you're immortal. How can a human kill you?" I asked.

"Like you, I'm not eighteen yet. Without any powers, any mortal can behead me."

That was one wicked curse. "How did you escape?"

"I knew what I had to do. Come back here to *my sanctuary*, my prison. I jumped in my car when people piled on my hood and banged on my windows. It was like *Night of the Living Dead* up-close and personal. I barely escaped with my life." She swallowed. "If I or Prince Rasputin take one step out that door, any human outside becomes possessed and wants to kill us."

I grabbed her hand, forcing her to look at me as I whispered, "I'll break this curse. I swear I'll find your destined love for you, but for that you'll have to give me your blessing."

"I'll give you my blessing anyway, Cass. You know that. Just promise you'll stay a bit longer. I've had enough of talking to a cat all day."

"Prince Rasputin's a demon."

She smirked. "A cat's more talkative." One of the ovens beeped. Clearing her throat, she walked over and opened the door. The flames retreated, revealing a thin layer of grey ash and four perfectly round tiers in various sizes.

"A wedding cake? I'm impressed."

"People from all over the world have been ordering here for centuries. I'm working my butt off fourteen hours a day, seven days a week. And for what?" A dangerous glint shimmered in her eyes. "So the last spark of hope in me doesn't die like a burned out candle."

"You should've told me. I could've helped," I said, softly.

She shook her head. "No. This is my battle to fight. You'll get to fight yours soon enough."

Not if I managed to avoid it. We returned with the tray, plates and hot chocolate to the living room. Patricia and Dallas engaged in small talk about the world outside as I tuned out with Dallas's fingers tracing circles in my palm. The cakes were even better than I anticipated. No wonder Patricia was so busy, which gave me an idea.

I pulled out a scroll and started scribbling my terms because in our family, nothing's fixed unless it's written down, preferably with one's signature chiseled in stone.

"So, I sort of stalked her, and the next day we moved in together." Dallas shot me a smile.

"I would've been freaked out," Patricia said. "Actually, anyone else would've been. She must've seen something special in you."

"You bet I did." I pushed the scroll and a pen toward her. "I know you agreed already, but I'd rather have it in writing if you don't mind."

She started to read, bobbing her head as she moved from one point to the next. "A TV show? I'd rather not, Cass. I'm busy already without the extra advertising."

I leaned back, regarding her coolly. "If you want to find him, you'd better get your picture out there."

"Find who?" Dallas asked. Patricia put the scroll aside and took another bite of her muffin.

I peered at her, amused. "Someone who'd better hurry come knocking on her door before she turns into a chocolate cupcake herself."

"That's mean." Grinning, she dropped the muffing onto her plate. "I see your point. You'll have my written agreement by tomorrow."

I'd rather have it tonight, but rushing anyone in my family would get me nowhere, so I shrugged. "Sure. Take your time." Obviously, I didn't mean that part.

Outside, a full moon rose against the canvass of a starry night. We spent another hour chatting, then retreated to the privacy of our bedrooms with their flowery wallpapers and comfortable bedding. We didn't get to share a room, which was probably Dad's doing, but that didn't stop us from engaging in some serious smooching before we said goodnight. I went to bed lightheaded, my skin still tingling from Dallas's soft kisses.

I'd barely managed to close my eyes and catch some snooze when the presence of a shadow woke me up again. Disoriented, I jumped up and headed for the kitchen in my sleepwear, barely able to resist the sudden urge of pushing some cupcakes into the preheated oven. I was never one to cook in the kitchen. Since I'd pick a microwave any day versus slaving away over a home cooked meal, I knew something was definitely wrong with this picture.

Patricia was already there, moving around at a swift pace. Sleep-drunken, she barely peered at me as I sat at the kitchen table and rubbed my aching head. A moment later, footsteps thudded down the stairs, and Dallas appeared in the doorway with hooded eyes and his hair in disarray, murmuring, "I want to help roll out the dough."

"Do you know what time it is?" I asked him.

"Can't sleep. Just want to help. So how do we make the batter?"

"This is barbaric," I muttered, fighting the urge to grab a bowl and help Dallas.

"What's happening?" Dallas asked. "I want to cook. I need to cook...to bake...right now."

Patricia stopped only long enough to wipe beads of sweat off her forehead, then resumed her work routine.

"The curse is making us a slave to this kitchen and to baking." Her voice came so low I wasn't sure I heard right.

"I'm nobody's slave." I grabbed a bag of flour and poured it into a giant, wooden mixing bowl while Dallas cracked two eggs. My words said I wasn't a slave, yet I was.

"I'm so tired, I need fresh air." Groaning, Dallas moved to the backdoor and yanked it open. A strong gust of wind blew in. The fires sputter. A spiral, like a black veil, whirred around us, hissing in our ears.

"What are you doing?" Patricia yelled. "Close it. Close it now!"

I peered from her furious face to Dallas's dumbfounded expression, then back to her. The wind wafted through the kitchen, blowing out one of the fires.

"Don't let Prince Rasputin get out." Patricia screamed and made a dash for the door, tripping on a blob of dough on the floor. I hurried to catch her fall, but it was too late. With a thud, she landed on her tummy, her arm hanging out the doorway into the shimmery snow. A deep menacing growl echoed in the darkness behind me. I spun around and met Dallas's eerie black eyes.

"Get him away from me," Patricia screeched.

Like a zombie, Dallas moved forward, reaching her in a few long strides. His face looked like a distorted mask of anger, no longer resembling the charming guy I fell in love with.

"Cass!" Patricia screamed, sliding across the floor into the snow outside.

Dallas let out another growl and lunged at her, grabbing her neck in a deadly grip.

Do something. He's killing her, Pinky yelled in my ear.

I didn't understand. Why would he do that? Yesterday, it seemed as though they got along like a house on fire, and today they were trying to kill each other. That didn't make any sense.

It's the curse, Kinky said, coolly. *Surely, you put two and two together by now.*

My brain kicked into motion. I had to come up with a plan, and pronto. I peered around, considering my options. Whacking him over the head with something was out of the question since I still needed my fiancé to marry me. The phone was in my room, so beaming him out of here wasn't an option either.

"Babe, stop it," I yelled. If he could hear me, he didn't respond. Patricia struggled in his iron grip, pushing against his broad chest, as she gasped for air.

Talking a possessed guy out of his killing ambitions is your plan? Kinky snorted.

"Obviously not." I closed my eyes and focused on Dallas, calling on my inner powers that had been lying dormant ever since my birth. The air around me stirred. Excitement washed over me. My breath caught in my throat. For the first time ever, it was working, or so I hoped.

Stop wasting time, Pinky cried. *Do something, Cass.*

Patricia's ear-piercing scream ended in a gurgling sound. Was he strangling her? I pried an eye open, disturbing my concentration. He *was* strangling my aunt, and quite successfully. I watched in horror her eyes turning in their sockets. Enough of my affable nature already. It was time to act.

With a shriek, I jumped on Dallas's back and covered his eyes. His breath came in short, angry heaps. He turned

213

like a raging bull, trying to shake me off. Clenching my teeth, I held on for dear life. I didn't know how long I could keep my grip on him. Dallas was a big, strong guy. He might throw me off any minute. I'd rather he didn't because from this height it looked like it might be an uncomfortable fall.

"Patty, get inside. Move it!" I shouted.

She made another gurgling sound as she pushed up on her knees and shuffled across the floor toward a kitchen counter, hiding behind it as if that could ward off a raging maniac.

A roar rippled through Dallas's chest. My arms turned to jelly, my whole body ached. I was going to take a tumble any second. And then he stopped struggling. I held my breath, unsure whether he was just bluffing.

"Cass?" His voice was anxious, questioning.

"Yes?"

"What are you doing?"

He was asking *me* what I was doing? "You don't know?"

"I think he's all right now," Patricia whispered.

"I figured that much." Sighing, I jumped off his back but my muscles remained tense just in case he decided to resume his killing.

Patricia appeared from behind the counter and slapped his shoulder. "What the heck's wrong with you? You almost killed me."

He frowned, confused. "What did I do? I just came down for breakfast."

"Leave Dallas alone. He didn't mean it." I rolled my eyes and intertwined my fingers with his. "You should know better than to venture out that door."

214

"I had to close the door so Prince Rasputin wouldn't run away. He wouldn't stand a chance outside these doors," Patricia hissed. "You'd do the same for that dangerous Hell hound you love so much."

Dallas cocked a brow.

"A pit bull," I explained. "And he's a sweetie."

Patricia snorted. "To you. Everyone else hates him. There's no way you'd stand by and watch him die."

"Good point." I loved that dog to death, red eyes and all. "The more reason to sign that scroll so we can get on with that campaign."

She raised her chin defiantly, eyes glinting. "You did it on purpose."

"What?" I laughed. "You think I persuaded my fiancé to kill you so you'd sign my plea. This is ridiculous. You're nuts. All that sugar must've messed with your brain cells."

She regarded me in silence.

"Cass, what's this about?" Dallas asked.

"The curse says I can't leave the house," Patricia said, ignoring him. "I didn't, so your little performance must be part of your scheme to get my approval."

She's not the brightest star, is she? Kinky said.

Annoyed, I retrieved the scroll from the counter and waved it in Patricia's face. "Switch on your brain, mate. If you can't leave the house, neither can your body parts."

She shook her head. "You're bluffing."

I shrugged. "Let's try it on the first customer then. Hold your arm out of the window."

For a moment, we stared at each other in silence.

"Give me that scroll then," Patricia said, snatching it out of my hands. I could barely breathe as she stretched it on the counter and signed below my handwriting, then handed it back to me. "Promise me you'll do everything in your power to find him. I don't want to stay here."

Smiling, I nodded. "You have my word."

She grinned back. "Can I have it in writing?"

* * *

"What the heck was that all about?" Dallas whispered as he helped me pack our bags to leave again.

"What?" Obviously, I knew what he was talking about, but I'd rather play dumb and stalk for time. Maybe I'd come with a good excuse in the meantime.

"Patty said I tried to kill her."

Laughing, I looked up at him. He towered a foot over me, a frown perched between his brows. I hated to see him upset, and yet knowing the truth would upset him even more. "It was a joke. I told you she's a bit strange. Come on, we need to hurry if we want to catch that train."

He shook his head, unconvinced. "Why would anyone make such a sinister joke?"

"Babe, there's something I didn't tell you." I pulled him on the bed next to me. Our gazes locked. "She's up here on her own because she has an antisocial personality disorder. She really doesn't like people much." I inched closer whispering, "I'm so sorry you had to see this."

"But last night she seemed so social and friendly."

"I know. The mood swings are part of her condition."

"No wonder you couldn't tell me." Dallas pressed me against his chest. I snuggled my head into his shoulder and held up my lips to meet his kiss, my guilt instantly forgotten. Surely Patricia would understand the need for my little, white lie. I mean, how could I possibly be of any help to her tied to Hell like she was bound to this house?

His lips pressed harder onto mine. A spark ran up and down my body, gathering somewhere in the pit of my stomach and wandering up to my heart. I savored the delicious taste of mint and chocolate as he drew me deeper into our kiss.

"You have no idea how hard this was for me," I whispered eventually against the warmth of his lips.

"I can only imagine."

You're milking it for all it's worth, huh? Kinky said. *I like your style.*

Clearing my throat, I peeled my lips off Dallas and resumed my packing. "We're meeting Aunt Krista in France."

"I hope she'll like me," Dallas said.

No doubt about that. She'll have him for breakfast. Kinky laughed. Yep, he might be right about that.

Chapter 20 - Seductress

A few hours later we arrived at Nice airport. Our designated driver was already waiting outside the arrivals hall, the silver BMW barely standing out from the crowd among the countless limousines, *Ferraris* and other luxury rides that wouldn't look out of place at a German auto show.

He bowed deeply and grabbed the bag from Dallas's hand, a leer playing on his lips. There was something strange about him, maybe the way he paraded cockily as though chauffeuring clients for a living was way beneath him. I regarded him from the corner of my eye, only then noticing the two tiny horns peeking from under a mop of black hair. Of course Dad couldn't just arrange for a mortal driver to drive us the few miles to the harbor. He had to send out one of his chaos demons, and an arrogant one at that. I motioned to the demon to put his cap back on...pronto. If Dallas got one glimpse of those horns, my cover could be blown.

If you pull a stunt on us, I'll send you straight back to Lavardos. Let's see whether you can take the billowing flames searing into your skin like a steak on a grill. I've heard it feels like being boiled alive in a pot of steaming hot water. My mind focused on him, lest he ignore my threat and pretend it was intended for someone else.

Hearing my thoughts, he obeyed, then grinned, green eyes sparkling with mischief. I wondered whether I should drive, just in case he decided a bit of fun might be worth Dad's wrath and consequent punishment after all. Come to think of it, Dallas might find my decision to jump behind the wheel strange though, so I decided against it.

"Do you have everything?" Dallas asked.

I nodded and jumped on the backseat, making room as he joined me. The demon started the engine and pulled out into the heavy traffic. After a few minutes, I relaxed against the cool leather and Dallas's stroking fingers on my arm.

"Would you like me to take the scenic route giving you a breathtaking view of the ocean, Princess?" the demon asked, peering through the rear-view mirror straight at my legs.

So he could stare some more and make Dallas jealous while he soaked up all the tension and drama vibes he could get his dirty hands on? This chaos demon had guts.

I let out a breath and narrowed my gaze. "No. Just keep your eyes focused on the road and take the quickest shortcut." Smiling, I nudged Dallas. "He thinks I'm royalty. Isn't he funny? Guess my childhood nickname will never go away. Maybe I should just attend The Princess

Academy, become a Princess, and make my five-year-old me so very happy."

"You look like a princess with all those waves in your long red hair and the way your beautiful eyes sparkle," Dallas said, pulling me against his chest protectively. His jealousy was cute because it told me he loved me just as much as I loved him. The knowledge made visiting Aunt Krista almost bearable.

Beaming, I peered out the window at the clear, blue sky and the scantily clad people. The car took a few turns and gained in speed as we drove up a highway. To our right I could already see sparkling water stretching in the distance. A few yachts sailed at a leisurely speed, the people sprawled on the decks enjoying the midday sun.

Half an hour later, the car pulled onto the promenade, almost running over a lamppost. I got out quickly and motioned Dallas to follow.

"It seems your aunt is already waiting," the driver said with a leer. I followed his line of vision to a blonde, busty woman wrapped in flowing chiffon that revealed a little too much, leaning over the railing and waving from a huge luxury cruise.

"Thank you." I grabbed the bag from the demon's hands and tossed it toward Dallas who caught it in one fluent motion.

The demon grabbed my hand and kissed it softly, leaving a wet trail on my skin. "If there's anything you need, Your Highness, I'm only a phone call away."

Dallas leaned into me whispering, "If he hits on you again, I swear I'm going to deck him."

I was flattered that my fiancé thought the guy was into me, but the truth was he stalled for time because he wanted to meet Aunt Krista. I couldn't believe the cheek. Then again, why was I surprised? Every demon in Hell would kill for a date with her.

The demon hesitated, gaze fixed on my approaching aunt who swayed her generous hips from side to side, ambling at the pace of a turtle. "Want me to get that phone fixed for you?" he asked.

"Oh, you tried to call." My fake laughter rang through the air. "I had it turned off on the flight. Trust me it works just fine."

The demon grinned. "Are you sure? Because you could've beamed yourself here in a flash."

"The *Star Trek* convention's in New York. If you hurry you might catch the plane on time," Dallas said.

My gaze narrowed at the demon to show him I meant business, and he jumped back at the sight of two bright flames burning in my eyes. "Go away," I hissed. "Or need I remind you of Lavardos?"

"What did you say?" Dallas asked.

"I told him he did a great job and Dad will have to 'toast' him." With fire. Loads of it.

"A great job?" Dallas whispered in my ear. "Put away the wine, babe. The guy stared at your legs the entire ride here."

With a sigh, the chaos demon bowed and jumped onto the driver seat, starting the engine as he shot Aunt Krista a rueful look.

"Come on." I grabbed Dallas's arm and pulled him across the promenade. "We might as well meet her half way, or else she won't reach us before dawn."

221

"That's your aunt?" Dallas whispered as we stood a few feet away. I nodded, regarding the curvy, heavily tanned figure balancing on six-inch stilettos. He laughed. "Oh, boy."

"Darling girl, look at you." A hint of expensive perfume wafted past as Aunt Krista air-kissed me left and right. She took off the huge sunglasses covering most of her face and pushed them between her ample breasts almost spilling out of her black *D&G* bathing suit. "What happened to your hair?"

"What?"

She waved a manicured hand in my face. "You need a cut. That color isn't doing your freckled complexion any favors either. You should sue the hairstylist."

"It's my natural color." I ground my teeth.

"Poor you. Luckily, Pierre's paying us a visit tomorrow. I'm sure he can squeeze in a few minutes to help out my unfortunate niece." She turned to Dallas, gaze wandering up and down. "Look at how big and gorgeous your brother's turned. I still remember him as a chubby little boy. Time flies, doesn't it?"

My jaw dropped. Was she for real? "Auntie, I don't have a brother. This is my fiancé, Dallas."

"Are you sure?" She pouted. "Who was the chubby, little boy then?"

I rolled my eyes. "There was no chubby, little boy. Only me." The woman found me fat as a kid?

Smiling, she inched toward Dallas, bosom pushed out, and held out her hand. "Aren't you a cutie? You might be inclined to feel shy since it's an honor meeting me." She clicked her tongue. "Well, don't be. I'm just a normal woman, albeit a very good-looking one, and—"

Grabbing her arm, I pulled her aside muttering under my breath, "He has no idea who you are, and I'd like to keep it that way."

"He's—"

"Mortal?" I nodded.

"Interesting. Let's enter my measly abode then." Aunt Krista sauntered back up the ramp of the huge luxury cruise. Dallas and I followed behind as she started showing us around as though she owned the place.

We passed the entrance hall, a large room with marble floor and several sitting opportunities, then took a right, down the stairs, to the sleeping quarters. Aunt Krista's *measly abode* was a large penthouse-style apartment with open rooms and a balcony overlooking the sea. The glass slide doors, golden candelabras and silk curtains gave it a regal yet modern flair. Everything looked so sparkling and immaculate. If it weren't for a pair of pink slippers with four-inch heels left next to a bedside table, I wouldn't think anyone actually lived here.

"How long have you been traveling around the world?" Dallas asked.

"A few months, maybe a year." Aunt Krista dropped onto a wine-colored chaise longue and rang a bell. A second later, a young man clad in silk, green pantaloons, a golden shirt and a large turban appeared, holding a tray with refreshments.

I snorted. "You can't be serious."

"You don't like my genie, dear?" Aunt Krista pouted, her forehead remained smooth where there should've been a frown. I wondered how much Botox she had injected to get that frozen, shiny skin.

"Did you just say 'genie'?" Dallas asked.

"That's what she calls her service personnel. They like it a lot." I glared at her, lest she dare contradict me.

"As you say, dear." She tapped a long, red fingernail on her bare thigh. "He's the boy you talked about on the phone." I nodded, thankful she remembered that until she continued, "Why would you marry a butcher?"

"What?" I peered at Dallas who shot me a confused look.

Aunt Krista moistened her lips. "I was married to one a few hundred years ago, and let me tell you, you'll never get used to the smell."

"A few hundred years ago?" Dallas asked.

"She thinks she's really old, hence the Botox," I whispered to Dallas. "Why would you think Dallas is a butcher?"

"I can tell when I see one." She turned to him, brows drawn. "How will you provide for my niece? Obviously, she won't be able to live on pork chops."

"I'm not a butcher," Dallas said.

I shook my head and made a cuckoo sign to Dallas. "He isn't. Now, drop it, Auntie. We both have jobs."

"You're not marrying a butcher," Aunt Krista said.

What was wrong with her? Last time I checked, she wasn't this loco. Must be all the Botox. Leaning back, I crossed my arms. "So, you're agreeing with Patty. I'm glad you've finally decided to work out your differences."

She narrowed her gaze. "You went to see Patty first and she didn't give you her blessing?"

I shrugged. "You know how she likes being the first at anything. She sets the pace and everyone else follows."

"Hm." Aunt Krista tapped her fingers against her shimmering lips. "We'll have a huge reception, and she's not invited. My friend, Donatella, makes the most stunning gowns. Of course, we'll need to do something about that hair of yours. I'm so glad I didn't inherit that red mop."

Actually, she did. Dad said peroxide was developed specifically so Krista could pretend otherwise though. "You're a natural blonde then?" I smirked and pulled a scroll out of my handbag. "Tell that to your roots. Now, if you could sign the dotted line so you can get back at Patty. We haven't got all day."

"Are you getting married in Hell?" Aunt Krista asked, inspecting the scroll.

"I wouldn't call marriage hell." I shot Dallas an amused glance as I mouthed, "She's been married one too many times."

"No, dear, I asked if you were getting—"

"You're talking about the weather? For someone who lives on a cruise you sure abhor the Californian heat." My fake laughter sounded forced. I had to get us out of here before my crazy aunt blew my cover. Dallas might be gullible in that he believed everything I said, but he wasn't stupid.

"What's in this for me?" Aunt Krista asked.

"You get to see your only niece married, living happily ever after." I groaned inwardly because I knew I'd have to come up with better bait than that.

Aunt Krista shook her head, her fake blonde strands swaying with the soft breeze coming from the open window. "No."

Let the bargaining begin. I took a sip of my cold water and cringed at the sour taste of lemon. "What do you want then?"

"I want to be featured on your TV show."

"How do you even know about it?"

She smiled, self-satisfied. "I have my sources."

Dad must have told her. "What would you need PR for?" I asked.

"Well, since I'm trying to set up my own business some exposure would come in handy." She rang the bell again. The genie demon popped back in, carrying a large tray with a selection of sequined handbags and shoes that glimmered in the sunny room, and dropped it on the table. The glittery stuff made my eyes ache.

"This is my life's purpose," Aunt Krista said, her throat choked with emotion.

"It's very—" I gestured with my hand, struggling for words. Horrendously ugly, non-wearable, and certainly nothing that anyone in their right mind would ever want to buy, or even be seen with, dead or alive. Fortunately for Aunt Krista, I was family, so it was only natural that I lie. "Creative," I finally managed to say.

Dallas nodded, wide-eyed. "Indeed, and so very shiny."

"That's the appeal. The more shine the better. It's all the rage right now. Don't you read *Cosmopolitan*, dear?" She picked up a garish red purse with faded stripes. It looked as though a toddler painted it. "I designed it all myself."

"I bet the stock's going through the roof," I said. Probably when someone threw the ugly handbag away, out of fright, and it smashed through the ceiling.

"Numbers don't lie," Aunt Krista said. "These things are selling like hotcakes."

To blind people? I nodded, eager to change the subject. "You're talented. Now can we get on with the scroll?"

Aunt Krista shook her head. "Not before you've agreed to a bit of product placement on your show. I wouldn't mind doing an interview or two, maybe even a model catwalk, in exchange for my signature."

It was all Dad's fault. If he only kept his mouth shut, we wouldn't have to give in to Aunt Krista's crazy demands. The truth was, the moment we featured cheap bags from the eighties we'd lose all credibility.

I sighed, considering my options to get out of this disaster. "You know we're not *Project Runway*, right?"

"Of course I do, dear." She laughed. "I'm already in the process of becoming a household name. I just need more traffic to my website." She had a website? Yet more clutter on the Internet.

"We'll find a way to fit you in," Dallas said, shooting me a doubtful look.

"Goody. Where do I sign then?" Aunt Krista clapped her hands. Several minutes passed as she took her time reading the scroll. Eventually, she grabbed a pen, hovering over the thick paper, as though she was about to sign over the family jewels.

I bit my lip until I drew blood. The pen moved, leaving behind a wet trail of cursive handwriting. She had barely finished putting the last touches in the form of a dot when

227

I snatched the scroll and pushed it into my purse for safekeeping. Two aunts down, one to go.

"See you on the set?" I asked, signaling Dallas to get up.

Aunt Krista nodded, flabbergasted. "Sure, dear. Let me check my diary for a free slot and—"

"Tomorrow, eight o'clock in the evening." I was almost out the door when I shouted over my shoulder, "We won't reschedule for you, so don't be late."

Chapter 21 - Who wants to be famous?

It's amazing how irritating and time-consuming travelling is when one has to rely on old-fashioned technologies such as planes and taxis. After getting back to California I was so tired I wished I could lie down and sleep off my jetlag, like Dallas. He'd be out for hours. Amber compelled him to sleep all day. She refused to let him see 'my' world. I was offended at first because I knew all the hard work he had put in. He'd want to be there to see it, but I figured it was for the best. How would I explain all those demons sitting in the studio audience anyway? Besides, there was no time because my personal assistant was already waiting in the studio. The studio Dad had created in the 5th dimension of Hell. He assured me there would be no problem catching satellite waves for the broadcast. I assumed he had some kind of trick up his sleeve but he refused to discuss it with me.

I walked into the large stage and stopped to peer around, taking in the eerie yet groovy atmosphere. Chairs with velvet lining were set up in rows facing a raised platform with two black, leather sofas surrounded by countless burning candles. On a coffee table, a silver tray with an embossed dagger, salt, various wood utensils and yet more candles waited to be used in our fake séance.

"What do you think?" Ginny asked, anxiously. I turned and smiled.

"I couldn't have done a better job. Time to get our guests then."

"They're gathered in the reception area together with the camera crew."

"What about Theo?"

"She's been debriefed," Ginny said. "I've just finished going through her list with her one more time. She's memorized everything for your reality show."

I nodded, impressed. Apart from arranging nicer clothes for himself, he had thought of everything. "Ginny?"

His eyes turned wide with alarm. "Yes, Princess."

"I'm taking over from here. Why don't you get yourself something nice to wear and sit down with a cup of coffee? You've earned a break."

If his skin, dark as coal, could flush, it would've for sure. His gaze lowered to the clean floor, fixing on his battered shoes. "But this is what I've been wearing for most of my life," he whispered.

I inched forward and placed a hand on his shoulder, giving it a light squeeze. The coarse material of his shirt felt like sandpaper under my touch. "I understand but you have an important job and need to look the part."

He bowed and scurried away. For a few seconds, I stared after him, wondering why I never exchanged more than a few words with him during the time he worked in our kitchen. What a shame I missed out on a wonderful friendship for so many years.

As Ginny said, Amber and Theo were waiting in an adjoining room together with at least a dozen people, ranging in age, I've never seen before. Frowning, I inched closer, ignoring Amber's greeting and the makeup artist wanting to put the last touch to my makeup.

A middle-aged man dressed in a business suit bowed, his dark hair almost touching the ground. The others noticed and followed suit. My gaze connected with that of a freckled teenager, and for a moment his magic broke, revealing a surprisingly human face with red skin and flames dancing in his black eyes. He must be one of the upper level demons employed to play audience. Ginny thought of every detail.

"Please, follow me," I said, pointing through the open door to the empty chairs. "Have a seat and try to behave like normal people."

"What do you mean?" Amber asked.

The teenage demon grinned and his appearance flickered for a moment, revealing what hid behind, all lobster-red skin and blazing eyes. Amber flinched and took a step back whispering, "What's that thing?"

I shrugged. "This and that."

"A vampire that isn't cocky? Every day harbors a new learning experience," Dad said from the door.

I turned to face him, my eyes shooting daggers, lest he annoy my guests, forcing me to spend days if not weeks searching for another necromancer to do Amber's job. It wasn't like they advertised their services on a website.

"I know a few who do freelance and—"

"Dad!"

"A dead person speaking to the dead." He shrugged. "I'm just saying it's a little weird."

"She's not dead like most vampires, okay? She's an upgraded version."

"Like Windows 7.0? Most upgrades come with a few bugs." Smirking, he looked around. "So where's Dallas?"

"Sleeping off the jetlag."

"This was his project too. He's blowing us off to sleep? That's lousy work ethic."

I pulled him aside hissing, "Keep it shut, Dad. This is my show. I'm the boss here."

"He's your father?" Amber asked. I rolled my eyes because I'd heard it so many times before it really ticked me off. Every one of my female friends fancied Dad. He must have some sort of magnet implanted under his golden skin. "He's so—"

"Handsome? Good-looking? Hot? Fit?" Irritated, I grabbed her arm and guided her to the leather sofas. "Stop drooling, Amber. It's not attractive. Just sit and do your job."

"I'm not staring." She ran a hand through her brown hair, peering at Dad from under long lashes. What was it with every post-pubescent girl developing a crush on his green eyes and mysterious flair?

"Thank you for helping us out," Dad said. His eyes twinkled.

"My pleasure," Amber stuttered, her pale cheeks flushed. "It's the least I can do for your hospitality."

"That was my daughter's doing. She has a rather persuasive nature." Dad shot me an amused look. "We're happy to have Dallas's family over."

Amber beamed as though he had just complimented her on her amazing taste in fashion. I gestured Theo to sit down, only now noticing the confidence in her stride. There was also a flicker of hope in her blue gaze that wasn't there before. I bet she wouldn't let Dad's charm distract her from her job. Or maybe it wasn't working on her because she hadn't grasped the magnitude of the power he wielded over the world. Looking at her, seemingly pale and frail in her oversized white gown, I felt sorry I hadn't bothered to visit her in Distros after our initial meeting. I just didn't feel I could take any more of that pain she felt inside.

"Theo, this is Amber. She'll be assisting you in contacting your sister," I said.

Amber nodded. "Hi."

"Thank you," Theo whispered, arranging her flowing gown around her. "I'll do whatever you say. All I ask for is that you persuade Sofia to stay away from him and his family. I don't want the same fate to befall her."

"Wait." Amber jumped up, wide-eyed. "Is she a—"

"A ghost?" I smirked. "Amber, you're a necromancer in a show about raising the dead. What did you expect? Eerie sounds produced by a computer and a few Hollywood actors in bad makeup? Please don't tell me you've never seen a real ghost."

She shook her head. "I thought I was going to speak to them...*not see them*!" Her skin paled again, giving Theo a run for her money.

"You're staying in Distros. How did you manage to avoid them?"

"Aidan keeps me inside," she whispered.

"Is he afraid you might catch a sunburn?" Talk about a control freak. I patted her knee. "Relax. Everything's going to be okay. If it helps, Theo's one of the good ghosts out there."

"She's no poltergeist then?" Dad asked.

I shot him a glare. "Stop freaking her out."

"Thanks for helping us, Theo," Dad whispered. "I know being in Hell isn't a thrilling experience." Yet Dad wanted me to run a campaign trying to promote this place he has just admitted 'isn't a thrilling experience'. Go figure!

She shrugged. "It's not that bad, sir. Maybe a bit lonely at times."

"You should come over for dinner. Cass would appreciate the company," Dad said.

I peered at him, surprised. Dad had never invited anyone over before because he wasn't keen on visitors. Maybe he had taken a liking to her. I didn't have time to ponder over Dad's change in attitude though because Aunt Krista's shriek rippled through the air, drawing everyone's attention to her.

Jumping up, I dashed in her direction, then stopped. What the heck was she wearing? It looked like a huge roll of pink spandex wrapped around her big bosom and round hips. I hoped she wouldn't bend forward because I wasn't keen on seeing her underwear. "What's wrong?"

She stared at me as though I was dense. "Your demon friend won't let me arrange my merchandise."

Ginny appeared behind her whispering, "You didn't say anything."

"I'm sorry. It's my mistake. I should've discussed my idea with you first, Auntie." I winked at Ginny and turned to face Aunt Krista.

"What idea?" she asked, eyes narrowed in suspicion.

"If we keep your designs on display, our audience might think it's all part of the visual merchandising." I pulled her to a seat in the front row and motioned the sitting demon to move to the back.

"So?" Aunt Krista cocked a brow.

"You want to surprise your audience." I pushed her down into her chair. "You want to go for that wow factor, Auntie. Why don't you talk about your bags during our five-minute break when everyone's focus is on what you have to say?"

"You know what people usually do during a break?" Aunt Krista paused for effect. "They visit the restroom."

"Not always. Sometimes they get popcorn or switch channels because they're bored," Dad chimed in, amused.

I threw him an irritated look over my shoulder. I thought this campaign was important to him. How could he not take my attempt seriously?

"Isn't he the jokester? Trust me, no one will channel-hop," I assured Aunt Krista. My phone had been programmed to broadcast the show on every channel in the world at the same time. Even if viewers tried to change the channel, they wouldn't get to see anything else.

"If you say so." Her voice betrayed doubt.

"What's worse? Losing a few viewers or people failing to notice your bags among all the candles and drama unfolding on the stage?" I cocked my brow and started counting to ten in my thoughts. I barely got to four when she nodded, excited again.

"You certainly know what you're talking about, dear."

Not really, but I gathered it was common sense. A bit like advertising hats during a football play. With all the action going on, who'd remember the hats?

"Who knows, if you do a good job you can pick a bag or two." Aunt Krista winked.

"Thanks." I smiled and turned away, hoping she'd forget about what she probably believed to be a generous offer. I wouldn't even dream of wearing something that hideous, not when I had my own style. The makeup artist hurried over to apply a layer of bronze over my face and flattened a few stray strands of hair, which jumped back into curls straight away. I motioned her to go because my hair was a lost cause anyway.

Three of Dad's demons aka the camera crew took position as Dad left the stage and took his seat behind a curtain, out of filming range. I'd rather he returned to his daily routine, but he seemed keen on watching our performance live and I didn't have hours to waste on arguing with him.

Lights, camera, action. Gee, I wondered if Oprah ever felt this way getting ready for a show. I adjusted the tiny push-to-talk microphone conveniently clipped to my collar. "Testing. Testing. Can everyone hear me?" My voice echoed across the room and every demon in the studio audience flinched. "Somebody fix the sound," I yelled. They covered their ears as the microphone screeched, piercing my ears. A blinding spotlight fell on me as I took position on the sofa. I raised a hand to cover my eyes against the glaring brightness.

A blinding spotlight fell on me as I took position on the sofa. I raised a hand to cover my eyes against the glaring brightness.

"Lower the light. She can't see a thing," Ginny yelled. The light shifted from my face to the floor and then back up to my chest. Dad must've skimped on hiring professionals, and now we were stuck with amateurs or, worse, beginners. I groaned.

"Hey, move back a few inches and try to keep that thing out of my eyes and away from my chest, otherwise you're fired. Got it?" I yelled. Dad laughed. Anger started to nag at the back of my mind. He must be having a lot of fun watching my first attempt at broadcasting. I was determined to show him I was a natural born director, and then he'd beg me for forgiveness for underestimating my talents.

"Is this it?" Aunt Krista asked. "Shouldn't we have a trial run first?"

I shrugged. "You know your lines, right." She nodded, so I continued, "Great. Then let's get going. You'll be fine. Who needs practice anyway?"

"I'm not talking about myself, dear." She pointed at Amber whose breathing came in ragged heaps.

"What did you do? Show her your handbags?" I muttered under my breath as I hurried over to Amber. "Are you okay?" I gestured at the makeup artist to hand

237

Amber a glass of water. She took small sips and bobbed her head, insecure. "It's only a handful of people. Apart from old ladies, I doubt anyone's going to switch on at this time of day," I whispered so Aunt Krista wouldn't overhear me. Starting an argument with Aunt Krista wouldn't ease Amber's nerves.

"You're right. I keep forgetting," Amber said.

"Is everyone ready?" Ginny asked.

Resuming my position on the sofa, I took a deep breath and nodded.

"Action on one. Three, two, one. Action." Ginny gave me the thumbs-up sign and I knew the camera was rolling.

"Welcome, everyone. Thank you for switching on to Messages from Beyond the Grave. I'm Cass and this is our visiting guest, Amber." I pointed at Amber who was staring at the camera, a smile frozen on her lips. This was her cue to explain her role in the show, but she didn't look like she'd be getting out a word any time soon.

"Many of us have lost a loved one too soon and wish they could have just one more moment to say what's been left unsaid. This show will give you a chance to do just that, and much more." On Ginny's sign, I paused and let the audience clap for a few seconds, before resuming my monologue. "Amber, you have the gift of communicating with the dead."

"That's right." Amber nodded, still frozen. Her voice sounded choked as though she was about to give a presentation in the middle of a panic attack. For the first time, I wondered why I didn't just employ a professional actress to do the job.

"I bet you never had to wonder what's on the other side, huh?" I joked. "Tell us something about it." My eyes implored her to kick her brain into motion and come up with more than a few monosyllabic words.

She laughed and shifted in her seat. "I did before I was granted the gift of seeing what's beyond."

"Thank you for sharing your unique experiences with us today. There must be many of them." I spoke out a silent prayer. Seconds ticked by. She just kept smiling. The silence became uncomfortable.

"Tell her about me," Theo hissed.

Amber turned to her right. "What?"

The camera focused on the space next to her. We saw Theo, but I knew viewers at home wouldn't because ghosts have no reflection and can't be caught on film. My pulse sped up as I decided to keep quiet and see where this might take us.

"Tell them about me and Hell," Theo prompted.

"What do you want me to say?" Amber whispered.

I leaned forward and stared into the camera, faking surprise, then turned back to Amber. "What are you seeing? Is it a ghost?" I rubbed my arms, hoping I wasn't going overboard with my performance. But the truth was I was enjoying every minute of it. The drama of not knowing what came next nourished my need for chaos. My skin tingled from all the excitement. "We're dying to know what you're seeing."

A frown crossed Amber's features and for a moment she just peered at me. "I see the ghost of a girl with blonde hair and blue eyes. She says her name is Theo and she lives in Hell."

"Distros," Theo corrected.

239

Amber nodded. "Sorry, Distros."

"That's one of the seven dimensions of Hell," I said. Like on cue, several people from the audience drew their breath sharply. For a second, a camera focused on their shocked faces. At Ginny's request, the attention returned to Amber and me.

"Ask her what Hell's like," I said.

Amber repeated the question as though Theo couldn't hear me only to echo Theo's words a moment later. "She says it's hot."

"Nothing new there." I laughed toward the camera but inched closer. My need for chaos and drama grew stronger.

"There's many people and they live in cottages, but most keep to themselves," Amber continued, unfazed. "She says it's very similar to a holiday cottage in the woods except that people aren't there to relax."

She paused. The candles flickered.

"Is she being punished?" I whispered.

Amber shook her head. "There is no punishment where she lives. Just waiting and thinking of her sister, Sofia, and hoping she'll get a chance to warn her."

"So, Hell isn't a bad place then?" I shot the camera a questioning look.

"No," Amber said. "It's a place of contemplation and reminiscence. Theo's happy for the chance to think about her life. Lucifer has made it clear once she's finished, she'll see her loved ones again. It's a necessary phase to go through in order to evolve spiritually. Some will be stuck in there forever because of the magnitude of their sins, but others, like Theo, only pass through."

"Lucifer and Hell exist then?" I stood and walked to the front of the stage, talking to the audience. "And it's all so very different from what we've been spoon-fed for centuries. Doesn't that challenge our perception of life and death and what lies beyond? Amber, can you prove you're telling the truth?"

Amber seemed to be slowly getting into her role. "Of course. I'm happy to summon any ghost you want." Whoa, that was a big lie. The girl couldn't raise the dead if her life depended on it. Not least because she'd probably end up fainting in the first place.

"Great." I turned to the camera. "If you have a secret no one else but a deceased relative or spouse knows about, give us a call and put Amber to the test. The lines are open now."

A telephone number appeared on the screen. I breathed out, thankful for the quick break. Next door, Dad's employees were sorting out through the first calls, picking a few genuine ones.

"You did great," I whispered to Amber and Theo. "Ready for the challenging part?"

"I've no idea how to raise the dead," Amber said. I figured that part.

"Don't worry, I do." I winked and smiled as my face appeared back on screen. "Thank you so much for staying with us." Not that they had a choice. "My assistant tells me we had thousands of callers." It was a lie. We only had ten of which eight called to complain they couldn't switch off their TV set.

"Hello?" Amber said.

"Hi," a thin, female voice said. She sounded insecure, as though she expected it all to be a prank and was ready to hang up any moment.

My smile grew wider. "You're Helen from New York. Tell us why you're calling, Helen."

"My mother died six months ago. I'd like to know whether she's okay."

Amber peered at me.

"What's her name?" I asked, stalling for time.

"Martha."

"Martha," Amber repeated. She reached for the salt and spread it over the dagger. "Yes, I can sense her presence. She's far away." Amber's forehead creased as she raised the dagger, holding it over her head. Her voice rose into a crescendo. "I'm reaching for her, pulling her to me, but it's a long tunnel."

"Who's that idiot?" a sharp voice asked.

My head spun toward the woman in rags inching toward us. The strong smell of sulfur hit my nostrils, making me gag. I pressed a hand over my mouth and shook my head.

"I did it," Amber whispered, amazed.

"You did nothing. I entered through that door." Martha planted her hands on her hips as she scanned the room. "What's going on? Why was I brought here?"

"Can you see her?" I whispered toward the camera.

Amber nodded. "She's one mean lady."

"Martha wasn't a nice person," Helen said. She sounded whinier than before.

"Is that you, Helen?" Martha hissed. "How dare you take that tone with me after all I've done for you?"

"Don't be shy or scared. You can ask anything you want," I said, softly. "Go on."

Helen hesitated. The candles flickered where Martha stood, staring at Dad's imposing figure. The fear in her eyes told me she must've met him before, so she couldn't be a temporary guest from Distros. Dad winked, but the way he regarded her resembled more a warning to play along than a friendly greeting.

"You amassed a fortune from your husbands. I want to know what you did with the money," Helen said.

Martha turned to face me, gaze ablaze with something I couldn't quite pinpoint. "You want the money for yourself, then."

Amber repeated the statement, wide-eyed.

"No," Helen said. "It's time to return what never belonged to you."

"You're lying, you righteous, little beast. It was all my hard-earned cash, and you're not getting any of it," Martha yelled, lunging for Amber to snatch the dagger out of her hands. Amber stumbled and dropped on the sofa, fighting the screeching ghost. Red trails of blood appeared on her skin where Martha's nails scratched the skin.

I stepped in front of the camera calmly. "What is Martha's secret? Don't miss your chance to find out after a short break."

The screen turned blank. At the same time, several demon guards jumped on stage and seized Martha's arms, pinning her down. From the corner of my eye, I noticed Aunt Krista slip into the adjacent room, which had been specifically decorated for her handbag infomercial.

"The phones are going crazy," Ginny said. "There are so many callers, the lines will fry."

"You said no one would watch," Amber whispered.

I shrugged. "Who cares? You're famous. I've heard everybody wants to be on TV."

"You don't understand, Cass. Aidan will be so mad."

"He's just jealous because you're getting all the attention." I squeezed her hand. "Just tell him to suck it up. He'll get the chance to be a necromancer at the next paranormal race in five hundred years. Until then, you get to be the star in the family."

Chapter 22 - Confessions

The phone lines were down. Ginny was trying his hardest to sort through the chaos and fix the mess while Aunt Krista was really getting into her marketing. She'd been talking non-stop for at least five minutes, holding up this and that bag. I had no idea what she could possibly have to say about her ugly designs, but apparently it was interesting stuff because there was so many hits on her website the server couldn't cope. Of course, it could also be our worldwide viewers searching for another way to reach us.

Dad leaned over Martha, probably talking sense into her. After her vicious attack on Amber, I doubted there was anything sensible about Helen's mother, but the show must go on. We couldn't afford people thinking we were phonies.

"They didn't see Martha, did they?" Theo asked. I shook my head, barely paying attention to her through all the chaos. "So viewers actually witnessed scratches suddenly appearing on Amber's face. I've got goose bumps just thinking about it. If I saw that on live TV I'd be so freaked out."

I tapped a finger against my lips, thinking. "You're right. No wonder everyone's eager to call and talk to the necromancer."

"Standby on the set," Ginny said. Everyone shifted into place and Ginny finally yelled, "Roll tape."

"I know where I've seen this guy before," Dad whispered.

"Your kitchen?" I peered at him, barely able to suppress my grin.

Dad shook his head. "No. I recently promoted him from guard to gatekeeper in Distros."

"I'm sure that's it, Dad." I rolled my eyes as he took his seat, then turned to Amber. "You've been doing brilliantly. We need you to continue with the show."

She nodded, jaw set. "No ghost's ever going to scare me."

"Let's go live then." I signaled Ginny to start before Amber could change her mind.

"Three, two, one. We're live," Ginny said.

I smiled into the camera. "Welcome back to Messages From Beyond The Grave. My name's Cass and this is Amber, our very gifted necromancer. Our last caller was Helen whose mother took a dark secret to the grave. Helen, are you still with us?"

The line crackled. "I am, Cass."

"Great. What did you say—"

"What happened to Amber?" Helen interrupted. "Did Martha attack her?"

I peered at Amber, unsure whether to tell the truth. Luckily, she made that decision for me. "She did, but I've got it all under control now."

Helen exhaled audibly relieved.

"Our viewers were enthralled. Why don't you tell the ones joining us now about your problem, Helen," I prompted.

"Martha stole a lot of money from people who trusted her. I want to know where it is so I can give it back." Helen's voice sounded more confident than before, as though being in the spotlight boosted her confidence as we spoke.

I nodded. "That's noble of you. Martha didn't seem to agree though, which is clear from the scratches on Amber's face. Did we catch that on camera?" I peered around me with exaggerated movement, then tapped against an imaginary earpiece. "My team says we did. Well, let's see it in slow motion then."

Ginny signaled and the pictures of Amber being assaulted by an invisible force appeared on the screen.

"If that looked nasty on camera, imagine catching it all live here in the studio. That's one messed up, scary ghost, let me tell you that," I said as soon as I was back on. The audience nodded. Murmurs erupted. By now our viewers must be glued to the screen, not least because the programming in my phone kept them from moving.

"I would've done far more than that if you didn't stop me," Martha shrieked. For a soul who had just spent years dangling from chains in the ceiling, she sure was mouthy.

247

"How did Martha die?" I didn't ask because I wanted to know. It was more out of a need to wind Martha up because her rudeness was slowly starting to tick me off.

"She killed herself," Helen said. "Probably couldn't cope with the guilt."

"I didn't *kill* myself, you moron," Martha growled, tossing a burning candle on the floor. Luckily, there was nothing nearby that could catch fire. I grinned because the camera caught it all live as Martha continued, "The street was icy and I lost control of my car."

"Did you see that?" I stared into the camera as it moved from the candle on the floor to me.

"She's always been nasty," Helen said. "I'm not surprised she hasn't changed her ways in the afterlife."

Martha shrieked and jumped on the table, kicking at the candles around her. I peered at Dad, waiting for him to stand and do something, but he remained seated, watching the scenario with an amused expression, a glint playing in his eyes.

"That's enough," I yelled, scanning the air as though I couldn't quite see where Martha cowered. "Tell us where the money is."

"No." Martha shook her head, vehemently. A guttural sound escaped her throat.

"She said 'no'," Amber whispered, raising the dagger.

"What do you think you're doing with that?" Martha asked. "You can't hurt me. I'm dead already." With the back of her hand, she flicked our water glasses from the table. They shattered into thousands of pieces at our feet.

"She said I can't hurt her because she's dead already," Amber repeated.

"Stop repeating everything I say," Martha shrieked, hitting the table until it toppled over.

The audience gasped. For a moment, the camera focused on them, filming the fake shock and dread in their faces, then turned back to us. I got up from my seat and shook my head.

"Dear viewers, we clearly have a poltergeist entity on our hands. Amber will try to retrieve the secret and send it back where it belongs. I certainly don't envy the poor guy in Hell who has to deal with this day in, day out. Do you?" I cocked a brow. "Amber, it's your turn."

Amber narrowed her gaze. "Where's the money, Martha?"

"Make me tell you," Martha hissed.

"Force her to say it," Helen whispered into the phone.

The anticipated broadcasting hour was almost over and we hadn't even gotten to Theo's plea yet. Research said viewers usually switched off after sixty minutes. If we didn't hurry up, we'd lose people's attention. Obviously, I could just read Martha's mind, but I wasn't the necromancer here. The information had to come out of Amber's mouth. I shot Dad an imploring look. He smiled back.

"Don't make me send you back to Hell!" Amber warned.

Martha growled. "Where do you think I am, you moron?"

"Tell her," Dad said. His voice was silent, barely more than a whisper, and yet everyone's attention snapped to him.

I watched Martha gulp, eyes scanning the room for an escape even though she probably knew there was no way out for her. One snap of Dad's fingers, and she'd regret ignoring his request for the rest of her existence.

"Behind the fireplace, on the right hand side just above her head, is a loose stone. She'll have to squeeze in the thin blade of a knife and jiggle it about to be able to pull it out. The money's there," Martha said.

Amber recited the ghost's words calmly.

"We don't have a fireplace," Helen said. "Maybe she's not telling the truth."

"That can't be," Amber whispered, mortified.

I turned to Martha as I forced my way into her mind, pushing aside memories of poison and cold-hearted apprehension, of a slippery street in the middle of the night, and the unfortunate car ride that consequently killed her.

Closing my eyes, I pushed harder, fighting to get into those parts of her life she had been desperately trying to hide from those around her.

The house came into focus; a shabby thing at the outskirts of town, with a back garden that had never been tended and a weeping willow that had seen too many secrets. Inside, old clutter covered every available surface. It made sense. Martha liked to hoard things, and so she collected her husbands' life savings, robbed children of their inheritance and stacked them all away behind a brick inside a large fireplace with a marble sill. Years later, the house still looked the same except that a thin wall covered the once magnificent fireplace.

I opened my eyes and leaned toward Amber, whispering in her ear. She nodded.

"What? What did you say?" Martha asked, warily.

"Helen," Amber said, ignoring her, "the fireplace is hidden in the living room, behind the wall facing your brown sofa."

"Let me check," Helen said.

We waited in silence as she thumped into another room, what must be a portable phone transmitting the sounds of a door opening and knocking on a wall.

"It's hollow," Helen said.

I nodded at the camera. "You can kick it in."

The line crackled. We heard a few bangs accompanied by groans. A chair or table shifted. Something clattered to the floor.

"There's something behind it. Yes, the fireplace is here."

I shot Martha a triumphant look. She dropped down on the floor, sulking. If I had a secret as big as hers and someone forced it out of me, I'd probably be sulking too, but I couldn't quite bring myself to feel sympathy for her. What she did was wrong.

"Get a knife and start digging," Amber instructed.

Ginny signaled we had five more minutes. I turned to Amber. "Didn't you say something about a message from beyond?" Amber's expression went blank. "Theo," I whispered.

"Right." Amber paused. The camera focused on her. "There's a girl, Theo. She wants her sister, Sofia, to know that she did something wrong and now she's in Hell, but the place isn't bad and she's safe."

I nodded, and she continued, more confident than before, "Sofia Murphy, if you can hear me, your boyfriend's the brother of the one who murdered Theo. He lied his way into your life with bad intentions. You

251

must get away from him this instant and never see him again."

It wasn't good enough. If I were Sofia, in love with a man I implicitly trusted, I'd never believe a television broadcast trying to convince me otherwise. "Tell her something only she can know," I whispered.

Theo tapped a finger against her lips, only now coming to life. "Let me think. When I was five years old, right after our mother's death, I thought I saw Mom's face and bent over to peer into the fountain in the backyard of our old house, the one we had to sell because we couldn't afford the upkeep. I almost fell in, but Sofia caught my leg. We swore to never tell anyone."

The camera fixed on Amber echoing Theo's words. I hoped somewhere out there a girl called Sofia was watching and remembered the incident, thinking of her little sister who died too young.

"The brick's out," Helen said. "I can't believe it." She laughed. "The money's here. There's savings bonds and deeds and what else not."

Ginny signaled we had only seconds before the hour was up. I smiled into the camera. "I'm glad we could help, Helen. We'll be back next week with more Messages From Beyond The Grave. Don't forget to tune in, same time, same place."

"That's it," Ginny shouted. "Well done, everyone."

I beamed at Dad who seemed impressed. I just wished Dallas were here to watch what a great job Amber and I did, but then he might not be so inclined to think we were still holidaying in Disneyworld.

Chapter 23 - The Seer

Dallas was awake and working when I arrived at the mansion. I found the office as I left it—a big mess. Countless sheets of paper covered every inch of surface. My notebook was switched on with yet more brainstorming ideas jotted down on virtual sticky notes for step two of our campaign, and empty cups littered the cabinet behind the desk because I hadn't yet found suitable replacement for Ginny. Even with a map, I doubted anyone could find their way around this place. I tiptoed around Dallas's chair and planted a sloppy kiss on my fiancé's cheek.

"So sorry I missed your big TV debut, babe. You should've woken me." He pulled me onto his lap, cupping my face in his hands. The sleeves of his black shirt were rolled up, revealing the tanned skin and taunt muscles of his forearms. A glitter sparkled in his honey eyes as he looked at me, making my heart skip a beat.

I moistened my lips. "No worries. You didn't miss anything. Barely anyone watched."

"Yeah? I'm sure you were great." A lazy smile spread across his lips. "It'll catch up next time."

"Maybe."

He pulled me closer until our lips met. "Your aunt's staying over for dinner."

"Aunt Krista?" I pulled away, narrowing my gaze. "Why?"

"Don't know, but your dad said if you want to escape the visit from Hell, you'd better make a run for New York now."

"Why? What's in New York?"

"Your aunt Selena."

I took a gulp of his water to calm down, but my temper flared nonetheless. "He told you the location?"

Dallas nodded, brows raised. "You seem upset. What's wrong?"

"Well." I ran my fingers through my hair and started playing with a strand just to keep my hands occupied so I wouldn't pull out my phone and beam myself wherever Dad was to give him a piece of my mind. "What else did he tell you?"

"Nothing." Dallas regarded me. I could see he was curious just as much as I realized I was overreacting, but I couldn't help it. If I could delay Dallas finding out what Aunt Selena was like, I would stall for time. The later he met her, the better.

"So, you didn't talk?" I finished his water and placed the glass back on the table with a little too much force.

"We did."

"About what?"

Dallas hesitated. "You don't like me spending time with him, do you?"

How could I when Dad was a fallen angel who could burst Dallas's bubble of living in Disneyworld any time? I doubted Dad had taken a liking to the idea of me getting married, so it was only a matter of time until he let something slip and Dallas put two and two together. "No. I'm just curious. You don't have to tell me if you don't want to."

"No secrets between us, remember?" He grabbed my hand. Our fingers intertwined. For a moment, I honestly believed he meant it. Guilt nagged at the back of my head, until I remembered he had been keeping a few secrets as well. I knew his sister was an immortal being, but not because Dallas confided in me. He still didn't trust me with that part of his life.

"He's invited me to stay here," Dallas said.

My jaw dropped. From all the things Dad could've said, this was the one thing that didn't make any sense. "Why?"

"Because he offered me a job."

"You didn't take him up on the offer, did you?"

Dallas avoided my gaze. There was my answer then. Groaning, I threw my hands up. "Why would you accept, Dallas? You know I can't wait to get away from here."

His eyes sparkled with curiosity. "See, that's weird. You have a beautiful home. Bob's a great guy, and the pay package is so much better than anything I could find in London. Why don't you want to stay?"

"Because no girl wants to live at home. Now drop it." I stomped out and slammed the door so he'd get my point. Aunt Krista said, once I started working in the 'family business' I'd never get out to see the world. She might be eccentric with the attention span of a five-year-old, but she probably had a point. I doubted I could break Dad's heart by raising his hopes and then crushing them again. Offering Dallas a job must be part of his plan to keep me here. There was no way in hell I'd let him take Dad up on the offer.

Furious, I burst into Dad's office without knocking and planted myself in front of his desk so he couldn't ignore me. He looked up and sighed.

"What's wrong?"

"You offered Dallas a job. How could you?" I took an accusatory step forward until my thighs brushed his armrest.

"The boy's looking for work and he likes it here." Dad shrugged. "You should be happy for him."

I couldn't believe the cheek. "Dallas hates the heat. He'd only accept because he wants to take care of me, and you know it."

"That's not what he assured me." Dad stacked away the loose sheets from his desk and turned to regard me. The expression on his face was serious, too serious even for him. "Cass, have you given any thought to your financial position?"

I snorted and rolled my eyes. That was Dad, always the practical soul with no romantic bone in him. "Don't worry about it. I've got it all covered."

He seemed unconvinced but didn't comment further. "As you wish. What about Dallas getting older and you not? Don't you think he'll notice?"

"Maybe."

"No, Cass. It could happen now or in ten years, but he'll start asking questions eventually." He rubbed his forehead. "I offered him the job because at least here, he gets to stay the same."

As in, he wouldn't grow old and die. That tiny detail must've slipped my mind. Nothing ever changed in Hell. How ironic that what once irritated me was actually the answer to one of my biggest problems: Dallas's mortality.

"Thanks, Dad," I whispered, burying my head into his shoulder.

He nodded. "Don't sweat it, kiddo. I want to see you happy. That's all that matters to me. You did a great job with the TV show."

Embarrassed, I smiled and ran a hand through my hair. "Thanks."

"You're so grown up and all." Dad slapped my shoulder awkwardly. "I've decided to give you a break from Kinky and Pinky. At least for the time being so you can spend some time with Dallas. But don't do anything stupid, or they're back in no time."

I gaped at him. "Are they gone?" I peered around me, looking for the tiny angel and demon, suddenly realizing I hadn't heard from them in a while. "What did you do to them?"

"Pinky's back in heaven on vacation and Kinky's, you know—" he waved a hand in the air "—around. I thought that was what you wanted ever since your mom and I decided to make them your companions."

I nodded because he was right. For years, I had been complaining, and yet, for some inexplicable reason, I felt sad. I pulled my nose and fanned myself air to dry my suddenly wet eyes. "I would've wanted to say goodbye."

"Don't be sad, Cassie. You can visit them any time."

I nodded again, the thought comforting me a little. I wanted to grow up and be alone for a change, without the constant yapping in my ears and watching over my shoulder. It was probably for the best. I smiled, pushing my melancholy to the back of my mind. "I'll invite them for my wedding."

"Don't you have a plane to catch?" Dad winked, smiling.

"Spending hours on a plane and the consequent jetlag sucks." I kissed him on the cheek and dashed out shouting over my shoulder, "Sorry about before."

"One last thing before you leave."

I stopped in mid-stride, suspicion washing over me again. "What, Dad?"

"When you travel together—" he cleared his throat, avoiding my gaze "—what are your sleeping arrangements?"

"Huh?" I laughed. "You're kidding." He inclined his head, his face remained dead serious. No kidding there, then. "You've kept us so busy it's taken us forever to even share a first kiss."

"Really? That's exactly how I like it. I gather you'll continue to be busy, yes?" Dad beamed up at me. His broody mood from before seemed completely lifted. For a fallen angel, he sure was conventional.

"We'll do our best." I headed for the door, hesitating because something didn't quite feel right. For a brief moment, my vision blurred and my ears picked up a piercing sound, like the cry of an eagle. And then it was gone again. I turned, shaky on my feet. "Did you hear that?"

"Hear what?" Dad asked, brows raised.

I shook my head, wondering whether all the stress from the TV show finally got to me. "Nothing."

"Have fun in New York, then," Dad called after me. Ignoring him, I went in search for Dallas.

The office was empty, but the door to his room stood open. He was leaning over his small suitcase, arranging his clothes meticulously. I wished I could tell him I could program anything into my phone and it'd all be completed by Hell's energy from which the phone drew its power, but firstly we hadn't reached that level of trust yet. And secondly, he looked so cute with his forehead creased in concentration, I wouldn't mind watching him for hours.

"Hey." I tapped him lightly on the shoulder because I didn't know what to expect after our first fight.

"Hey." He turned and smiled, pointing at his luggage. "Want to give me a hand? I was never good at this stuff."

"Sure." I didn't point out I'd never manually packed anything in my entire life.

"Are you okay?" He sounded so cool and nonchalant, as though we hadn't just argued less than half an hour ago. His easy-going attitude sure beat the drama and shouting I was used to from past boyfriends.

"Yeah. Are you?"

He shrugged. "Why wouldn't I be?" I started tossing his clothes in haphazardly, my mind a million miles away. "On a second thought, you might want to get your own packing done," Dallas said, pushing me away.

"You're right." For a moment, we stared at each other. The air was charged with something, making my mouth dry. My hands turned clammy as he leaned forward and planted a kiss on my lips. My skin tingled, my heart raced. He broke off the kiss too soon. As usual, apart from the golden speckles in his eyes, he seemed unfazed.

"When's the flight leaving?" Dallas asked.

He was too observant for his own good. In all the drama, I completely forgot to check.

"There's plenty of time," I said, hoping he wouldn't persist. "See you later."

Outside, voices carried over from the ground floor. I leaned over the balustrade to get a better look when I realized no one was there. It was the same whispering—countless voices speaking at once—from before, all in my head. After seventeen years, I was used to reading minds, but usually they were accompanied by a mental picture of the person speaking. This didn't make any sense.

I closed my eyes and took a deep breath, willing the mysterious voices to go away. They persisted. My phone rang. For a moment, the piercing sound competed with the sudden screeching in my head. I didn't feel like talking to anyone, but it might be important, so I picked up.

"Cass, someone broke into Distros." The tension was palpable in Dad's voice. "I need you to stay inside until we've found the intruder."

How could anyone break into Hell? There were only two gates in Distros, one leading to the lower and upper plane, the other to the world of the living. Both were heavily guarded by the Keepers aka Dad's winged demons.

"The TV show did its purpose then. You're famous. Everyone wants a piece of you," I joked.

"Not me, your friends," Dad said.

"What? How do you even know about them?" I asked, but he'd already hung up.

Chapter 24 - Mortal

For the first time in years, I actually missed Kinky and Pinky. Truth be told, I was starting to feel kind of lonely without the tiny devil and angel. If only they were here, they might know what the voices in my head were all about and advise me how to get rid of them. I realized, without my companions I was completely on my own.

Only after we were out of Hell and on the way to the airport did the murmurs drop to an unobtrusive level that could be ignored. I was finally able to sustain a conversation with Dallas, but he seemed engrossed in his phone, typing furiously.

"You okay?" I asked, leaning closer to get a glimpse.

"Sure. Just busy." He turned away from me, hiding the screen from view.

My trust in him instantly evaporated into thin air. He was hiding something. Once again, I wished Kinky were here so he could peak over Dallas's shoulder and spy on him.

"Anything important?" My attempt to sound nonchalant failed. Dallas put his phone away and sighed.

"Nothing worth mentioning."

"Ah." I nodded, scolding myself for not having the guts to ask him straight out. The problem with being too interested in his matters was that he might misinterpret it as being snoopy, or insecure. That isn't a message one wants to convey so early in a relationship, so I kept quiet and put on my poker face, ready to pretend all was well with the world and I wasn't in the slightest bit obsessed. But I was so very desperate to know his secret. Would my phone be able to find out?

I tapped my fingers on my thigh, considering whether to give the tiny device a try at mind reading when the car pulled up at the airport. We got out and headed for the check-in area, followed by the driver, a six-feet Schwarzenegger-type of guy who seemed to be glued to us. It wasn't the poor guy's fault Dad was obsessed with the idea we were not safe after someone broke into Hell. Now I knew from which part of the family I inherited my tendency toward OCD.

"Franz, tell Dad we got on the flight in one piece," I whispered to the driver.

"But, Princess, you haven't boarded yet." For such a big guy, he sure sounded whiney.

I glared at him, marveling what the air must smell like up there. "Do as I say."

"My instructions—"

"We'll be fine," I hissed. "Now chop, chop. Or you'll be looking for a new job once I get back home."

He bowed, his brows furrowed. "As you wish."

As soon as he was gone, Dallas and I purchased a latte macchiato and headed for our gate, ready for our final adventure aka visiting Aunt Selena.

* * *

It was a half-hour drive from the airport to Aunt Selena's bungalow in a suburb of New York. I paid the cab driver while Dallas grabbed our bags, then we headed up the front porch, my heart hammering in my chest. Two aunts down, one to go, but any previous success could pulverize into dust with a snap of Aunt Selena's fingers. She was the dragon among my aunts, the stubborn one, the spinster that kept changing her mind like the weather. Heck, a hurricane was more predictable.

"How old is she?" Dallas whispered.

"Old," I muttered. "Why?"

"I'm trying to figure out which charm to use."

"You have more than one kind?" I snorted. "Don't waste your breath. Whatever you sell, she probably ain't buying it."

"Why?"

He'd see soon enough. Ignoring him, I pressed the bell, peering around as we waited for someone to open. The hedges were trimmed to perfection. Wild rose bushes stretched from the ground to the windowsills, their gigantic thorns sending out a menacing message to any prospective burglars. I stretched out my hand, watching the thorns move toward me as though they were alive.

This was definitely good ole magic because no thorn I'd ever seen could do that.

The wall was painted a dirty white. A huge box blinked in the upper right corner. The door looked like not even a medieval battering ram could kick it in.

"She's into security big time, isn't she?" I whispered.

Dallas nodded, grinning. "You could say that."

A door bolt slid open, followed by a loud rattle, then the door opened with a heavy groan, and my aunt appeared. I stared at her, dumbfounded. She couldn't be serious. What was wrong with my wacky family? If Dallas didn't make a beeline for the nearest exit already, I wouldn't be surprised if he did now.

"Cassandra." Aunt Selena's thin lips curved downward as she grabbed me in a loose hug. The countless wooden yin yang pendants dangling from various chains around her neck clattered against each other. Her once black hair shimmered grey and golden in the sun.

"What happened? Did you turn into a pumpkin?" I pointed at her garish orange dress, tight around the waist and buttoned up to her chin. She laughed, but it sounded more like the cawing of a crow. "And the hair." I couldn't keep myself from staring, horrified. She used to look so polished and well dressed. As a child, she was the epitome of my fashion world, thin but not too skinny, and always so stylish. Peering at her hollow cheeks, I wished I could order some hamburgers from the nearest McDonald's.

"Come on in," Aunt Selena said with a pained expression on her face. I walked past, getting a better glimpse of her skin. Was that grey, smudged eye shadow right beneath her cheek? I squinted, but she turned to close the door.

"Thanks for having us, Auntie." I followed Dallas to drop our bags on the thin rug. Aunt Selena let out a pained huff, as though she was mortally ill or something. I frowned. "What's wrong?"

She turned from the door, her shoulders slumped, her mouth pressed in a tight line. "Nothing, dear. You're just interrupting something rather important."

"Want us to come back later so you can get on with whatever you were doing?" What was wrong with her? I'd never seen anyone so—serious, beaten, and depressing. I could only hope it wasn't contagious.

She sighed again. "It's too late."

Dallas shot me a questioning look. I shrugged and walked into the living room, halting in the doorway because what I was just seeing was beyond macabre. Every inch of the walls was covered in pictures of statues, goddesses, the yin and yang sign and passages of what looked like Chinese. The place was a fire hazard with wax dripping from the huge candles in the chandeliers, leaving shiny imprints on the breakfast table and the floor. The few bookshelves were stocked with nothing but copies of yet more Chinese books. The flowery, discolored sofa looked like it was created in the sixties and went through a few car boot sales.

I inched closer and picked up a picture of a fat man dressed in an orange tunic in a blinking plastic frame. "What is this? A shrine?"

Aunt Selena appeared behind me. "Don't be silly. Having a shrine is blasphemy. Do you want some water? You must be thirsty."

Looked like a shrine to me. I smirked. "I think I need something stronger. Maybe tea or coffee." Preferably something that would wake me up from this nightmare and I realized it was only a dream.

"Water it is." Aunt Selena turned on her heel when I grabbed her sleeve, forcing her to face me, my gaze searching for answers in her big, green eyes. Something glittered there before she pulled away and ambled out to the kitchen, cowering slightly as though her back was hurting.

"Whoa," Dallas whispered behind me. "You could've told me she was this—"

"Fanatic?" I turned to face him.

He shook his head, grinning again. "Devoted."

"Right." I shrugged and headed out after her because there was no way I wouldn't confront her.

I found Aunt Selena in the kitchen, hovering over a glass of water. As soon as I entered, she flinched and hid the glass behind her back. I narrowed my gaze. "Let me see that, Auntie."

She shook her head. I walked around her and snatched the glass out of her hands, then took a sniff. That didn't look and smell like water to me, more like plum juice or something stronger. She wasn't so holy after all. I gave her the glass back and put my hands on my hips, regarding her intently. "What's going on?"

She cocked a brow and shook her head lightly, as though she didn't understand my question.

I sighed. "What's with the fat guy in the picture frame? Do you have a new boyfriend?"

"No." She slapped my hand, shocked. "That's Buddha."

"Ah." I clicked my tongue. "Think I heard of him at school." I trailed off, leaving her room to elaborate. She didn't. So, I sighed. "Listen, as much as I'm enjoying our Q&A, I'm a rather busy girl, meaning let's get this over and done with. Why are you being so weird?"

Aunt Selena's back straightened, her jaw set. I grumbled inwardly, wondering whether I could just take out my phone and force this woman to start speaking or sign the dotted line, so I could return to my beloved, and she to her shrine.

"Strange things have started to happen, Cassie," Aunt Selena whispered. I cocked my head and inched closer, unsure whether I had actually heard her communicate, or my imagination was just playing tricks on me. Her green eyes pierced into mine.

I gestured her to continue. When she didn't, I said, "What things?"

She shook her head. "Bad things. You can smell it in the air. You can hear it in the wind. It's coming over the waters and riding the surface of the earth."

"Sounds like Doom's Day's near." I laughed. "You shouldn't believe everything you watch on *YouTube*, mate."

Aunt Selena's gaze remained glued to the floor. When she lifted her head again, something flickered in her eyes. Fear. Nervousness. Confusion. With tense strides, she reached the high-tech fridge in the corner and retrieved a bottle of water, which she tossed my way. I caught it in mid-air and unscrewed the cap but didn't drink.

"You're not getting married," Aunt Selena said.

I stared at her, stunned. My anger flared but, to my surprise, my mind remained clear. "Dad told you." He could kiss his beautiful campaign goodbye now.

"No, dear." Aunt Selena shook her head. "I can sense the bond between the boy and you, but there's more. Something dark and twisted."

"Yeah, it's in the air and all that." I rolled my eyes. "Let's get back to the marriage thing. What makes you think I won't be marrying him?"

"It's not happening."

I regarded her coolly as I bobbed my head slowly. No point in losing my temper now. If I wanted to win this particular battle I had to come up with a strategy and give it my all. Her green gaze bore into mine for a second too long, then she turned away and started wiping the already sparkling counter.

Why would she do this to me? Surely, my own family should be concern about my wellbeing. I peered at the small yet modern kitchen. White plates were arranged in neat piles in a glass cabinet. The oven showed a few droplets of dried grease where she had forgotten to scrub. There was only one mug left out to dry on a kitchen towel. No flowers from an admirer, no Valentines card. Maybe she was lonely...or jealous of my happiness, which wouldn't surprise me given how bitter she seemed.

I curled my lips into a smile. "If you help me out with this one I'll sign you up on an internet dating site, or even better, come with you speed-dating. Bet you'd have so much fun." Her jaw dropped like someone had just pulled a string. I shrugged. "Not your thing? I'll find something else then. Bingo, maybe?"

"This isn't about me, Cassie." She sighed that long, exaggerated sigh of hers again that made me want to pour a bucket of cold water over her head just to shock some life into her. "He's mortal."

Heard that one before. "So?"

"If he dies, bad things will happen to you," Aunt Selena said softly.

I leaned forward, all ears. "What bad things?"

"You'd turn into a reaper."

"A what?" I laughed, but it sounded forced even in my own ears.

She cupped my hands in hers, and for the first time I noticed concern in her eyes. "Your dad's guardians were once fallen angels, just like you and I. Now, look at what they've become after their bonded mate's death."

My mind travelled to the winged creatures transporting souls in and out of Hell. I was somehow connected to them because the moment I pictured them, the strong smell of sulfur invaded my nostrils, making me gag for a brief second. "I thought they were demons," I said, pushing their image to the back of my mind.

Aunt Selena shook her head. "I know you think guarding the gates and smelling a bit isn't that bad. But that's not all they do." I opened my mouth to speak when she held up a finger to stop me, eyes wide as she continued, "They tear the thread that binds the ethereal body to the physical."

Didn't sound particularly gruesome to me. I nodded, motioning her to continue.

"Hasn't your father told you anything?" She sighed again. It was starting to get on my nerves. "With every thread they destroy, they become slaves to their own nature, living for nothing but death. They start to ache when death's not around, so they linger around hospitals and the ill, waiting in pain and anticipation until someone dies. Then their own suffering disappears for a brief time, until the cycle repeats itself."

My mind went blank. I was rarely lost for words, but this story gave me the creeps. When my brain recovered a bit, I said, "What makes you think I might ever turn into one of them?"

"The boy's mortal, is he not?"

I nodded, suddenly seeing the connection.

"Then it's only a matter of time until he dies," Aunt Selena said.

Aunt Selena's words sank in, leaving an uneasy feeling in the pit of my stomach. "I'll do anything to keep Dallas young and alive," I whispered.

"You can try and keep him with you at your father's, but he will want to venture out one day. Every man does eventually," Aunt Selena said.

I swallowed past the lump in my throat. If only Kinky and Pinky were still here, they might know how to get through this. "Give me your blessing, and I'll find a way to make him immortal."

"Cassie." Aunt Selena's face neared mine until our noses almost met. I could smell her breath, the faint scent of plumes and mint. "I never said you don't have my blessing. I would never stand in your way."

"You said I wouldn't marry him."

She nodded, gravely. "I meant it literally. He will be gone by the time your curse takes effect and you're bound to Hell. After that, it's only a matter of years before he dies."

So, basically, what Aunt Selena implied was that the guy would make a beeline for the nearest exit as soon as I revealed my identity. But we were so loved up. It didn't make sense.

Aunt Selena filled a glass of water from the tap, then headed out the kitchen, probably to offer Dallas a drink. I stared after her, my heart unwilling to believe her words, and yet I knew she was right. Like Patricia and Krista, Aunt Selena had the seer ability, only Patricia had yet to turn eighteen and get her powers. And Aunt Krista couldn't be bothered to ever use it because she said all the thinking gave her wrinkles.

I knew I had to tell Dallas the truth eventually. So, was it really a matter of time until he left me? Would he still leave me if we were already married by the time I told him? Either way, I wouldn't give up on the love of my life without a fight. Not least because I wasn't going to be stuck in Hell forever.

"You said you'd give us your blessing. You can start by signing the dotted line," I said, stomping into the living room and tossing the scroll on the coffee table.

"Sure, dear." Aunt Selena didn't seem surprised. With slow movements, she grabbed the pen out of my outstretched hand and scribbled her name on the parchment, then handed it back to me, smiling.

Dallas shot me a questioning look, which I ignored. I clutched the scroll to my chest, relieved. Getting her signature had been easy, as though she couldn't even be bothered to argue.

"How are you going to save yourself from your fate?" Aunt Selena said.

"What fate?" Dallas asked.

I scowled at her, lest she say more and mess up the whole situation. "She thinks we're too young to marry and that we won't last." I scoffed. "Since my birthday's in a few weeks, we'll have to hurry up a bit with the wedding. Let's say, next Friday?"

Dallas's brows shot up. I flashed him my most gorgeous smile, ignoring the shocked expression on his face. Yeah, well, if he had cold feet, he could just suck it up. We were destined to be together, hence, why wait?

"I'll make sure to come," Aunt Selena said. "It'll be a rainy day, what with all the tears and sorrow."

Chapter 25 - The Plan

"What was she going on about?" Dallas said as soon as we exited Aunt Selena's house. "And why the hurry to leave?"

I hesitated, considering my words. What could I tell him? That Aunt Selena couldn't keep her mouth shut if her life depended on it? That her words of caution had made me worried and I wanted to return to the safety of Hell ASAP because I had a plan?

"Cass, what's wrong?" Dallas insisted. "I know you're hiding something. Think me weird, but I can feel it."

I smiled and gave his hand a squeeze. Of course he could feel it, and soon he would start to sense other things, like the fact that I wasn't ordinary and the ghouls outside Dad's mansion didn't blink and turn their heads because of some special effects. I had started to see what he was seeing when he wasn't around. Soon, my lies wouldn't keep him from putting two and two together when I couldn't explain the pictures flashing through his mind.

"Dad sent me text." I tried to keep my voice nonchalant. "He said the campaign was such a success that he needs us to work on step two straight away." It wasn't even a lie. Dad had called and left a message to return home, but not because of the campaign. Someone had broken into Hell. While he hadn't thought it necessary to bother me then, the situation apparently escalated when one of the guards was attacked. As much as I hated to waste my time on yet another flight, I vowed it'd be the last and just got on with it.

"You sure that's all?" Dallas asked, unconvinced.

Nodding, I flashed my most sincere smile. "Come on. We have a plane to catch."

* * *

We arrived in Hell the same day, jet-lagged and tired. I left Dallas in his room to get some sleep while I went in search of Dad. I found him pacing his room up and down, a deep frown set between his brows. He was dressed in jeans and a crumpled shirt, barely resembling his usual suit-clad, composed self.

"Your vampires sucked one of the reapers dry," Dad said.

My jaw dropped. "What makes you say that? I told you Aidan doesn't drink blood."

"And the girl?"

I couldn't answer that one because I didn't know. I had long guessed Aidan turned Amber after she almost died from her journey to the Otherworld in order to retrieve the book of Shadow incantations and magic that was now in my possession since I stole it from the immortal warriors. It never occurred to me that while Aidan's ritual had transformed him and his dim-wit brother, Kieran, into vampires who no longer needed blood and darkness to survive, the same might not apply to Amber. And yet I had seen her walking around in broad daylight. What Dad was implying didn't make any sense.

"There's my answer then." Dad rubbed a hand over his face. I noticed dark circles around his eyes that weren't there before.

"It wasn't Amber or Aidan," I said.

Dad turned to face me. "And how do you know that?"

"I just know. Trust me." I grabbed his hand. "There must be someone else, Dad. Just think about it. Why would anyone drink a reaper's blood?"

"To get their powers?"

"Is that possible?"

Dad shrugged. "Of course it is. At least for a time."

All the talk about reapers reminded me of something I had pushed to the back of my mind ever since Aunt Selena mentioned it. "Why didn't you tell me if something happened to Dallas I'd turn into one of them?"

Dad groaned. "Selena and her big mouth."

I nodded, annoyed. "Were you ever planning on spilling the beans?" He hesitated. "Tell me the truth, Dad."

"Obviously, I didn't want to worry you," he said, eventually. "I know the boy and you have a bond, which is about the only reason I let him stay here with us. Let's just say, now he's here, leaving Hell isn't an option, not without a few bodyguards and constant supervision."

That certainly explained the chauffeur demon's unwillingness to let us out of sight. I thought Dad was worried about me, but apparently it was all about Dallas. If Dad went that far even though he barely knew Dallas, then Aunt Selena spoke the truth and I had yet more reason to carry on with my grand plan.

"So, if something happens to Dallas I'll turn into a reaper?" My laughter died in my throat. "Seriously, could my life suck even more?"

"It's a myth. Might not even be true." I could tell from the way his gaze shifted uncomfortably across the floor that he was lying.

"Yet another legend with plenty of truth to it." I sighed and jumped down from my usual spot on Dad's desk.

"Where're you going?" Dad asked.

I shrugged. "Here and there. Listen, I need some candles from the ritual room. If you smell a bit of incense and hear strange voices tonight, don't mind them. This girl's one busy bee." I beamed at him, but he didn't seem to share my enthusiasm for the plan slowly forming in my head. Maybe because he didn't know it yet. I wasn't ready to share my brilliance with him. Better to keep everyone in the dark and just let them marvel once I was done.

"Why do I smell trouble?" Dad said.

"'Cause trouble's my middle name?" I grinned.

Dad's shoulders slumped as they always did when he just couldn't be bothered with prodding and prying. "Sure, Cassie. Just don't burn the house down."

I gave him a peck on the cheek and headed out again in search of the one thing that might just put an end to all of my worries and this awful curse.

Chapter 26 - Grimoire

Dad tried to free me from my compulsion to stack up everything I've ever bought or been given throughout the years. His attempts remained fruitless and I'm still the hoarding kind. I knew bringing home all sorts of stuff would come in handy—like today. A strange sense of wellbeing enveloped me as I went through my cluttered closet, pushing clothes and shoes and what else not to the side to reach a loose panel in the floor. I pulled it out to reveal my secret lair where I kept my most previous possessions such as letters from Mom, jewelry I made in Kindergarten and a particular book I acquired a few weeks previously. Acquired may not be the right word, more like pinched from the Shadows. Since at that time I was still harboring ambassador aspirations, I figured the book was safer in my hands than in those of a hoard of immortal warriors who might just tip the balance in the Lore court in their favor and win the ancient fight against the vampires. Balance acquired through domination, now where's the fun in that? Like every fallen angel out there, I wanted to keep this battle as blood-free yet on going as possible.

I pulled the bundle out of the hiding place and retreated to the couch in the living room where Ginny had already arranged black candles in the chandeliers. Thick smoke rose from a golden bowl; the heavy scent of incense hung heavy in the air. I removed the coarse cloth with a flick of my wrist, revealing the old book hidden inside.

It felt dusty in my hand and smelled like it was retrieved from a grave. I hoped it was more interesting than the Necronomicon in Dad's library and offered something more useful than a quick spell on how to make a fire.

I turned the pages one after another. A ritual to fortify a door. Easy. Even my phone could do that. A ritual to read the minds of others. Oh phuleeaaaase. I've had that particular skill since birth. Did I pick up a book for beginners? I turned it in my hands to check the cover. Nope. The title said 'advanced.' Seemed like the vampires and Shadows still had a lot to learn. Flicking through the pages, I noticed rituals for love, beauty, wealth, mind control, and what else not, but nothing useful like how to build a successful fashion label or remove an annoying curse. Not even something like transforming a girl into a domestic goddess, which would've really helped me score brownie points with Amber, who didn't know how to tidy up a room if her life depended on it.

After a few minutes, I finally found what I was looking for: an incantation for immortality. The instructions were pretty clear: get twelve Shadows to murmur what looked like gibberish to me while the high priestess was supposed to yell yet more mumbo jumbo. Simple enough, except that we didn't have twelve Shadows hovering around Hell. I figured, since Shadows were immortals, I could surely replace them with a few of Dad's demons, which was a bit like replacing sugar with artificial sweetener when baking a cake to save calories. I did that all the time and the cake tasted just the same.

Focusing my mind, I called up a few Operandes and went through the instructions yet again, only now realizing, the person one wanted to turn immortal had to be present. Shoot. I tapped a finger against my lips, thinking. The Operandes were little green demons with tusks on their heads, skin that tended to shed off like that of a snake and a tendency toward attention deficit disorder. Dallas might believe they were Hollywood actors were it not for the fact that they also tended to literally cling to a mortal because they liked all the different emotional layers that characterizes humans. Once they met him, they'd pursue him for the next couple of years. But the book clearly stated the object of experimentation had to be present. Kinky would know how to solve this debacle, but he wasn't around.

My glance fell on a picture frame featuring Dad and me posing in front of an Egyptian pyramid, and that's when the answer to my dilemma came to me. I could just use a snapshot of Dallas, which I had taken a few days ago when he was asleep. I flicked open my phone and typed in a command to make the snapshot magically appear in the form of a print photo. A second later, I held a picture of Dallas in my hand. The same moment, the door opened and twelve Operandes flooded in, bowing before me, their black gowns brushing the floor in a wide arc.

I nodded, eager to start my work, and commanded them to gather around the sofa and coffee table in a circle, then lit the candles and resumed my sitting position. The Operandes commenced their chanting. Gathering my voice, I started reading from the book, stumbling over all the gibberish, wondering whether I was reading any of the words right. Halfway through, the flames started to flicker. I smiled, confident I was doing everything right, and continued. My voice resounded from the walls as I gained momentum. Somewhere outside, I thought I heard a bird's call, but I couldn't be sure.

Dallas's picture began to glow at the edges, the soft light spreading to his hair and face. I quickened my pace. From the corner of my eye, I noticed the photograph glimmering stronger. It was definitely working. Finally, I spoke the last line and leaned back against the sofa as I gazed at the picture. A last flicker and the light disappeared.

The room fell silent. I sent Dad's demons away and went to look for Dallas, ready to test his new immortality, even though I had no idea how. Piercing a dagger into his heart wasn't an option. For one, I couldn't stand the look or even the smell of blood. Come to think of it, I felt sick even *thinking* of anything gory. I figured observation was the best way to go. If he just gained immortality status, he sure felt differently and he'd show it. Maybe he walked more upright like Amber, so I had to look for tiny details that would give away the changes in his body.

I knocked on his door. No one answered. Frowning, I peered inside all rooms on the ground and first floor, my boots thumping against the wood panels as I ran around, frantic. Dallas was nowhere to be seen. Where could he be? Had my little incantation made him disappear? I considered summoning Thrain to help me search when my vision blurred. Stumbling back, I grabbed hold of the railing. My view changed from the soft light illuminating the hall to darkness. The moon cast a glow on the dead trees to both sides of a narrow path. It was so dark I could barely see a few feet in front of me. The smell of burned flesh wafted past, making my stomach turn. For a moment, my brain switched off and I just bowled over, ready to puke. And then I saw him: Dallas dashing through the trees in the distance, his breathing coming in labored heaps. Someone whooshed past him, grabbing hold of him and whisking him high in the air. I raised my gaze up to the winged figure flying away, but the vision broke.

The hall came back into focus. I realized my back was pressed against the wall, sweat drenched my clothes. Wearily, I peeled my aching body away and forced my legs into action, taking two steps at a time as I flew down the stairs. I had no idea where Dallas was but, judging from the fact that he couldn't travel between the planes, I figured he must be around.

The entrance door squeaked under my shove. I left it open as I hurried out and almost bumped into the winged being, Octavius—Dad's best gatekeeper in Distros and a reaper I would become if Dallas ever lost his life.

Octavius released Dallas from his clutches and bowed deeply. In the soft moonlight, his pitch-black skin almost blended into the night. Even bent forward he was taller than Dallas, and twice his size; his strong arms with claws as sharp as a hawk's peered from beneath a thin shirt that molded around his muscly chest. His black eyes shimmered in a surprisingly human face, reminding me he hadn't always been a reaper. I shuddered. No way would I turn into something like this.

"What happened?" My gaze wandered to Dallas's pale face. His wide eyes betrayed shock. His expression seemed lost, and I wondered whether he even recognized me.

"Something chased him," Octavius said. "I had two options: either save the mortal, or charge after the creature. Since I didn't know whether there were more than one, I chose to save the mortal."

I nodded. "You chose wisely." I didn't even want to think what could've happened if the reaper decided the other way. "Did you see the thing? What was it? A demon? A soul?"

Octavius shook his head. "It moved too fast. I didn't get close enough."

"It must've been a demon," I muttered. "Maybe one of the guards confused Dallas with a straying soul."

"That was no guard," Octavius said.

"What then?" I snapped, regretting it instantly. He wasn't to blame. Fear rose inside me as realization kicked in. Was Dad right and Amber and Aidan weren't the dieting vampires they pretended to be after all? I mean, with Dallas being the only one mortal snack around, he might just be the obvious choice.

"I don't know, Princess."

Narrowing my gaze, I peered at the reaper. "Did you see anything at all? Even if it seems insignificant."

A frown crossed his forehead, creasing his smooth skin into thin lines. "When I descended to grab him, the moonlight caught in something long and red. I thought it was hair."

"Red hair? That doesn't make any sense." Not when Aidan's locks were dark and Amber's a washed out brownish color. I tapped a finger against my lips. "I guess they could've worn a wig." But that didn't make much sense either. For one, how could they possibly leave Distros without my help? And then why would they use such a bold wig and risk being seen?

"Shall I inform the big boss as soon as he's back?" Octavius asked. My attention snapped back to him and I noticed the lines of impatience around his mouth. He wanted to get going and fulfill his duty. I nodded and muttered a thank you as he bowed and took of through the air.

"Come on. Let's go inside." My hand clasped around Dallas's. As though waking from a trance, he took a step forward, then stopped. "Come on, Dallas." I pulled but he didn't budge.

He opened his mouth to speak, then closed it again, and I realized all the secrets I had been trying to keep from him were about to be revealed now. Even if I tried to pretend he hadn't just flown over the hills and dying woods clutched in the iron grip of a large, winged demon, something inside me protested. I was sick of lies and deceit. Aunt Selena had predicted Dallas's departure. Well, I was ready to find out.

Chapter 27 - A deadly acquaintance

The gargoyles shifted in the darkness, sniffing the air like guard dogs, ready to raise alarm with their wailing at my command. Dallas and I were inches away from the gate when his voice boomed through the silence of the night. "What's going on here?" Even though some sort of paranormal creature had hunted him less than half an hour ago, his tone betrayed irritation, as though nothing could shake his cool.

I took a deep breath and turned to face him. Our eyes connected. I moistened my lips, still considering whether to tell him the truth or not. Dallas cocked a brow. He wasn't making this any easier on me. Where should I even begin?

"Do you remember when I said Dad's name was Bob and that he ran Disneyworld?"

"Yes?"

I brushed a stray lock out of my eyes, averting my gaze. "Well, it's not exactly the truth."

Dallas inched closer and lifted my chin, forcing me to face him. "Where are we, Cass?"

I winced. Why couldn't he start with an easier question, like why a paranormal being had just flown him over the woods? Or why it had two huge wings on its back and looked like it just stepped out of a *Terminator* movie?

"Promise me you won't freak out." I shot him the most confident smile I could muster even though inside I was shaking.

Dallas didn't return my smile. "Just say it. I'm sure there's a reasonable explanation for all of this." The frown on his face told me he was just trying to convince himself.

"Hell," I whispered.

"Huh?"

Biting my lip, I took in the various emotions running through him. Confusion and excitement intermingled with a bit of mistrust. I breathed out, relieved. It wasn't that bad.

"Well, are you going to tell me?" Dallas prompted.

"I just told you." I did, didn't I? Unless my scattered brain had just played a trick on me.

Dallas laughed uncomfortably. "You said 'hell'." I nodded. "You can just spit it out. There's no need for cussing."

He thought I was just cursing. Laughter bubbled up inside me, rippling out of my throat. I wiped away the tears in my eyes at his confused look, then shook my head. "No, you don't understand. By 'hell' I mean we're in Hell. Literally."

"As in Heaven and Hell?" Dallas asked. I bobbed my head. "So we actually died during that mugging?"

"Not exactly." I faltered, searching for words. "See, we're in Hell because my dad runs the place. We were never mugged."

Dallas stayed silent. Why wasn't he saying anything? I searched his face but he remained expressionless, regarding me coolly. No drama wafted from him, no fear or repulsion. My throat bottled up, insecurity washing over me.

"You were lying, I knew it all along. Your stories were too far-fetched, and yet I desperately wanted to trust you. That's why I didn't confront you," he finally said. His tone came so low I could barely hear him in the eerie silence of the night.

"No." I shook my head, wide-eyed.

"You lied, Cass, over and over again." His lips curled into a smile, but it didn't quite reach his eyes. "You said we were going to California and that your father ran an amusement park. To find out we're in Hell and your father's what everyone would call the devil makes everything you told me a big, fat lie. You should've trusted me the way I trusted you."

He didn't even blink at mentioning Dad's name. "I'm sorry," I whispered because for once no words could betray my true emotions. I was so disappointed at myself, at him, at everyone. I had never been one to feel sorry for myself, and yet here I was swallowing down on the unshed tears that threatened to choke me any second. Maybe not being the crying kind was a blessing for a change because I didn't want to humiliate myself even more.

"Being sorry isn't good enough." He let out a huff and ran a hand through his hair. "What are you?"

Now he made me feel like a freak, which ignited my defensive nature. I pushed out my chin defiantly. "I'm Cass, but you may call me Princess of Darkness."

"I'm going home," Dallas said.

"No." My eyes started to burn. Aunt Selena had been right. Dallas would leave. Why didn't I lock the house so he couldn't venture out? What had he been doing outside anyway? "Just look at me. I'm like you," I said softly. "It's not my fault my dad's a fallen angel."

Dallas's eyes pierced into me, making my heart bleed at the contempt I saw in there. "You're not like me, Cass. I'm not a liar. When Amber warned me, I should've listened. Aidan ruined her life. I'm not going to add a *fallen angel* to our sorrows. As much as I like you, I want nothing to do with all this paranormal stuff." Throwing me a last glance over his shoulder, he walked down the narrow path into the house. I stared after him as he departed. He was probably packing his belongings this instant, ready to leave me behind like it had been his plan all along. Tears clouded my vision and spilled onto my cheeks. My emotions threatened to choke me. Somewhere at the back of my mind I remembered the ancient book and the ritual I had just performed. The thought registered that, unless the spell hadn't worked, he was a paranormal being himself now, whether he wanted it or not. He had yet another reason to hate me forever.

It was my nature to be good at deceiving, but all this time I hadn't really wanted to lie to him. I just thought he wouldn't understand. No one ever did. Not even Aidan and his friends, whom I had tried to help for years, yet they still despised me because I wasn't like them. I thought Dallas would be different because we shared a bond. As it turned out, not even the one with whom I shared a bond wanted me.

Wiping my tears off with my top, I trudged down the narrow path away from the house into the nearby woods, seeking some solitude. Already I felt the comforting silence of the night enveloping my mind. Dad was right. I didn't belong among the other immortals and certainly not among humans. I belonged here, with the other fallen angels and demons. It was time to take my position seriously and embrace my place as Dad's successor. Better stuck here forever where people actually liked me than where my heart would be broken over and over again. Although, after the fight with Dallas, I doubted anyone could ever hurt me more.

I reached the trees and kept going. The canopy of thick branches filtered most of the moonlight, but some rays found their way through, casting a golden glow on the dry earth. My steps thudded through the eerie silence of the night. Twigs snapped under my feet, the sudden noise jerking me out of my thoughts. I peered around me and realized I had walked farther than I intended. The air smelled of burned flesh here, probably gases from the volcanoes in the distance, and yet I had never noticed it before.

My tears had long dried on my cheeks. Stopping, I inhaled and scrunched up my nose. I focused on my latent abilities waiting to be released soon and turned my head, smelling all directions. The bad odor seemed to come from up in the trees. Peering at the dark canopy above my head, I squinted. For the fragment of a second, I thought I saw a shadow in the distance, jumping from one branch to the next. I took a step forward to get a better look. Nothing stirred, but a twig snapped, the sudden sound cut through the silence like a knife. Someone was out there. Maybe a dying bird or one of Dad's demons. Only too late did I remember Dallas had been chased in those same woods just half an hour ago.

The creature charging me came out of nowhere. One moment I was staring at the trees towering over me, and the next something knocked me to the ground. I raised my arms to protect my head as my back hit a large branch. Throbbing pain rippled through me, making me choke on my startled yelp. Groaning, I turned to the creature leaning over me. A long mane of hair encircled a tiny, shriveled face with yellow eyes floating in their hollow sockets. Her loose skin looked as though it had been put through a shredder, hanging from her in chunks. Her long nails pierced the skin on my throat, probably ready to stab me if I moved.

I opened my mouth to speak when she fletched her teeth, and for a moment I thought she'd bury her long fangs into me like a dog into a bone. Whatever this thing was, I knew I should be worried, but all I could think about was the burned smell that wafted from her and that made my stomach clench, ready to puke. The blood bond between Dad and me kept me from contacting him, but my mental abilities could reach out to the others. Focusing, I called out to Ginny and communicated where I was so he could raise alarm. There was no answer, but I knew help would arrive in a heartbeat. This was Hell, where nothing ever happened. An event like this wouldn't go unnoticed for long.

My mind searched the creature's, probing forward through foggy layers of conscious thoughts until I reached what I wanted to know. She had come for me, but she wasn't alone. My mind penetrated further. I flinched at the memory of leaping flames and the onset of unbearable pain. As the creature's body seemed to catch fire, my whole body began to burn. I forced my awareness away from her mind and the pain stopped. There were so many things I needed to know, but I figured I'd find out soon enough.

"Get up," she hissed. Her voice sounded like a long screech. I had difficulties understanding her because much of the flesh around her mouth was eaten away, revealing the white bone beneath. If I could only reach for my phone, I'd be able to punch in a code and knock her out or beam myself onto another plane. But her scary eyes watched me like a hawk. Maybe if I played along she'd become careless.

Pushing up on my elbows, I did as she ordered, sweat trickling down my spine as her odor hit my nostrils again. My heart hammered hard in my chest, but my mind remained clear. I was an immortal, I had nothing to fear, and yet I wasn't comfortable turning my back on the creature to walk up the path back to the house. My footsteps thudded across the dry earth, but the sound couldn't mask the creatures whistling breathing. I wondered why I didn't hear it before.

Dad's mansion came finally into sight. I frowned and shot the creature a look over my shoulder. "In there?"

She didn't answer, just gave me a push forward. I squeezed my hand inside my pocket.

"Don't," the creature hissed. I pulled my hand out again, realizing she knew about my phone. Either she had watched me, which couldn't be since I would've noticed the smell, or someone had told her about it. But who?

We reached the gate. I scanned the darkness stretching over the back garden. Nothing stirred. The gargoyles didn't move. Concentrating on the little demons, I sent my thoughts out to them, ordering them to pierce the creature's eardrums with their wailing, but the statues didn't move.

Out of the darkness stepped two figures dressed in black with hoods covering their heads and faces. The first one's hand was clasped around a dagger he held to Dallas's throat. My heart sank in my chest as I lunged forward, ready to defend him with my life. The creature's claws wrapped around my arms and pulled me back. I fought against her tight grip and the sudden wave of pain invading my arm where the thing bit me. Kicking her in the gut with a strength I didn't know I possessed, I sent her flying a few feet away. She scrambled up to her feet quickly, fletching her teeth, but before she could charge me again the second hooded figure pulled out a sword and held it to my throat whispering, "Move back, Rebecca."

I stared in awe at him. Rebecca. The vampire who had turned Aidan and his vampire clique, Kieran and Clare, a few hundred years ago, way before I was born. The one who had almost killed Amber. The one after whom I had sent Dad's reapers. Why didn't I recognize the hair or see the connection?

My hand wandered to my pocket again, eager to use my tiny device and get Dallas and me the hell out of this mess.

"Don't dare take out your phone or your boyfriend's dead, and you with him," the first hooded guy said. I blinked at the next surprise of the day. I wouldn't mistake this voice in a million years.

Chapter 28 - Et tu, Brute?

Seriously, what was it with me and my inability to make anyone actually like me? As I peered from Dallas's face to the one hiding behind the hood, seemingly satisfied in his belief it kept him anonymous, I couldn't believe the irony of the situation. I had told Dallas Hell was the safest place on earth, and yet one of the craziest hunters had forced her way in together with the one group of immortals I thought were my friends. Thinking back to Dad's warning and staring at the sword cutting into the fragile skin of my neck, I figured I was lucky if the Shadow didn't spill my blood for one of their grotesque rituals.

Where the heck was Dad anyway? Surely he couldn't be sleeping like a stone and miss all the drama of his only daughter being slaughtered on his doorstep in a freaky attempt at voodoo, or whatever these people practiced. Even the gargoyles seemed engrossed in their slumber, slacking off in their job, or why else wouldn't they raise? If I could only get nearer and kick them out of their dreams. I took a tiny step toward them. The blade pressed harder into my skin. Something hot and sticky trickled down my neck, and I almost fainted from the smell of blood. Behind me, Rebecca screeched hungrily.

"Cass, no!" Dallas yelled. I shot him a tentative smile, my heart bleeding at the worry I saw in his eyes. For a mortal, he was surprisingly calm. Then again, I wasn't surprised given that he had been gifted an immortal mate. Well, a soon-to-be immortal with the powers of Heaven and Hell if I only made it alive to my eighteenth birthday. Either way, Fate had chosen him wisely.

I raised my gaze to the hooded guy holding the blade against Dallas's throat. "You know the timing couldn't suck more. My life's in ruins already, but you surely added to the fire. How did you even get in here?"

"You underestimate everyone," Connor said. "Your kind always does." Heard that one before, but I couldn't remember where.

"Where's the book?" the other Shadow asked. My head turned sharply toward him. Devon. He was the one who helped Amber retrieve the book from the Otherworld.

I groaned. "Et tu, Brute?"

He kept silent, but I knew he understood Latin and my insinuation at him being like Brutus, Caesar's best friend and the one who betrayed him.

"The book belongs to us," Connor said.

"That book should've never been written so, from that perspective, it belongs to no one. You want it so you can take control of the whole immortal world." I shook my head. "Fat chance, mate. I'd rather die."

"What about your boyfriend?" Connor asked. "Would you rather see him dead?" Connor's robe shifted as his hand clenched tighter around the dagger in his hand. My heart started racing a million miles an hour. It was nothing but an empty threat. He couldn't mean it because the Shadows didn't kill mortals. Or did they? The blade cut into Dallas's skin. I peered at his widening eyes and the blood trickling onto the white of his shirt, almost black in the darkness. My mouth turned dry, my tongue stuck to the back of my throat. All reasoning stopped. I jumped forward, forgetting the sword cutting into my own skin, but Rebecca's grip held me back, snarling and spitting, probably crazed by the scent of Dallas's blood. Why didn't anyone hear us? Seriously, it seemed like nothing could interrupt Dad's rejuvenating sleep.

"Get the book and he'll live. You have two minutes," Devon whispered. "If you try anything funny, he's dead. Now hand over the phone."

Groaning, I fished it out of my pocket and tossed it across the ground to the guy's boot. "Don't worry. I'll be right back," I whispered to Dallas, then headed down the path into Dad's mansion.

"One minute and fifty seconds," Connor hissed. I didn't hurry my step because I wouldn't give him the satisfaction of seeing me follow their orders. Whatever they were, I was a hundred times stronger, or so I'd be...soon. I groaned. Soon wasn't good enough, I needed my powers now. Or a kick-ass plan. If only Pinky and Kinky were here, but it was all my fault. I wanted to be rid of them before turning eighteen so I could spend alone time with Dallas. That hadn't turned out so great either.

Counting the seconds, I thudded through the hall into the living room where I had dropped the book onto the floor just a few minutes ago when I hurried out to help Dallas. The house was quiet like usual, but something wasn't right. Ginny hadn't replied to my message. I focused my mind on Thrain and Octavius but received no answer. Had my meager abilities somehow deserted me? Halting to listen, I scanned the room.

The grandfather clock had stopped ticking; the lamplight cast dark shadows on the walls. I averted my gaze, then turned back. The shades on the walls seemed to shift with me, just like the gargoyles outside, but less obvious. I inched closer and reached out. A thin layer of fog covered the wall. My fingers disappeared inside an inch before I touched the hard surface. I pulled back, then tapped it slightly. The fog gathered around my finger and enveloped my hand. Even though I had never seen anything like this before, I knew instinctively it was some kind of Shadow magic. They could perform Voodoo stuff and astral travel, which is why no one even noticed them entering Hell, or standing in front of the house, threatening me and the love of my life. But I figured I could wonder later. Time was running out. Connor had said two minutes. I had to hasten my pace to get back. For some stupid reason, I actually believed since they were my friends they'd let us go once I handed over what they wanted.

I grabbed the book and took off down the hall and out the house, stopping in front of a gargoyle near the door.

The little stone demon's eyes were closed. I squeezed its shoulder, then gave it a shove, but he didn't move.

"Ten seconds." Connor's voice jolted me out of my thoughts. I sprinted down the path to the waiting Shadows.

"Now let go of him." I tossed the book at Devon's feet and crossed my arms over my chest. Connor picked it up and opened it, then nodded. Holding my breath, I peered at Dallas. Our gazes connected. He didn't speak, but I could feel he was trying to say something—mentally. I raised my brows, signaling I didn't understand a word. You'd think a bond would actually gift one the ability to hear the other person's thoughts, which might come in handy in a deadly situation, or when the guy's harboring dirty thoughts about the pretty neighbor. But as usual, Fate had messed up big time.

Dallas dropped his shoulders slightly. I squinted, still not getting what he wanted. Was he about to feign unconsciousness? Did he need to visit the bathroom? His gaze wandered past me to the woods and then back to me, and then I understood, or so I hoped. Someone was coming. What were they waiting for? A sloppy handshake and an invitation to dinner? Time to get this over and done with.

"You got the book. Now, go away." I pointed at the bundle on the ground. Rebecca hissed greedily but I paid her no heed. Ignoring me, Connor retrieved the book and flicked through it, then stacked it under his baggy robe. How they could even walk with that thing around their ankles was beyond me. "You know what should feature on your priorities list? Developing a fashion sense. That thing you're wearing looks like an ox could hide in there and no one would find it for a week."

Dallas laughed. I peered at him from under mascaraed lashes, my heart bursting with happiness. The man of my dreams had just laughed at one of my jokes. Maybe he didn't hate me after all.

"You used it," Connor said, pointing at the book. "What have you done?"

I blinked. How did the guy know? Did I somehow spill my coffee, leaving a stain behind? That happened all the time. "Nope. Don't think so."

His black, liquid eyes regarded me intently. I returned his stare, my mind penetrating his to find out what he thought. There was nothing there, just glaring emptiness. Either the guy knew to keep me out, or he was a big dummy who just liked to switch off the big computer every now and then. Eventually, he turned away without another word. I shrugged, wondering why no one had arrived yet.

"You're going with her." Devon pushed Dallas forward until he bumped into Rebecca. My heart skipped a beat. That's what he had been trying to say. He knew Rebecca would take him with her.

"No." I shook my head. "You said you'd let him go."

Connor nodded gravely. "Yes, and we'll keep our part of the bargain. However, she never agreed to it."

My gaze wandered from him to the scary vampire. He was right. How could I be so sloppy in my bargaining? My blood turned to ice as I saw the hungry look in her eyes. "Don't you dare touch him," I hissed.

A guttural sound escaped her throat. It took me a moment to realize it was laughter. I lunged forward when something hit me hard in the back and I stumbled to my knees, for a moment unable to breathe. The pang of pain brought tears to my eyes. Through the wet haze, I noticed blood spreading across the ground around me, the dry earth sucking it up greedily. It was just a bit of blood that would heal quickly. I might not be endowed with supernatural strength or speed, or any other fancy ability, but at least my body could heal itself.

"Cass!" Dallas's voice rang through the silence of the night, reaching me a moment before I raised my head and watched Rebecca disappear with him in the distance. Ignoring the pain, I stumbled to my feet and took off after him.

My legs seemed to move of their own accord. I had never run so fast in my entire life, ignoring my burning lungs and the branches grazing my arms and face as I pushed through the dry thicket. Blinded by darkness, I switched off my brain and just followed my intuition and that tiny silver thread that would pull me to my mate no matter where I was.

Rebecca's red mane appeared in the distance, then disappeared again an instant later. Her abilities included teleporting. I could only hope she was too weak to move from one place to another in an instant because in that case I might lose her tracks. I wished I had retrieved my phone from the ground where I had dropped it, but it was too late to return for it now.

My breathing came in ragged heaps as I felt my legs slow down, ready to buckle under me any minute. My brain screamed to keep on going, yet I knew if I didn't stop I might just pass out. Telling myself it'd only be a short break, I leaned my back against a tree trunk and scanned the area. I was deep inside the woods now with trees all around me. A soft wind howled through the air, swaying the dry leaves hanging from narrow branches, its whistling sound making me shiver. The moon had hid behind a curtain of dark clouds. Rebecca was a hunter, used to tracking and sprinting after her prey. Even if I wasn't completely out of shape since I stopped frequenting a gym two years ago, without any abilities and my high-tech phone I couldn't take down a blood-crazed vampire. But I figured she was on my territory, so I still had one major advantage: she might've found a way into Hell, but no one ever left this place without Dad's consent.

The Shadows must've spun their magic around this place, or why else would no one answer my calls? But I wouldn't give up without a fight. Closing my eyes, I focused my mind and descended into the lowest fractions of myself, like Dad always told me to. I could feel the dark walls closing in on me, the ones that usually made me run for a mile because I was so scared of what might be lurking down there, but this time I didn't hesitate. Something snapped inside me and darkness rose, a freezing sensation enveloping my body and soul. I realized my fallen angel nature was about to take over. Just one more tiny step into that dark abyss of my soul. Taking a deep breath, I faltered and then plunged right in.

The Shadows' magic broke and the bond with the others returned. Hundreds of thoughts invaded my head, cries and laughter, commands and defiance. The instant I sent out my order, the world in my head fell silent. And then all Hell broke loose.

Chapter 29 – Heirloom

I don't remember what happened between summoning Dad's demons and someone yanking at my arm, imploring me to return from that dark abyss that seemed to keep me hostage. Confused, I peered from the spot on the ground to the tiny demon cowering next to me, his tusks shimmering in the pitch black.

"Ginny?" My voice came so low I wasn't sure I had even spoken.

"You raised alarm. Everyone's now looking for the intruder." His eyes were filled with terror as he helped me to my feet.

"Where's Dad?"

"The guards said he left earlier this evening." Avoiding my gaze, he seemed uncomfortable talking about it, so I didn't press him for details, but I wondered where Dad could possibly have gone. However, finding out wasn't my priority.

"We need to find Dallas. Do you still have the phone I gave you?"

Ginny nodded and reached inside his pocket to retrieve it. Through the haze in my mind, I noticed he was wearing new clothes and boots, which gave him a confident flair. I opened my mouth to compliment him when he pressed the silver cell into my outstretched hand. Whispering a thank you, I punched in the numbers and letters that would lead me straight to Dallas, then grabbed Ginny's hand to take him with me through the portal.

The surrounding changed from dense woods to Distros' sparse hills. "How did they get here?" I mumbled.

"She drank a reaper's blood," Ginny said.

"Dad thought it was Aidan." I remembered Dad mentioning it and the consequent argument when he wouldn't believe me it couldn't be Aidan because he no longer needed blood to survive. Instead of investigating, I had forgotten all about it. Now Rebecca could probably travel through the various dimensions of Hell. That certainly wasn't good news. "She must be here somewhere. But where?" My phone had malfunctioned again. Instead of taking us straight to Dallas and Rebecca, it seemed as though we were in the middle of nowhere.

"Maybe over there." Ginny pointed to a bush. I inched closer until I could see the opening hidden behind it.

"It's a cave. You stay here and inform the others." Without waiting for Ginny's reply, I flipped my phone open to illuminate the opening, cowered down and squeezed through.

The space was big enough to crawl but not to walk upright. Dallas was a big guy, I wondered how Rebecca got him in here unless she had done something to him—

Pushing forward harder, I forced the thought to the back of my mind. I had never been one to picture the worst-case scenario, so I wouldn't start now. Besides, if something happened to Dallas, wouldn't the bond we shared warn me?

The sickening odor of blood and bones hung heavy in the air. Several times, I almost bowled over to vomit so I focused on the pain in my back and where the uneven terrain grazed my palms and arms. A few minutes of taking shallow breaths through the mouth and I finally reached an opening. With a sudden burst of energy I squeezed out into a clearing.

The sky was sprinkled with countless stars casting a soft glow on the nearby trees. Something pulled me forward. I sniffed the air, taking in the scent of morning dew gathering on the dry grass. And then the tiniest hint of Dallas's aftershave hit my nostrils and my heart started to hammer in my chest. I took off through the trees and bushes until I could make out the slim silhouettes of cottages. The first one I reached looked surprisingly familiar with its newly redecorated porch and the pretty curtains covering the windows. Even though I still lacked half the puzzle, my brain started to put the pieces together. Rebecca had dragged Dallas here to get back at Amber and Aidan. An angry yell rippled through my throat as I pulled out my phone and yanked the door open. The air crackled around me, freezing everyone inside into place. I had no idea how long it would work for, but I hoped it was long enough to come up with a plan.

Inside, several lamps were lit, giving the cottage a homely touch. I hurried through the tiny hall into the living room where I found Aidan standing in front of Amber protectively. Her gaze was fixed on the hideous creature cowering next to Dallas's unmoving shape in the opposite corner. Something wasn't right about the scene. Why wouldn't Aidan just charge Rebecca? Surely, two vampires were stronger than one? But maybe not since she had drunk the reaper's blood. If I wanted to get Dallas out of here in one piece, I had to stop analyzing and just get on with my rescue mission. Gagging from the stench of burned flesh wafting from Rebecca, I peeled off her claws from Dallas's neck and tried to pull him away, groaning. The guy weighed way more than I expected. We barely reached the door to the hall when the air crackled again and the unmoving vampires stirred.

"Cass?" Dallas said. He didn't even sound surprised to see me. Maybe he had felt my presence as much as I had felt his.

My breath caught in my throat. I took in his smile, forgetting the other immortals as I got lost in his golden gaze. "Yes?"

"I always figured I'd carry my bride over the threshold, not the other way round." A flicker of amusement crossed his brows.

I grinned, wishing I could just plunge into his arms and plant a kiss on his delectable lips. "Sorry, you lost me at 'bride'."

He stood and planted himself in front of me as though to protect me. I noticed Rebecca behind us only when she kicked me, sending me flying against the wall. She must've teleported. Rubbing my aching head, I pulled out my phone again.

"If you so much as move a finger, I'll snap his neck," Rebecca hissed, digging her deadly nails into Dallas's throat where the aorta beat frantically beneath his fragile skin.

"She means it," Amber said.

My fingertips hovered on the keyboard, but I knew better than to ignore the magnitude of Rebecca's threat. She had killed before, she sure wouldn't hesitate now.

"A family reunion, how lovely." Rebecca laughed. I cringed at the guttural sound.

"Let him go, Rebecca. He hasn't done anything so don't take our unfinished business out on them," Aidan said.

Rebecca turned her head sharply, regarding him through eyes that seemed to smolder with maliciousness. "Who said my unfinished business involved you? Do you really think I'd go to all the trouble for a man?"

Yet another spat between Aidan and one of his exes. I rolled my eyes. Seriously, it was getting annoying. Time to change the subject before they started throwing dishes at each other. "How did you get into Hell, Rebecca?"

"She didn't need to because she was here all along. You just didn't know," Amber whispered.

I blinked, putting two and two together. That's what Aidan had been looking for during his 'strolls' when I came visiting Amber and he wasn't around. During the Shadow ceremony, when Amber retrieved the book of the Shadows from the Otherworld, she had in fact travelled to

Distros where Rebecca had been hiding. "Apart from the Shadows, she has another companion," I whispered to myself.

"You broke the case wide open, Sherlock Holmes," Aidan muttered.

"Is that why you agreed to come to Hell?" He nodded. My gaze travelled to Dallas, taking in the guilty expression on his face. The guy had blamed me for keeping secrets and yet he seemed to have plenty of his own. "Did you know?"

He shook his head as much as Rebecca's iron grip would let him. "Not everything."

"We told him the person we were looking for was here and that you weren't who you said you were. That's all," Aidan said.

My mistrust from before returned. The Shadows got the book and Rebecca found what she came for: an opportunity for revenge on the one who killed her hundreds of years ago. She could just attack him or suck Dallas dry to get back at Aidan by hurting his mate's brother. That she should just wait in the doorway, her feet tapping on the carpet impatiently, didn't make any sense. So, what was she actually waiting for?

"What do you want, Rebecca?" I asked when no one else did.

Soft footsteps moved outside the window and the entrance door opened. "Hello? Is someone here?" a girl's voice called.

Rebecca's gaze met mine as she whispered, "Your answer's just arrived."

I opened my mouth to warn Theo to get away from here as fast as possible, but it came too late. Theo stopped in the hallway, confusion crossing her pale face. I could hear the hundreds of questions racing through her mind as she sorted through them in the hope to make sense of the display before her eyes.

"Come on in." Rebecca pointed at the living room. Theo shot me a questioning look. When I nodded, she did as Rebecca said. "I believe you have something I need." I regarded her with mistrust. What could she possibly need from the girl?

Theo's long, flowing dress brushed my bare arm as she walked past me. She barely stepped over the threshold when Rebecca dropped Dallas and grabbed Theo's neck. Only too late did I realize what she was about to do.

It happened within seconds. Rebecca's fangs bore into Theo's skin, tearing through muscles and tendons, red blood soaking the girl's white dress. I lunged forward the same moment as the others did, but Rebecca was faster. Still holding on to Theo, her nails tore through Dallas's neck. Amber's scream filled the air. Like in slow motion, Dallas's surprised gaze met mine and then realization kicked in. I caught his fall, my hands bathing in his blood as I pressed my palm against the gnashing wound spreading from his neck down to his torso. Something dark, like black fog, gathered around us. His mouth opened into a smile and more blood gathered at the corners of his lips.

Her name's Sofia. Rebecca's thoughts penetrated my mind. I wasn't sure whether she had spoken to me or whether it was just a statement as she flicked through Theo's memories. She tossed Theo's unmoving body aside and disappeared before my eyes.

"Cass, I really love you," Dallas whispered.

A curtain of tears clouded my vision as I pressed my mouth against his, whispering, "I love you too." My fingers glided over my phone to punch in the commands that would save my mate. He drew in ragged heaps of air, the blood spilling out of his mouth making a gurgling sound. The air crackled with electricity, but his wounds didn't heal. No technology could stop fate.

"Don't leave me," I whispered through silent sobs and tears streaming down my face.

"Never," he said softly. My heart ripped inside my chest. His body began to shake. I tried to pull him into a sitting position to make breathing easier as my hands patted his wounds as though to stop the blood flow. His skin turned a few degrees colder under my touch. From the corner of my eye, I noticed Aidan struggling to hold Amber back, but she kept screaming, begging and cussing to let her go. I knew Aidan wouldn't let her turn her brother into a vampire, and I couldn't blame him when turning a human meant a sure death sentence from the Lore council. He wouldn't risk losing his mate just as much as I'd do anything in my power to save mine.

"You're going to be okay," I chanted over and over again as I brushed his hair out of his face, desperation washing over me. I peered at Aidan, imploring him to let Amber help Dallas even though I knew he wouldn't. "Please." He shook his head slightly in response, his jaw set, his hard gaze avoiding me.

Dallas's eyes rolled back. I pressed his palm against my mouth to hold back my sobs. It wasn't supposed to end like this, and yet somewhere, deep within my heart, I knew it would. As the bond between us drew me closer to him, I could feel something happening to my body. My top tore at the back where a cold and hard sensation moved beneath my skin. My jaw quivered with pain, my gaze turned sharper.

"No, Dallas! Don't you dare die on me!" Amber's angry words were barely audible through the sudden buzzing in my head, the unnerving murmurs I had tried to ignore before, only a thousand times louder now. The earth began to shake beneath me. I could feel the dark abyss at my feet, telling me my time had come. But I wasn't ready. Not now, not when our love was still hopeful. It wasn't time to give up yet. I shook my head, fighting the changes in my body: the nails growing into sharp claws, the wings tearing their way out of my skin. My whole body felt like I was being burned with fire and cooled with ice-cold water at the same time, the pain unbearable and yet so much more bearable than the aching in my heart.

Dallas's eyes closed and with a last breath, he gave into my embrace, his still warm body a mere shadow of the living being he had been only a few minutes ago. A painful scream pierced the air. It took me a while to realize that it was mine.

Chapter 30 - Accommodating changes

Dad said I had been in and out of my dark abyss for days, but I couldn't remember a single lucid moment. All I remembered was the cold seeping through my clothes and the constant shivering no matter how much I tried to shift my position on the hard floor with the dark tower around me rising into the night.

Eventually, I opened my eyes, expecting skin as dry as tires and flapping wings. The wings were there, but my body felt as smooth as before, albeit a bit battered and bruised. Dad reached for me. I pushed him away so he wouldn't touch me. No one should. I was an abomination now. A demon gatekeeper. A reaper, waiting for death until that's all I'd ever know.

"I'm sorry I wasn't here when you needed me, kiddo," Dad said. "Your mother saw the TV show and she wanted to see me in Heaven." He didn't mention he'd been away all night, probably hooking up or something. Urgh. I'd rather not picture that so I pushed the disgusting thought to the back of my mind. I could hear the excitement and guilt in his voice. Excitement at the prospect that his plans to woo Mom might work after all. And guilt because he hadn't been here to stop the events that would've happened anyway because they were part of my fate. I patted his hand to signal it was okay, then pulled my fingers away quickly, burying them beneath the torn sheets to hide the sharp, deadly claws that were my nails now. A reconciliation between Mom and Dad was what I wanted all along and yet my happiness for them couldn't quite melt the thick sheet of ice enveloping my heart.

"Dallas?" I barely dared to speak the words. I knew Theo would live because she was a ghost already, but Dallas had been mortal at the time of the attack. He was dead, so what was the point in torturing myself with his memory? And yet I had to hear it to find closure because in my heart, our bond still burned bright.

Dad shook his head, a deep frown replacing the hesitant smile from before. "In the physical realm he'd be considered dead."

"And here?" I bit my lip to stop it from quivering.

"It's only a matter of time until—" Dad's voice broke off. He didn't need to finish what he had to say because I knew it.

I nodded. "So I'll be a reaper and bound to Hell forever now." Staring at the torn sheets around me—my sharp claws' doing—I avoided his gaze. I didn't want to see the pain in his eyes. With my own pain shredding my heart, it might just be too much to bear.

"As long as his soul continues to search for his physical body, you won't completely transform." Dad's finger moved beneath my chin, forcing my gaze up to face him. His eyes searched mine, and for a moment hope flickered in them. "Through your life force, I can keep Dallas's soul alive for a while. But you'll have to find the girl soon."

"The girl?"

"Theo's sister, Sofia." Dad leaned forward and cupped my face. "There's something I never told you about Distros." I bobbed my head so he continued, "We don't frequent it because it's the plane where we keep paranormal beings, and we don't get involved. When Amber travelled to the Otherworld to retrieve the book of the Shadows, she entered Distros and raised Rebecca." I blinked, confused.

"That's why the reapers arrived so quickly to take Amber back to the threshold of the living."

"The threshold of the living aka the East Gate in Distros," Dad said. "But that's not important. What matters here is Theo. She's a direct ancestor of a very powerful woman, but it's her sister, Sofia, that's inherited all the power. You need to find her to help Dallas's soul return into his body."

"You mean she can raise the dead?" My eyes widened at Dad's grave nod. No angel could grant life, but a girl could? "What is she?"

"That's for you to find out, kiddo." Dad rose from his position and pulled the curtains aside, bathing the room in glaring brightness.

My body felt stiff and worn as I followed after him. My eyes squinted against the midday sun casting a shimmering

315

hue over the erupting volcanoes in the distances. "You knew this would happen."

"Sometimes it helps to have a seer in the family. You may think your aunt Selena's a nutcase, but deep inside she cares for your wellbeing." He turned to face me. "Thrain's waiting outside to help you find Sofia. Get packing, Cass. I've been missing the kid."

And by kid I knew he meant Dallas. I rose on my toes and planted a kiss on Dad's smooth cheek. A smile spread across my lips and my heart started to race. With a new purpose came new hope.

Sofia.

I would find her, no matter what.

THE END FOR NOW...

Voodoo Kiss (Ancient Legends Book Three) Preview:

1678
Prologue

He came after the fall of darkness when all was quiet and the relentless heat of the late August sun had long waned into a freezing night. I wrapped my shawl around my aching bones and opened the door to let him in, but he just lingered in the doorway, his black hood covering most of his pale face, smooth as marble, and shiny black eyes.

"Esmeralda."

For a moment, my breath caught in my throat. The time had finally come, meaning there was no going back now. I shouldn't be scared. After all, it had been my decision to call for him. I had no choice than to go through with it because Death was already lurking in the shadows.

A breeze blew across my face; the cool air felt good on my hot-burning skin. I hoped against all odds I wouldn't pass out before the deal was sealed. It was time to hurry so I pointed behind me. Without my invitation he would never be able to cross the threshold. "Come on in, Warrior."

He bowed before me and stepped past into the dimly lit hut with dried lavender hanging from strings attached across the ceiling, his boots barely making any sound on the naked ground that hadn't received a good scrub ever since the fever got hold of me.

"Over here." I pulled a chair for him when white spots filled my vision and I collapsed into a heap on the cold floor.

His piercing eyes met my gaze. "Time is running out for you."

"You think I don't know that?" Laughing bitterly, I scrambled to my feet and pointed at the chair. He nodded but didn't take me up on the offer. Instead, he marched over to the hearth with the burning logs and pulled out a scroll from under his coat, then handed it to me.

My eyes scanned the handwriting, soaking up the beauty of the cursive and the words I had never learned to read.

"Is the agreement not to your liking?" the warrior asked.

"All is well." Drawing a deep breath I grabbed the dagger from his outstretched hand and pierced its tip into my thumb, letting two drops of blood stain the paper. "Then it is done?"

"Not yet. Reincarnation requires personal sacrifice." He pushed the scroll back under his cloak and removed the hood. I stared at the pale skin covering high cheekbones and the unnaturally black eyes, dark as puddles, soaking up the light in the room. He seemed young, maybe eighteen summers old, and yet I knew it couldn't be. His race would only send a master to deal with my proposition.

"You will inherit this sacred land and all the souls I have bound to it throughout the years. I have fulfilled my part of the bargain, now it's your turn." My voice shook because his eerie eyes made me nervous. I hid my wringing hands behind my back.

The warrior inched closer, his gaze prodding into mine. "And so we shall. As agreed, you, Esmeralda, Priestess of the Seventh Order, will be reborn as the seventh daughter of the seventh daughter of the Romanov dynasty. Your powers shall know no boundaries for they were bestowed to you by the Goddess herself."

I nodded. "Yes, that was part of the agreement."

He held up a hand to stop me. "There is more, however. As we grant life, we're also owners to take it. Nothing but the Blade of Sorrow will be able to kill you. Once it does, your skills will pass onto the owner of the blade and your soul will be forever bound to the Cemetery of the Dead."

"No." I shook my head vigorously. "That wasn't part of my offer. I will not agree to it."

"It's too late. See your mark?" He pulled out the scroll and unrolled it. I peered mortified at the blood soaking the paper, dripping onto the ground. A sudden flash of light blinded my eyes. I blinked and returned my focus to the contract. The blood formed a perfect hexagon across the entire scroll. I couldn't help but gasp. The warrior continued, "The goddess has accepted your sacrifice."

Outside, a strong wind began to howl through the nearby trees, rattling the windowpanes. The warrior started to whisper in a language I didn't understand. A sharp pain, like that of a knife, pierced my heart and I dropped to my knees, clutching the rags I had worn for more years than I could count. My breathing came in labored heaps, but my mind remained surprisingly sharp.

The door opened with a creak and he flew in, his great wings flapping softly. The reaper—a creature of Heaven and Hell who lingered around me for many months, waiting for me to draw my last breath so he could transport my soul wherever he was meant to take it. He stood directly before me—seven feet tall with a surprisingly human face. Its dark gaze sharpened on me as he let out a piercing scream coming straight from the pit of hell. It was the first time I got a good look at the creature, all skin as dark as coal and eyes as deep as the ocean.

I turned my head to look at the chanting warrior, begging him to save me, but he averted his gaze. On my knees, I pulled myself to the far side of the wall where a stack of hay covered by a thin sheet served as my sleeping chamber. The reaper lurched, his enormous wings fluttering behind him. Sharp claws cut into my chest, the pain intensifying until I could no longer breathe. I knew then that I was about to die.

My scream found its way out of my throat a moment before my vision blurred and the room became darkness. What would be the purpose in fighting with a body wrecked from age and disease? I sighed, ready to succumb to my fate. Instead of fighting, I let go willingly.

I had been deceived by the ones I had trusted.

End of sample. VOODOO KISS by Jayde Scott...out September 2011

22956007R00204

Made in the USA
Middletown, DE
12 August 2015